A Simple Tale of Ink and Bindings

Kami King Larsen

For everyone who ever felt slightly out of place

Come Fairies, take me out of this dull world, for I would ride with you upon the wind and dance upon the mountains like a flame

-W. B. Yeats

ONE

It was as good a day as any for Fia to disappear. The streets were crowded, the people jovial, and the sun bright in the sky. The air held the barest trace of damp cobblestone under the heavier aromas of horse manure and fresh baked bread. Not the best olfactory combination, but also not the worst.

Pulling her cap lower over her brow, Fia stole a glance up the bustling lane. From her spot against the wall near the bakery's side alley, she could just make out the profile of her brother's face several shops away and farther up the high street. His expression was one she'd rarely seen when they were younger but seemed to be a frequent fixture in the past six months. Oscar clearly thought it was a placating smile, but to Fia it was much more akin to a grimace. This expression meant his wife was unhappy. And when Claire Walsh was unhappy, those around her became unhappy too.

As Fia was the most frequent cause of Claire's unhappiness, to her mind, her disappearance should ensure the grimace would alight on her brother's face far less frequently. In her heart, Fia knew Oscar would miss her just as she knew she would feel wretched not seeing him. For a moment her resolve was tested, and she almost changed her mind. Perhaps she could stay a wee bit longer and endure a wee bit more. As the thought came to her, Claire said something which caused Fia's gentle brother to hang his head and sigh.

Fia had seen it all before. Claire was always worse after spending any length of time in Fia's presence. It was decided. Staying would do none of them any good.

The street was full, but not so much that Fia's view of Oscar and his wife was obscured as they entered the butcher shop—Claire no doubt planning a dinner they couldn't afford. It was the chance Fia'd been waiting for. If she was quick, she could hustle up the street, be in and out of the bookseller's before either of them realized she wasn't in fact at the bakery, and be off before they knew to look for her. One night at a small inn on the city's outskirts and gone on the train at first light.

Slipping her hand into her satchel, she felt for the book that would buy her ticket out of the city and buy her brother the quiet life he so deserved. The leather binding was smooth and worn under her fingers, and her heart gave a little dip in her chest. It would hurt more than she cared to think about to sell the treasured volume, but it was the only item she owned of any real value. Fia withdrew her hand and scrubbed the water lining her eyes. She hoisted her small bag tight against her chest and wished her brother a silent farewell.

The mild weather had brought the people of the city out in droves. It was both a blessing and a curse. Businessmen in tidy tweed jackets, mothers pushing prams smelling of egg yolk and slightly sour milk, gaggles of children, and even the occasional man of the church served her well in masking her escape, but the throngs also kept her from moving as quickly as she'd have liked. She sidestepped around a group of giggling adolescent girls and hopped over a steaming pile of horse dung as she crossed the busy thoroughfare, all while occasionally looking back over her shoulder for signs of Claire or Oscar.

As she reached the stately gold and ivory painted door of her destination, Fia pulled the book from her bag. As if the heavens were plotting against her, a gust of wind rushed up the street and snatched at her cap at the same time the shop door opened outward with the tinkle of a bell. Cursing softly to herself, she grabbed at the thick brown wool with one hand and cradled the leather and vellum treasure with the other. She was able to slap the cap back on her head, but the movement caught her off balance and sent her pirouetting on the slick cobblestones. She righted herself in time to avoid crashing to her knees but not soon enough to avoid careening into the man exiting the shop.

Fia's ankle twisted as she stepped on the man's foot, and the air was knocked from her lungs as something firm and pointed connected with her ribs.

"Watch it then, lad," a terse voice admonished. "These are worth more than my boots, and certainly more than yours."

She had a good view of the boots in question, doubled over as she was, trying to catch her wind—one hand still clutching her cap as the other hugged the green leather volume to her chest.

"Sorry, sir." She didn't look up. Let him think she was a boy—all the better for her.

"What's that you've got?" the man asked. If she hadn't been doubled over, he would have stood only a head taller than her.

Fia drug in air but didn't stand upright to answer. "Nothing, sir, just an old book I was hoping to sell." She didn't think he could see what exactly she was clutching and felt safer giving as little detail as possible.

"Well, then, let's see it." He extended a hand in her direction. Despite her unwillingness to reveal it to him, it wouldn't do for her to outright refuse and cause a scene. The sooner she got on with her business, the better. Reluctantly she straightened but didn't immediately offer the tome for inspection.

He stood waiting, arm outstretched and balancing a stack of at least eight other volumes against his side. His gaze remained focused on the leatherbound book she cradled against her, never lifting to her face. Any other day, she'd be happy to avoid someone looking at her, but the hungry expectant expression in his pale blue eyes made her uneasy, and she willed him to drag his gaze from the book even if it meant him looking at her instead.

"Come on, lad. I haven't got all day." He blew an inpatient breath upward, trying and failing to get his chestnut locks back from his face.

"It's precious to me, sir," she mumbled, getting her breath back.

"If it was so precious, you wouldn't have been about to wander in there with it, now would you?" he mused a moment, eyes still devouring the bits of leather not covered by Fia's arm. If they'd met under other circumstances, she'd probably find him attractive, but given both his tone and his insistence, she felt only a wary kind of discomfort. "You do mean to sell it, I'm guessing. Not precious. No, I think valuable is more likely."

She thought of turning and running back to where she'd last seen Oscar. The book—and her escape—would have to wait for another day. The trouble was, she had no idea when another opportunity like this would arise.

"Look. There's no need for this reluctance. I'm in the market for good books. Unique ones too." He dipped his head toward the stack under his arm. "And I can pay just as well as dry old Mr. Watiker—likely even better. So let me take a look. I promise not to saunter off with it. You'd undoubtedly be more than able to trip me up, even should I try."

Fia thought about it for a moment, still hesitant but also still desperate. She cautioned a glance up the road, and though it was still choked with people, there was still no sign of Oscar or Claire. That wouldn't remain the case for long. She handed over the book.

It wasn't in his hand more than a second or two before he blurted, "Did you steal this?"

The biting accusation stung Fia. "I'm no thief," she snapped back.

"Sure you aren't." Still he had eyes only for the book. If he'd looked up, he'd have seen the color high in her cheeks and the fire in her eyes. "It's only every day an urchin such as yourself is popping in with a prize like this."

"Good then that not only am I not a thief, I'm also not an urchin." Despite her ire, she couldn't help the hint of a laugh in her words. While she was neither a lad, nor a thief, nor an urchin, she certainly couldn't blame him for his ignorance. In scruffy boots, cap down around her ears, trousers and an ill-fitting sweater, she was easy to mistake for a boy half her age. Most of the time when she ventured out, she dressed similarly. Oscar didn't mind and let her dress as she saw fit. It was only on the rarest of occasions she wore a dress or dared to go about with her head uncovered.

She'd been called any number of cruel names in her life, but being accused of theft was new to her.

Perhaps it was the laugh in her tone that struck him. The man finally glanced at her face briefly, back to the book, then back to her almost instantly. A widening of his eyes and a faint flush on his cheeks were the only signs of his surprise before he spoke. "I beg your pardon, miss. I . . . Is this book in fact yours then?"

"Since the day of my birth, or at least for as long as I can remember. Now if you don't mind, I really need to get on with my business." She glanced down at her book and back at him, raising her eyebrows. A silent request to return it.

"But why on earth would you think to sell it? It's extraordinary." His voice held clear reverence.

"I have my reasons."

"I can't imagine ever parting with it. Do you not know what it is?" He raised one perfect eyebrow in a decidedly appealing way, despite the accusation in his voice. It irked her that he was wasting her time, but it irked her more that she'd grown up with the book, knew it was special and rare and *important*. Unfortunately, she did *not* know what it was. Only that it was hers and that it might be worth enough to see her on the road.

She had to get moving. "I'm sorry. Is it every day you insult a person and then carry on with such a personal interrogation?"

He had the decency to look momentarily abashed, and she realized he wasn't all that much older than her. Certainly not more than a handful of years over twenty.

"No." The barest shake of his head accompanied his now furrowed brow. "Not every day."

"Well, just call me lucky then!" Fia felt distinctly unlucky, but she would never let it show on her face. Her life might be challenging at times, but she refused to let the world view her as morose as well as odd. Plastering on a smile, she dipped her head and glanced at the shop door once again. "I really must be on my way."

"Fia!" Her heart plummeted at the sound of Oscar's voice. "Fi! There you are!"

She'd been close. So very, *very* close.

"So much for that plan," she muttered. Taking one last longing look at the door to the bookseller's, she shoved the beautiful green leather tome back into her satchel and raised her chin, a bright smile on her face. If there also happened to be the sheen of tears in her eyes, she could always blame the brightness of the sun bouncing off the glass.

Fia raised her hand and waved at her brother, then turned to the man standing at her side. "Please don't mention the book to my brother."

The stranger ran a hand through his hair, momentarily pulling the untidy locks from his face. The small furrow of his brow deepened as he looked at her.

"I realize I have no right to ask a favor. It's not really a lie, just an omission. Oscar, well, he simply would not understand."

The man nodded, mouth turned down, but did not argue.

"Fia, for the love of the heavens, you gave me a start. I thought you meant to visit the bakery, not the bookshop. When you weren't there, I realized I must have misheard you." Oscar didn't look overly concerned. In fact, he looked as happy and chipper as he often did back before he'd married Claire. Or more correctly, since before Claire had met Fia.

"It's likely my fault, Oscar. I may have misspoken. You know how I am sometimes."

The man at her side shifted his stack of books from one hip to the other.

"Are you done then? We should be getting along, but if you haven't had enough time to window shop we can probably linger." He raised his brows toward the window in silent question but dropped them just as quickly, a sour look taking over his face. "But then there'll be the bread. I don't suppose you got a loaf, did you? Claire was planning on it with dinner. And she's waiting in the square."

He needn't say more. They both knew this was one more thing for Claire to hold against her.

Fia sighed. "No. I did *not* get the bread. Sorry."

He nodded. "Ah, Fi, don't look so glum. Didn't figure you had. She'll just have to make due. She's not as bad as all that."

Fia was skeptical and mumbled, "I beg to differ." Smiling, she grabbed Oscar's arm. "But we should be going either way. No sense delaying the inevitable."

It was then that the man at her side stepped forward and extended the hand not balancing the precarious stack of books toward Oscar. "Tieg Connolly. I don't believe we've met. I was just having the most enchanting conversation with your *sister*." The inflection made it almost a question, and Fia understood why. She and Oscar didn't particularly look like siblings. While Oscar was solid and broad, Fia was—as Claire called her—willowy. Tall for a woman but slight. Where Fia was pale, Oscar was golden and tanned. Her eyes the grey green of pond water in winter and his a deep loamy brown. But while they differed in appearance, their mannerisms and outlook were nearly identical. They shared a love of laughter and a warm disposition. Oscar shared his smile with the world— at least when his wife was happy—while Fia loved to smile but often found it serving as armor as much as anything else.

Oscar looked momentarily confused, either because Fia had been having a conversation with someone or because he simply hadn't noticed the tall stoic man standing at his sister's side. He thumped his hand to his forehead and grimaced, then shook Tieg's hand vigorously. "My feckin manners. Sorry, mate. It's been a day. Oscar Walsh, and Fia you've met apparently."

"I have indeed. This might be a bit unconventional, but could I interest you both in coming round for tea? Tomorrow perhaps? I'm staying with a friend, and it gets quite dull at times." If the words were meant to be inviting, he was failing miserably. It came out forced and more than a little stiff.

Fia squeezed her brother's arm in what she hoped would be a silent plea to decline. "We really must be getting along, Mr. Connolly. Thank you, but I think we'll decline."

Tieg looked from Fia to her brother. "Are you certain? He's a great fellow. Simon Beck? Perhaps you know him already?"

"It's a big city, Mr. Connolly," Fia stated.

"Ah, Mr. Connolly," Oscar said. "It's a great invitation, but well, Fia—or rather we—aren't, well, very social."

"I understand." His eyes flicked to Fia in her tattered clothes and stodgy cap. "But if you change your mind, just send word. The invitation stands." He dipped his head as the siblings departed.

Fia looked over her shoulder just once as Oscar escorted her up the cobblestone roadway. The glance was brief and the sun bright. She couldn't tell if Tieg Connolly's expression was one of confusion or irritation. Either way, her plan was shot, in no small part because of him. She felt more trapped than ever.

"What do you mean, you declined the invitation?" Each word was clipped and sharp. Fia refused to be outright rude to Claire, but in moments like this, it took all of her inner strength to keep her chin up and her lips tight.

"Now, sweets, no need to get upset." Oscar stood near the mantel and gave his wife a pleading look.

"Don't you 'now sweets' me." Claire hauled herself up and out of the threadbare armchair she'd been occupying. Fia noticed two bright scarlet blooms on her sister-in-law's otherwise pale cheeks. "In what world would you decline an invitation to Simon Beck's home?"

"In this world. You know Fia isn't comfortable—"

"I care for a city rat's whiskers more than I care about what does or does not make Fia comfortable. In case you hadn't noticed, few in the city would extend an invitation to her and here you've gone and done this ridiculous thing. Turned him down?"

Fia sat, hands folded in her lap, on the small bench she often occupied when all three were in the tiny reception room. Having not grown up in the city, she wasn't sure how detrimental the rejection of an invitation to tea could be. "I'm sorry, Claire. But who is Simon Beck?"

"*Who is Simon Beck?*" Claire raised her blond eyebrows toward her even blonder hairline. "How have you never heard of Simon Beck? Not that it matters. In your circumstances, any invitation should be considered a good one."

Fia didn't flinch at the words the way she might have in the past. She was more than used to her sister-in-law belittling her. Claire had never particularly warmed to Fia, but with her belly swollen with the couple's first child, she'd completely abandoned any pretense of love for her husband's sister.

Fia often found it easier to simply agree and move the subject along. She nodded. "Of course the invitation was a lucky one. But could you at least tell me a little about him?"

Claire proceeded to inform them that Mr. Simon Beck had a reputation as a bit of an eccentric businessman with ties to various shops and endeavors across the city. He was both admired and respected for his charity and willingness to assist those who worked hard. She did admit she'd never heard of Tieg Connolly but assumed any friend of Simon's was a friend worth having.

Claire placed her hands on the small of her back and looked at Oscar. "Send word first thing in the morning that we shall take Mr. Connolly up on his offer for tea."

Oscar sat next to Fia. Leaning forward, he rested his elbows on his knees, earnestly avoiding his wife's gaze. "I'm just not convinced it's a good idea, Claire. What do you think, Fi?"

Claire pursed her lips and paced the short distance from the window to the mantel. Fia looked at them both. The last thing she wanted was to cause Oscar any more trouble than her general presence did already. Knowing there was no good solution no matter what she chose, she opted to placate Claire for now and worry about the unusual invitation tomorrow.

"Of course we can attend." She smiled brightly at her brother. "If Claire believes it's for the best, I'm happy to oblige." Absently she reached up and placed a hand behind her ear, running her fingers through the short curls there. "My emerald cloche might be suitable."

Claire snorted. "Unlikely. But it'll have to do."

TWO

When the sun's rays carried through the gaps of Fia's worn shutters the next morning, they fell on an empty bed. Never a deep sleeper, she had been awoken by the noise from the street below, as it typically did. In that part of the city, the working class rarely had the luxury of sleeping in.

Oscar had gotten permission to close the glassblower's shop early enough to escort his wife and sister to tea. Technically he was still an apprentice, but Fia knew the term was merely a formality. She'd seen the miracles he could work with a tube and lathe. Mr. Hastings—the shop's proprietor and Oscar's mentor—rumbled around in the back near the kiln most days, but Oscar did all the real work that needed doing, both with the blowing and the sales. When he'd asked for the extra time, it was also just a formality. The old artisan never denied Oscar if he could help it, and Fia adored the man because of it. Still, her brother felt a duty to be present and busy, so he was bustling out the door earlier than usual in an effort to regain the time he'd lose later.

Fia sat in the kitchen, bleary eyed and clutching a mug, as he gathered his things to go.

"I'm sorry about Claire," he said as he scooped up his jacket.

"No need to be." Fia smiled and blew on the steaming tea in her mug. "I'm a burden on her household. It's only right she wants me moving on."

He paused at the door. "You're no burden, Fi. Don't ever think it. She knew she was getting both of us when she agreed to marry me."

"Thanks." Fia looked down at the tea rippling from her breaths. If she'd had her way, she would have been gone by now and this conversation wouldn't be necessary. "Well, you better run! Tell Mr. Hastings hello for me and be careful not to singe your eyebrows again!"

After her brother left, Fia tidied up the kitchen and went back up the narrow stairs to the tiny room she occupied. It wasn't much—really just a lumpy mattress on a wooden frame and a small chest of drawers alongside a leaning cabinet where she hung her three dresses. But it was clean and it was safe. Her brother did what he could for her, despite everything.

Fia thought about the afternoon to come. It was sure to be a strain on all of them. Was there still a way for her to get to the bookseller's? She dismissed the idea. She retrieved the book from her satchel and sat on the bed, stroking the soft leather binding. Fia opened it to the front page and ran her fingers over the words so elegantly penned there—not in the same bold print as the body of the book, but in swooping handwritten swirls. *Life may be dark, let your inner light guide you always.* The page was thin and the ink faded from the number of times she'd run her fingers over the handpenned words. As she flipped through the following pages, the words seemed to dance across the paper until she came to the center of the book with its brightly inked illustrations. More than once Fia had tried to read the text, but it always jumbled in her mind—words easy to read but at the same time elusive in their meanings. Even the painted panels in the center, while beautiful to look at, lacked any meaning. It was like listening to an opera sung in some unknown language; she knew it was beautiful even if she couldn't understand a word. She'd just make out an image and it would blur—her mind unable or unwilling to hold fast to it. She was mesmerized by them while having no idea what they were meant to represent.

Noise from downstairs signaled Claire was up and about. Fia had no desire to interact with her brother's wife, knowing the conversation would be uncomfortable at best and miserable more likely. The worst part was knowing Claire wasn't a terrible person. She could be charitable and joyful at times, and Fia knew Claire genuinely loved Oscar. She had been over the moon when he'd proposed, and now that the baby was on the way, she was even happier. Unless, of course, Fia happened to be in the room.

Often Fia would hear bits of laughter or singing from an adjoining room or behind a closed door. But the moment Claire's eyes would catch on Fia, it was as if all the joy and good humor would rush from her like water from a pitcher, leaving in its wake a cold hard shell.

Fia Walsh was different. Not just in appearance, but in the very core of her being. She wasn't sure why or how, but she knew it and so did Claire. Unfortunately, Oscar's wife was unable to accept Fia's differences. And therein lay a huge problem.

So Fia avoided her as much as possible. That morning was no exception. Not wanting to subject either of them to the dramatic change in mood her presence was sure to insight, Fia elected to stay in her room and attempt to assemble an outfit suitable for tea. The emerald cloche was a must, and luckily her best dress—a dove grey frock with delicate green embroidery at the collar—was both appropriate and clean. She added the long string of cerulean and silver handcut beads Oscar had gifted her on the occasion of her last birthday. They must have taken him hours to shape and string. She kept them wrapped in thin muslin and brought them out when she needed a cheerful reminder of all the beauty in the world. It was a perfect day to wear them.

The given address was a short ten-minute walk from Oscar and Claire's tidy home, but the neighborhood could have been in a different world altogether. While Mr. Connollly's friend didn't exactly live on *the* wealthiest street in the city, it wasn't a far cry off. The home featured pale stonework across the front and ornate sconces large enough to illuminate the entire walk from the street to the manse when the sun went down.

Oscar rang the bell, and the trio was escorted into a wide spacious entry complete with marble floors, hardwood wainscoting, and a high arched ceiling painted a lush dark burgundy. Fia tilted her head back and stared at the milky glass globes of the fixture dangling above their heads. Like an inverted tree dressed in fairy fruit, it was beautiful in its simplicity. A perfect balance to the rest of their surroundings.

"Fia! Your hat!" Claire hissed as the felt slipped from Fia's crown.

She reflexively tugged it down, and color rose in her cheeks. As a maid led them through to a warm but equally elegant reception room, they were greeted by Tieg Connolly and a man perhaps a decade his senior. This, then, must be Simon Beck.

Both men rose from leather armchairs as Fia, Oscar, and Claire entered. Side by side the two men made quite a pair. Mr. Beck was relaxed yet stately and Mr. Connelly rigid but quite handsome. His clipped and severe tone the day prior must have kept it from becoming evident.

"Thank you, Gwen. We'll be taking tea in here, I believe," Mr. Beck notified the maid. She dropped her head and slipped out, shutting the door behind her. "Welcome to my home. It's a pleasure having you join us." His voice was full-bodied and warm.

He stepped forward, and Oscar shook his hand a touch too vigorously. "The pleasure's all ours, Mr. Beck."

"Please. Call me Simon. I don't go in for all the formalities."

"Right then. Well, I'm Oscar and this is my wife, Claire." She stepped forward, and Oscar placed a hand on the small of her back and simultaneously nodded in Fia's direction. "And my sister Fia."

Simon dipped his head to each of the ladies in turn. "It is so lovely to meet you all. Tieg was quite insistent we have you for tea, and I see he was right in his excitement."

Tieg Connolly, however, looked anything but excited. The two men couldn't have been more different in their affect. While Simon was all smiles and warm welcomes, Tieg remained reserved and stiff.

Claire beamed at Mr. Connolly. "It was so kind of you to extend the invitàtion. Particularly after what sounds like quite a brief encounter." Claire's cheeks were rosy and her face full of good humor. Fia recognized a flash of what had attracted Oscar to his wife. When she wasn't looking at Fia with a scowl, she could be quite enchanting.

Mr. Connolly dipped his head in acknowledgment.

"Please, please. Do sit." Simon motioned toward the sofa and chaise. Once the ladies were comfortable, he and his friend returned to their chairs. "It's one of my favorite things, meeting new faces. In a city of this size we can all just blend in if we aren't careful. Walk past one another on the street and never know what kinds of interesting friends we might have made if we just stopped for a moment to chat."

Fia couldn't disagree more. She *wanted* to blend in and be lost in the crowd—a bubble of isolated happiness in an ocean of careless people. Still, she found herself smiling at the sheer joy Simon exuded when he spoke. Already she felt herself warming to the man.

"Now tell me, Oscar, what it is you do in this fine city of ours. Tieg was a bit miserly with the details yesterday."

"I'm a glass smith, Mr. Beck." When the other man twisted his lips, Oscar amended, "Er. I mean Simon."

Simon's smile was charming as he asked, "A glass smith and not a glazier? There are so many windows, I'd imagine you could find ample work as a glazier."

"Yes, but it lacks the creativity I crave."

"How fascinating. And do you run your own shop?"

"No. Well, really I'm an apprentice, but—"

Claire cut him off. "No need to be so modest, Oscar. He practically runs the place, and you should see his work. It's the most amazing glass you've ever encountered. But he's too good-natured to admit it."

"I can appreciate a modest man and an artisan to boot. I myself was modest once." He chuckled. "Now not so much."

"That is quite contrary to all I've heard," Claire said.

Simon waved her off. "Don't listen to all the chatter on the street, Mrs. Walsh. I'm not quite what the good people of the city make me out to be."

"So you *are* modest. And I thought you didn't go in for all the formalities. Please, I insist you call me Claire."

Fia blinked. Was her sister-in-law flirting with this man? The very thought seemed inconceivable. She really must have wanted to make a good impression in the hopes of ridding herself of Fia.

"And you, Miss Walsh? Shall Tieg and I address you as Fia then?" He glanced at his friend, who didn't appear overly amused. In fact, Fia had yet to see the man come within throwing distance of a smile.

Fia found her voice. "Of course. It seems we are all friends now." She looked at Mr. Connolly. "Tieg then?" He gave the barest nod. "And what is it you do in our fair city?"

"Oh, I don't actually live in the city. I'm only visiting and on the kindness of Simon. I'm collecting a few things before I head back home."

"Where do you hail from then?" Oscar asked.

"It's a small town. About a day's train ride up the coast. Folks are calling it Feyport these days. It's unlikely you'd have heard of it."

Fia's breath caught and she sat forward. *She'd* heard whispers of Feyport. In the small café she occasionally visited, groups of young men and women talked in hushed voices about the small coastal town. Things there were *different.* Occasionally the word magical was thrown in. And once she swore she heard a girl tell her friend in wonder that the *Fey* in Feyport meant sprites and elves walked the streets in broad daylight.

She'd dreamt of the place even though she'd known no such town could truly exist. She'd never imagined she would actually meet someone from the mysterious place let alone be invited to tea by him.

"I've recently come into a small inheritance, and I'm using it to open a shop of sorts. Part library, part bookseller, and part . . . well something else."

Does Feyport not already have a library?" Oscar asked.

"Sadly no. We generally get books from the school or the church. Every now and then, if there's something really special, the local sundry shop will order it in. I'm trying to acquire enough of the popular titles—and a few rare ones." His eyes flicked to Fia. "It's why I was at the bookseller yesterday when I bumped into your sister."

Fia gave a slight shake of her head and widened her eyes. The last thing she needed was for him to inadvertently let slip why *she* was in that particular location the day before.

Maybe he missed the silent plea, or he simply wasn't interested in keeping her secret, because he carried on without missing a beat. "In fact, that's partially why I extended the invitation for tea." Fia's heart raced, sure he was about to reveal her desire to sell the precious leatherbound book she'd had longer than her first memory.

The door opened and the maid entered carrying an enormous tray laden with all manner of small sandwiches and dense cakes. She was followed by a younger woman, carrying a similarly sized tray. The younger maid's hands weren't quite as steady, and the five porcelain cups she ferried clattered into one another with each step she took. The matching pot and jars also bounced, and Fia was sure the whole thing would soon crash to the floor. The maid made it to a small oak table, however, and seemed relieved when she finally deposited her tray on the highly polished surface.

Fia felt almost as relieved as the poor maid had appeared. Hopefully, Tieg wouldn't return to his conversation and she could rest easier. As the women went about setting up the tea things, Fia glanced around the room. The light from outside was streaming into the space, and she caught her reflection in the clear glass pane.

If either of their hosts had thought it odd she hadn't removed her cloche at the door, neither mentioned it.

She only realized she'd been staring at her reflection when Tieg cleared his throat. "It's a bit more posh than what I'm used to as well."

Fia flushed and looked down at her lap. When she looked up again, Tieg handed her a delicate porcelain cup filled with warm amber liquid, the same slightly bemused look on his face. "Cream and sugar are there if you'd like." He nodded toward the table.

Claire glared at her when Fia didn't immediately reply. "Thank you, Mr. Connolly," she finally managed. "It is all a little more than I'm accustomed to."

The tea was warm and soothing, and Fia was happy to nibble the dainty sandwiches and treats. A divine little cake filled with lemon curd and luscious cream had her reaching for a second before she could control herself. Simon and Tieg made excellent hosts and kept the conversation flowing smoothly. As a bonus, Tieg didn't mention their brief encounter again.

Claire appeared to revel in the attention. Oscar was cautious but cordial. And even Fia found herself relaxing bit by bit as the afternoon progressed. When the maids came to clear away the dishes and sweep up the occasional crumb from the table, Claire recounted the story of the day she and Oscar had met. As much as Fia knew Claire disliked her, she still found the story beguiling. Who wouldn't love a tale of a young hardworking craftsman leaving a single daisy each day for two weeks on the bench where he knew a certain young lady sat every morning after walking her siblings to school? The young lady—Claire—began to look forward to the small token and hoped to catch sight of whoever was leaving them. Finally, one morning an entire bouquet was waiting for the young lady, and when she looked to see if she could spot the person responsible, Oscar stepped from around the corner holding a single pale pink rose which he tucked into the center of the arrangement.

Fia sat forward, drinking in each of Claire's words, chin in her hand and twisting a single short curled lock just below the edge of her hat. The magic of the story was broken when Claire gave her a sharp angry look. Realizing her mistake, Fia jerked upright and tugged the felt lower on her head. Thinking she'd gone unnoticed, she gave a slight sigh of relief. Then she caught Tieg Connolly staring at her. His mouth was slightly agape, and a small line had formed between his brows. He drew his unruly hair back with one hand, and his expression was once again clear.

Claire at least didn't react. "And that," she told Simon, "was the happiest day of my life." She beamed at Oscar, and Fia could almost forgive every horrid thing she'd ever said to her.

"You are a lucky man, Oscar Walsh," Simon said earnestly. Claire's smile grew even wider. "Don't you agree, Tieg?"

"Very much." Tieg looked thoughtful for a moment. "Not to change the subject so drastically, but I wonder if I might bring up a proposal I've been contemplating since yesterday?"

"Please do," Simon responded and looked to Oscar.

Oscar, still unsure of the current company, said "Of course."

"Really it's a question for Miss Walsh."

Fia grew uneasy.

Oscar frowned.

Claire raised her eyebrows.

"I'd very much like you to come work for me," Tieg stated.

Fia wasn't sure she'd heard correctly. "Come work for you?"

"Yes. In my new library. And the shop as well I suppose. It's all one large space."

"But you said you didn't live in the city," Oscar stated.

Tieg nodded, face still impassive. "That is correct. I don't."

Oscar shook his head in what was a frantic dismissive gesture. "Oh, I'm afraid that really isn't the best idea."

"No?" Tieg studied him. "Why not?"

"Because I can't just let my sister go off to some little town no one's ever heard of with a man I've only just met." In very un-Oscar-like behavior, his voice was rising right along with the color in his face.

Fia, not having the heart to tell him *she* had heard of the town, and had almost slipped away unnoticed the day prior, sat quietly. The placid smile on her face disguised her rapid heartbeat quite nicely.

"Are you her guardian then?" Simon asked as if he hadn't thought of it before.

"Our parents passed several years ago, but I am an adult," Fia said.

"And an unmarried young woman," Oscar added as if it weren't already obvious.

"Of course I don't mean to spirit her away this afternoon," Tieg said. "I'll be in the city for several more weeks, and I could use an assistant who's familiar with the shops. I'd like to visit some local artists as well. It's important I do some additional purchasing, and Fia could assist me with looking in the right places. Simon has his connections, but he's a busy man and certainly has more important things to do than escort me all day." This was perhaps the most Fia'd heard Tieg speak since they'd met. He delivered his words with a quiet confidence she decidedly admired. "If the work suits you," he addressed her directly, "and you're agreeable to the employment, you can then decide if you'd like to try things out in Feyport."

The way he looked at her as he said the last words made Fia feel as if he knew exactly why she was at the bookseller's the previous day. Had he read the desperation in her as she'd handed over the book for his inspection? Did he know she had intended to use the money to flee the city and the sister-in-law who barely tolerated her presence? It seemed impossible, but Fia had no other way to describe it.

"If you—and I suppose you, Oscar—agree, I can send word home to my sister. She and her husband run the inn in town, and she can let you a room that'll be both respectable and easily covered by the wage I'll be paying."

"Well, it seems you've got this all figured out, haven't you?" Claire remarked, her tone somewhere straddling relieved and incredulous.

Tieg didn't answer, but Simon smiled and gave his hands a clap. "I think it's a brilliant idea. If in fact, Fia here is willing! If she finds you to be a bore in the weeks to come, there's no harm in her saying so and remaining in the city. I for one would be happy to run into her on the street every now and then."

"I really don't think—" Oscar started but Fia could see the conflict in his eyes. His desire to protect his sister and her secrets was warring with his desire to make his wife happy and free up some space in their cramped home. His family was growing, and Fia was old enough to be taking care of herself.

She did wonder why Tieg would make such a offer when they'd only just met. Was it the book he was after?

In the end, she didn't need to think on it overly long. This plan of Tieg's provided a partial solution. Even if she ran away and disappeared, she would need a job eventually.

Before she could accept, however, there was something she needed to do. It would be bold to accept and move to a new town and away from Oscar, but it would take even more bravery to do it the right way. Tieg Connolly needed to know exactly what he was agreeing to. Someone somewhere was sure to see her at an inopportune moment and learn of her oddity.

Best to get everything out in the open now rather than waste everyone's time. If Tieg and Simon reacted as she expected they would, she would find another opportunity to slip away. At least if they were uncivil now, she'd have Oscar here to bolster her. It was preferable to being alone in a strange town when the inevitable time came.

Stealing herself, Fia took a deep breath. She reached up and plastered on her brightest smile. Then she removed her hat.

THREE

"I don't mean to be forward, Fia, but you are quite a lovely sight. Much better without the atrocious hat." Fia felt heat rising in her cheeks as Simon's kind words flooded her with a mixture of embarrassment and gratitude. "Would you not agree, Tieg?"

The younger man appeared to be at a loss for words, and Fia's heart fell. He simply looked at her, that odd bemused and slightly confused look on his face as if she'd told a rather odd joke and he was trying to work out the punch line. After several agonizing heartbeats, the confusion cleared into blank neutrality before he spoke. "Indeed, Simon. Miss Walsh is quite something to behold. Not sure how I initially took her for a lad." She wondered why he'd slipped back to the more formal address and if his tone was meant to be mocking or simply unimpressed. He was from Feyport after all. Maybe he saw young women with all manner of oddities.

It was too much for her to hope he truly wasn't taken aback by the sight of her without the camouflage her emerald cloche provided.

She knew what they saw. It was the same image that greeted her in the mirror every morning. A slender woman with delicate features, a slightly pointed chin, upturned nose and large pale eyes somewhere between moss and grey in color. Her ivory skin contrasted beautifully with the thick fringe of lashes and strawberry lips. Most would call her lovely and others beautiful. Until they noticed her hair—such a dark shade of green, it was almost black. If that wasn't bad enough, it was iridescent in the light—a rainbow of colors shimmering and shifting—not unlike the shell of a beetle. She'd dealt with the unusual shade of her hair all her life and had become adept at both keeping it hidden and accepting the reactions of people when she was occasionally caught out. She kept it short enough to tuck under a cap at all times but not so short it revealed her other peculiarity. The new one. The one she hadn't yet learned how to deal with completely. The one thankfully still hidden from those in the room.

Just above the apex of her ears, hidden among the green and polychromatic curls, the beginning knobs of boney keratin grew from her skull.

Fia wasn't singular in her odd appearance. Perhaps once a week she'd catch sight of someone in the city with oddly colored hair—pink or chartreuse, lavender or lime. She'd seen ladies with slightly pointed ears or mismatched eyes. She even witnessed an entire family with small tufted tails poking out of their trousers. But each time she noticed someone who seemed to have a touch of fey, she also noticed how they were kept at a distance by those around them. People in the city might be aware of these folks, but that didn't mean they accepted them. Fia had no desire to test the kindness of her neighbors and acquaintances. It was easier to hide among them.

"I understand, Mr. Connolly"—if he was going to be formal now, then so would she—"if you'd now like to rescind your offer of employment."

He tilted his head to the side, a furrow on his brow. "Why would I do that?"

Fia reached up and touched her head—patting her hair to ensure the nubs of horn were still hidden. "I think you'll find when I'm not conscientious with my appearance, I can be quite distracting." The number of times she'd heard the words *unnatural, demon, devil,* and *witch* in her lifetime were constant reminders of her difference. It didn't matter that she was also pleasant and kind, witty and generous. From the time of her earliest memories, it was the hair others saw. Not the smart and chipper young woman. Never that.

And now—saints help her—she'd begun sprouting horns in the past year. Only Oscar knew about them, but she suspected he might have told Claire. It would explain her more recent escalation in the dislike she held for Fia.

Oscar had offered to take her to a doctor when she'd finally worked up the courage to show him the lumps on her skull. He'd even suggested a surgeon in the hope they could be removed somehow. But Fia had adamantly refused. For now they could still easily be disguised under her hair, and until she knew more about herself and what they meant, she wasn't doing anything more drastic than wearing a hat.

"I'm not easily distracted," Tieg answered evenly, pulling Fia from her thoughts.

She dipped her chin slightly. "Perhaps not. But I'll wager your patrons are."

"On occasion, yes. It's a small town. People talk and some of them think it's their job to judge those around them. I'll not pretend otherwise. It's the way of people in general. I think you might find, however, for the most part, the good folks of Feyport have recently become a more welcoming lot. At least more so than some other places I've visited."

Fia wanted to smile at the idea, but she wasn't entirely convinced. In fact, she was certain she would never feel entirely comfortable anywhere. Occasionally she could get away with not wearing a hat at night, when the shadows hid her hair and the lack of sunlight dampened the iridescent sheen, but in any well lit place, she preferred to keep it covered and avoid any wayward glances or shocked slips of composure.

"But," Tieg continued, "if you're more comfortable in a hat, by all means, please wear it."

Claire stared at him and turned to Simon. "Are you not uncomfortable having her in your home?"

"Not in the least! I can assure you, Fia is more than welcome in my company."

Claire deflated a little, the smile replaced by a tight grimace.

Fia didn't understand. Claire clearly wanted her to meet Simon Beck and Tieg Connolly. Had insisted on it. She had to know they would eventually learn about Fia's appearance. If Fia didn't know better, she'd think their easy acceptance made Claire feel bad or at the very least concerned it cast her in an unsavory light.

Fia pulled the cloche back into place, snugging it down around her ears and the back of her neck. Simon and Tieg might say they were comfortable with her appearance, but Fia had no reason to either trust or believe them. Even if she did, one of the maids might enter at any time, and she certainly didn't want to invite any further discussion of her uncommon appearance.

Tieg Connolly described what he was looking for and what he'd already found. He also laid out a schedule of wages, timetables, and other items of only minimal import to Fia. She listened closely and asked a few additional questions, most of them trivial.

"We really should be getting home," Oscar said as he stood and helped Claire to her feet.

"Of course. But please consider yourselves welcome to call again." Simon smiled and walked them to the door, Tieg a step behind him.

"I'll be round to your place at half past eight in the morning. If you could compile a list of spots to visit tomorrow, it would be grand." Fia hadn't actually accepted the job, but she couldn't tell by Tieg's confidence. He nodded at Fia and dipped his head to Oscar and Claire before retreating back into the entry.

Fia walked behind her brother and his wife on the way home. She hadn't accepted officially, but she knew in her heart she would. The job was something, at least. Maybe she wouldn't need to part with her beloved book after all. She only hoped Tieg Connolly might forget she had it. Or, at the very least, make no attempt to buy it from her again. She didn't want a refusal to sell to jeopardize her opportunity. Either way, she was one step closer to giving Oscar and Claire the space they needed and one step closer to escaping the city. She couldn't decide if the idea thrilled or terrified her.

FOUR

As promised, Tieg arrived to collect Fia midmorning the following day. She'd never had a steady paying position before, only doing odd jobs and helping Claire around the house in exchange for a small allowance. As far as she understood things with Tieg, his offer didn't really sound like work at all. He simply wanted Fia to share her knowledge of the city and accompany him to various shops and studios. His plan was to purchase books and other items for transport back to Feyport. To her mind, that sounded a whole lot more like shopping and less like work.

Fia gleaned from the previous conversation that he'd been in the city for a few days already and had visited a handful of establishments—most on the main street running through the busy downtown district. Fia had mentioned a few other hidden gems, and he'd been eager if not exactly excited to see what she could recommend. In truth, Fia couldn't imagine Tieg being excited about anything. She'd yet to see the man emote more than a slight lifting of the brows or downturning of the lips. He seemed to have various degrees of bored, stern, and confused but no trace of happy or joyful.

She'd thought about that grim façade of his during several fitful hours in bed the night prior, worrying over her decision to accept this non-strenuous offer. She'd finally composed a list of suitable shops to visit and fallen asleep in the early hours of the morning.

When Tieg arrived at her doorstep, she was dressed simply in a knee length skirt, a soft blue cardigan, sturdy comfortable boots, and her favorite cap.

"Good morning, Mr. Connolly." She smiled as she pulled the door shut behind her.

Tieg pursed his lips. "Apparently I've offended you and the day is yet to begin."

Fia furrowed her brow. "Not offended, no."

"Then why the formality? I thought we'd come to an agreement yesterday." He walked beside her, hands clasped behind his back.

"I thought we had as well." *Until you saw my hair and got spooked.* "But as you are now my employer, I thought it best I not seem too familiar."

His lips tightened further, forming a hard line in his otherwise handsome face. "I can't argue with you obviously. So, *Miss Walsh*, have you the list I asked for?"

"I do."

"Can I see it?"

"Not unless you can read minds, Mr. Connolly." She tapped the side of her head. "It's all right in here. If I'm to go with you, I thought it was a waste to write it all out." One side of her mouth lifted then just as quickly fell as his brow furrowed further. After walking on in silence for another block, she sighed. "All right. I have several spots in mind, but it would help to know what exactly it is you're looking for."

"So you're accepting my offer then?"

"I am for the time being. Thank you."

He nodded.

"And I reserve the right to decide not to accompany you to Feyport."

"Of course."

It was Fia's turn to nod. "Well then?" She raised her brows in expectation of an answer to her earlier question.

"Books mainly," he said. "But any interesting artisans who might have small trinkets and baubles would also be nice. Reasonably priced art might be warranted, but that isn't top of the list. Anything slightly unusual or intriguing. I've no desire or need for the standard fare. Our local mercantile is well stocked, and the owners are friends of mine. I've no wish to compete against their business."

Fia gave a brief nod. "Three other bookshops spring to mind. All within an easy walk. It makes sense to try those first. Then there's a beautiful candlemaker and a shop that sells the cleverest little clocks and wind-up toys." She glanced sidelong in his direction and noted the cocked angle of his head. He was listening to her at least. "And then, there's my favorite shop in the entirety of the city. However . . ."

"However?"

"I'm not certain it will be exactly what you're looking for," she answered.

"Perhaps you'd let me be the judge of that."

"Right." She smiled broadly. "Gillian's. It's no bigger than a garden shed, tucked away on the alley behind the bakery with the warm sticky buns. It sells the most scrumptious soaps and lotions, bath salts, and oils."

"The bakery sells sticky buns and bath salts?"

The undiluted look of confusion on his face was too much, and Fia felt giggles bubbling up. "No. Gillian's sells the soaps and things. The bakery it sits behind sells the sticky buns."

Color rose on Tieg's face, and his frown deepened as he mumbled, "I'll keep it in mind." Fia did her best to stifle her laughter, but her cheeks ached with the effort. All the merriment left her when Tieg asked, "What about Oscar's establishment?"

"What about it?" she asked.

"Does his glass shop carry interesting things?" he replied, as if it should be obvious.

"Firstly, it isn't his shop. He's still apprenticing there. Secondly, I'm not sure you would call them interesting, but they *are* beautiful. Both those done by Oscar and those by Mr. Hastings. Though to be honest, Oscar does most of the work these days. I suppose if it's beautiful baubles you're after, it makes a certain amount of sense to add it to your list."

"Did Oscar make your necklace?" When Fia looked at him blankly he added, "The one of glass beads you were wearing yesterday?"

"Oh." She was surprised he'd noticed the small detail of her outfit. "Yes. He did."

"We should definitely add the shop to our list then."

A horse and cart rattled by on the cobblestones to their left, and Tieg held out his arm to pause Fia's steps lest she get splashed by the spray of murky puddle water thrown up in its wake. When the offending wagon had passed, they began walking again.

"Has he always been artistic?" He asked it casually but avoided looking at her directly.

"In a way. But he didn't really start to flourish until a few years ago. At least, not that I know of."

"That you know of?"

Fia paused. Talking about her childhood wasn't something she did often. Before she could think what to say, they reached the corner. Tieg stopped. Fia wasn't sure if he was waiting for an answer or for a break in the steady stream of wagons, carriages, and the occasional petrol-powered truck.

"The first bookshop is just this way." She pointed around the corner—a direction which didn't require the pair to cross the busy lane. Tieg nodded and sidestepped around a lamppost before regaining his place at her side. If he noticed she evaded his question, he didn't let on.

"I'll never get used to it." His voice was distracted as his eyes took in the city around them. "The noise and the crowds. So many people in too little space. And always in such a hurry."

As if to emphasize his point, a group of school-aged boys dashed around them from behind. They cackled and screeched. More like a flock of birds than children, Fia mused.

"It takes some getting used to," she said.

He glanced at her. "I'm no stranger to the city, mind you. I've visited often. Starting when I was young. But there's just something *overwhelming* about it all that I don't believe I'll ever love."

"I understand," Fia said.

"Do you?" His voice was thick with skepticism.

"I do. I wasn't raised here. I grew up in a small village."

"Oh?" He frowned.

It didn't curtail her enthusiasm at all. She continued to smile as she explained. "Mmm-hmm. I'm not really a city girl at heart. My parents had a small piece of heaven outside the village of Bodkin Green. Right along the brook. Not really a farm, but we had a couple of goats and some chickens. I loved it there." She'd loved the tiny stone cottage and the wide verdant fields, the little meandering brook where she grew up playing with pollywogs and the smell of animals and wild flowers in the air. Mostly though, she loved the time she'd spent with her parents and Oscar.

Before everything changed. Before the happy memories came fewer and farther between. The smile fell from her face and she stopped walking. She shook the memories from her mind and forced a half smile to her lips. "Never mind. Not important. Here we are."

She stopped in front of a faded navy door. The brass number 3 on the side frame was tarnished and off kilter—the bottom screw having vanished from the job.

Tieg rocked back on his heels, taking in the soaped-over windows and dust-coated lamp glass affixed to the post by the door. One large chunk of the globe was missing from view.

"Here?" The furrow between his brows was the deepest she'd seen yet.

"Yep. Here." Fia didn't know why, but the thought of proving his doubt unfounded made her smile even wider. She grabbed his elbow and guided him toward the door. "Come on, Mr. Connolly. I hardly think you'll be disappointed."

A bell warbled as they stepped over the threshold into the dim interior. It took a moment for Fia's eyes to adjust, but once they did, she turned and studied Tieg. Just as she'd predicted, he seemed anything but disappointed. In fact, as he stood wide-eyed and mouth slightly agape, she thought he finally looked like the young man he was.

He seemed to realize the expression he wore and quickly schooled his features back to calm and stoic. "This is . . . something, I'll admit."

Stretched out before them were row upon row of towering shelves. Each was packed with books of all shapes and sizes. Large tomes with three-inch bindings, miniature leather-clad volumes smaller than Fia's hand, slender books no more than fifty pages long. Some texts were bound with string and ribbon, others old and withered with cracked spines and yellowed pages. Any form or fashion a book could come in, there was sure to be an example in the ample shelves. Scattered among the texts, various bits of junk and ephemera peeked out. Glass globes, strange quills of brightly colored plumage from some undetermined species of bird, brass scales, and even a telescope complete with tripod inhabited the stacks.

"There's a hedgehog in here somewhere," Fia whispered. "I saw it the last time I visited."

Tieg only nodded as if a hedgehog in a bookshop was the most common thing in the world. He never once took his eyes from the row upon row of cases and their many parchment and leather treasures.

"What are we looking for specifically?" Fia asked, still not raising her voice. She was suddenly sure if she didn't direct him, they'd be standing in the entrance all day.

"No need to whisper. It's not a church. Nor is it a funeral," a cracked and scratchy voice called from behind the massive counter to their right.

Fia turned toward a woman who was neither old nor young, straightening from where she'd been bent over. Her arms were laden with books all jacketed in the same deep umber cloth. A worn tabacco stained pipe was clamped between her lips. She was squinting at them, either due to the dimness of the light or poor eyesight. Her hair was pulled back in the most painfully severe bun Fia had ever seen.

"How can I help ya?" The words were spoken from the side of her mouth not holding the pipe in place.

Tieg retrieved a sheet of cream paper from his jacket pocket and handed it to the shopkeeper. "Have you any of these titles?"

The woman squinted down at the list. "Oh aye. I've got several of 'em. A few though—these to the bottom of your page—are rather rare." She looked from the paper to Tieg, scrutinizing him.

Fia couldn't be certain, but she thought Tieg might be avoiding looking at her as he replied. "Yes. I'm aware."

"I've not got those. Not sure anyone in the city does." The pipe bobbed up and down with her words.

"I understand. I'd like to purchase the ones you do have." The shopkeeper nodded and disappeared into a back room, mumbling as she went.

A bit of movement accompanied by a low snuffling sound caught Fia's attention, and she looked down at a pale creamy grey hedgehog between Tieg's feet. She bent down to pet it along the bridge of its snout, and the animal cocked its head to observe her. If she didn't know better, she'd swear the soft spikey bundle was trying to communicate something to her with its eyes. What that communication might be, she could not guess. As she stroked between the animal's brows, it twitched its nose and scurried off. The hedgehog disappeared under a case brimming with books covering everything from animal husbandry to medieval medicinal herbs.

As she stood, she couldn't keep the smile from her face. Tieg, however, wore the same expression—a mixture of anger and confusion—she'd seen the previous evening. Her smile faltered, and she reached up to secure the hat on her head.

"You don't need to do that," he said, crossing his arms.

"Do what?" she asked.

"Fidget with the hat."

"I wasn't fidgeting," she argued. "And you don't have to scowl all the time."

He pursed his lips.

"I'm guessing you've never had to endure the types of taunts and foul looks I have." While Fia appreciated his unusually easy acceptance of her, she found it frustrating he didn't seem to realize how hard it could be to walk around in her skin.

"Maybe not, but you shouldn't let it get to you."

"Oh, I shouldn't, should I?" His frown deepened at her rising voice. She forced a smile and lightened her tone. "Maybe you haven't noticed, Mr. Connolly, but people have an inherent ability to be exceedingly cruel. Forgive me for not wanting to subject myself to it, every minute of every day."

Despite her false cheerfulness, Fia's eyes stung as tears threatened. Tieg Connolly opened his mouth, but whatever words he intended—apology or argument—never came. The shopkeeper returned with a heavy burden of books and thumped them down on the counter, and Fia wiped at her eyes and turned toward the shelves.

Tieg inspected each book individually—opening jackets, scrutinizing spines, and flipping through pages—as Fia silently browsed the shelves, one eye reading titles and the other searching for wayward hedgehogs.

Eventually Tieg agreed to all but two of the books and negotiated a price with the seller. He asked that they be delivered to Simon's residence, and for the money he was paying, the woman had no cause to refuse.

Fia and Tieg visited three other establishments over the course of the day, stopping only long enough to have a quick lunch of beef and potato hand pies which they—or more accurately Tieg—purchased from a vendor on the street. Sitting on a worn metal bench in a small square garden park, they ate in silence.

As the lamps began to pop to life up and down the city, Tieg left Fia at her door with a promise to return the following morning.

The pair passed several days in similar fashion. Fia provided locations and jubilant good humor while Tieg provided frowns, scowls, and the coins needed to complete each purchase. Several times Tieg voiced his concern they had run out of shops, but each instance resulted in Fia surprising him with a new spot to visit. Despite Fia's reluctance to be out in society, she'd wandered the streets of the city alone so many times and visited each small out-of-the-way shop often, quietly getting to know them and their proprietors over the years she'd lived in the city. Some of her ideas were more successful than others, and often they'd leave empty-handed or with only the smallest trinket to show for their efforts.

On the afternoon of the fourth day—after maligning his ability to locate some of the rare books he'd been seeking—Tieg suggested they call it quits early.

"Surely I've enough to be started with. Even if I lend out several of the popular titles, there will be plenty to make a go of it."

"But I've still got several more spots I think you might like," Fia informed him. "And we haven't visited Oscar's glass shop yet."

"Yes, well. We do know where to find him, don't we? It can rest a day or two." He ran a hand through his hair. "Besides, I have plans for the evening and could really use a washing up first."

"Oh." Fia blinked at him. "Oh, yes. Of course."

Tieg continued walking but said indifferently, "You could join me if you like."

"It's a business meeting then?"

"Yes and no. You'd need to wear a nice dress and maybe the beautiful string of beads." He slid a sidelong glance at her.

Fia pulled out the hem of her sweater and studied the worn wool. "What kind of business meeting are we talking about?"

"Not a meeting. A poetic reading. At the Krenshaw."

Fia's eyes grew larger. The Krenshaw was a small but very upscale theater nestled in the heart of the art district. It was frequented by the elite of the city, not glassblowers' sisters and small town librarians.

"If I'm not mistaken, for the Krenshaw I'd need a bit more than a clean dress and some glass beads."

"Believe me, on you a simple dress will be more than fine."

Fia looked at him from the corner of her eye. *Was that a compliment?*

"I'm not planning on mingling with the posh city crowd," he continued.

Apparently not.

"The poet is a fellow I knew growing up. I'm just planning to listen in and see if his new work is worth ordering copies." He looked away as he spoke, and Fia got the impression he wasn't being entirely truthful. "If you'd rather not attend, I understand. I simply thought if I had to go, I might try to enjoy myself."

"And you think having me along will make it more enjoyable?" Her voice was laced with skepticism.

"Is that hard to believe?" he asked.

Yes, she thought. *It is.*

Fia contemplated declining, but honestly, when would she ever receive an invitation to an event at the Krenshaw from a handsome man again? Even if it was to stand in the back in a shabby dress with a man who never smiled and happened to be her employer.

She smiled broadly. "I'd be delighted."

This time, Tieg couldn't keep the surprise from his face. It gave Fia a bubble of joy to watch his brows lift and his eyes widen before settling back into the placid mask he favored.

FIVE

The Krenshaw was everything Fia had imagined and more. Despite the gilded moldings and luxurious rugs, she couldn't call it opulent exactly. Opulence would degrade it somehow. No, the Krenshaw was sumptuous and extravagant and so much more. It was *magical.*

Even positioned in the back as they were, Fia could still take in the rich texture of the teal wallpaper and the tiny twinkling lights dotting the high ceiling. She could smell the oak banisters and taste the perfume and cigar smoke flavoring the air. The acoustics alone were a marvel, but altogether it was a gluttony for the senses and she couldn't feast enough. Hiding became difficult when all she wanted to do was reach out and explore.

The poet lounged in a velvet throne atop a small stage centered in a round open atrium. Occasionally rising to his feet to read from the small book clasped in his hands, his voice carried in the space, reaching even to the back. He wasn't much to look at—of middle age, black hair greying at the temples and a body gone soft around the midsection. He was dressed casually with his shirt undone at the collar and trousers a little sagged in the seat. And even though Fia found his voice to be a touch too nasally and pinched, he held the room in rapture at his words. One woman was near swooning as he spoke of love and despair, ruin and triumph. Others dabbed their eyes with silk squares. Men offered eager applause following a ballad of sorts.

Fia didn't understand the reaction. It all seemed a little too melodramatic, but what did she know? She was no scholar or artist. Didn't study languages or hold degrees. But somewhere, deep in her core, she thought she knew what true beauty was. This was not true beauty. Yet the words seemed to reach out and grab every other person in the room by the throat. Every other person that was save Tieg.

More than once she'd heard a sigh of boredom or a snort of derision. At one point, he'd even chuffed out a bark of what could only have been laughter. She couldn't be certain, however, having never actually heard Tieg laugh. The noise had earned him several disgruntled looks from the patrons crammed in around them.

It was this more than anything else that caused Fia to loose her own snort of surprise when the reading came to a close and Tieg informed her he wanted to join the queue forming to speak with the poet.

"I mentioned I knew the man, didn't I?" he said by way of explanation.

"You did. You aren't going to waste your coins on a copy though, right?" He didn't respond. "*Right?*"

She didn't know why, but something about the reading had left her unsettled.

Tieg chuckled and Fia's breath caught. He'd actually laughed. Not that she was trying to be particularly funny, but he had laughed. Would wonders never cease.

"What?" he asked.

"Careful. If you were to actually smile, your face might freeze like that. Then what would you do?" She smirked in his direction.

The furrow returned to his brow.

Fia looked at her feet—clad in barely passable heeled oxfords—to hide her amusement.

After endless minutes of waiting, the pair finally made it to the front of the line. The poet chatted happily with an older man and his much younger companion. The poet's words were lazy and his smile smug as he described finding inspiration for his work while traveling abroad.

"How lovely. I'm sure the freedom was exhilarating," the man commented. "Lived like a bachelor, did you?"

"Never," the poet replied. "Brigid is my muse." He gave a small wink. "And where I travel so too does my charming wife. And of course our son, Glendon."

The poet accepted a handshake before the couple moved along, and Tieg and Fia took their places. Fia watched with some fascination as the smug smile melted from the man's face at the sight of them. Or more accurately—for he hadn't even glanced at Fia—at the sight of Tieg.

"Connolly," the poet said, and there might have been a tremor in his voice.

"Owen Johnston," Tieg replied. "You've come up even further in the world. Folks do love a good story, it seems." If his voice was generally cool, this was downright icy.

"They love a good *poem*," Owen Johnston replied.

Tieg's lips thinned to a straight line, and he gave a short jerk of his head. "If you say so."

"I do. Well, I hope you enjoyed the reading." They were being dismissed, yet Tieg made no move toward the door. They stood there for a moment before the poet turned to Fia, perhaps to enlist her help in removing Tieg from his presence. She noted the change in the older man's eyes. The barest sharpening. Tieg must have noticed as well.

"My assistant," he said. "Fia Walsh." And did she imagine the slight recoil at her name? Surely not. "Fia, this *talented* poet is Owen Johnston."

"It's a pleasure to meet you, Mr. Johnston." Fia extended her hand.

"Yes, well, I am always eager to meet those who are patrons of the arts." He tilted his head and studied her. "No, surely not. . ." he muttered then caught himself. Clearing his throat, he extended a hand waiting for a book that would never materialize. "Can I sign a copy for you?"

Fia frowned. "I'm afraid I don't have one, but the reading was enjoyable." She hated to lie but could think of nothing else to say.

"Perhaps we can pick one up. Stop by the studio and have you sign it?" Tieg ventured. "I'd love to see Mrs. Johnston and catch up with Glendon."

Owen's face tightened even more as he grimaced. Fia had seen a similar expression from Mr. Hastings when he suffered bouts of rheumatism. "Of course. That would be fine." He bit the words out. "Glendon would be thrilled to see you, I'm sure."

He flicked his eyes to Fia one last time before turning his back on them completely and addressing the young woman in the line behind them. Conversation over.

Fia and Tieg made their leave. As they waded through the sea of people clogging the lobby, Fia could feel the eyes upon her. She looked down at her simple dress. It was a plain shift of pale lavender with a satin trim. It had been her mother's. Along with the green leather book, they were the only things she had from her parents. Fia had worn the shift only once before—to Oscar and Claire's wedding. It made her feel pretty, but looking around, her confidence wavered.

Several women whispered to one another behind silk gloved hands. Several men drank her in as she passed.

Their appreciative glances were tampered by the knowledge that the stares would turn to looks of disgust were she to remove her cloche.

Everywhere she looked, glittering beaded gowns and crisp starched jackets filled her vision. She reached to adjust the felt hat she wore, but before she could touch it, a warm strong hand engulfed hers.

"Chin up, Fia. You look quite captivating. More so than any of these lacquered birds." Tieg tucked her hand into his elbow and continued toward the door.

A curious flutter erupted somewhere between Fia's breastbone and her stomach. She lifted her chin as her employer suggested—a bright and brilliant smile on her face.

SIX

"Well my friend," Simon drawled lazily. "You've done a bang up job of it."

"Of what?" Tieg lifted a brow.

"Getting under a certain poet's skin." There was a twinkle in the older man's eye as he sat sipping whiskey near the fire.

Thank all that is good he's on my side, Tieg thought. *He's enjoying himself entirely too much.*

Keeping his voice level, he responded, "I can't help it that the snake finds my presence uncomfortable."

Simon rested the crystal glass on the arm of his chair. "I dare say he's a tad more than uncomfortable."

"His state of distress is none of my business," Tieg replied unconvincingly.

"And yet, you not only attended his big event, but you just happened to bring Fia along with you to parade under his nose."

"Fia has nothing to do with it."

Simon scoffed. "Doesn't she?"

"Simon. I've known the woman all of a week. My *dislike* for Johnston stretches back years."

Dislike was so mild a word it was laughable. Disdain. Disgust. *Hatred?* Each was true, yet the swirling black emotion that flooded Tieg anytime he thought of Owen Johnston was so much bigger than disdain. So much darker than disgust. So much more searing than hatred. It was all of those things and none of them.

"I am aware," Simon said. "However, you easily could have gone alone. You simply chose not to."

Tieg sighed and tipped his head back against the top of the wingback chair. "I did. I'd tell you the reason if I understood it myself." He thought for a moment, trying to find the best way to explain. Still staring at the ceiling, as if the answers to all the world's mysteries were spelled out in the cream tiles, he said, "There's something about her. Something familiar but intangible. It plays at the edges of my brain, and I keep hoping if I take her out of focus for just a moment, it will snap to and I'll understand."

Simon frowned at his friend. "I thought it was quite obvious. The hair on the girl alone is enough to make the connection, is it not?"

"Yes, of course there's the hair." Tieg tried to sound less exasperated than he felt. "Clearly it's similar, but there's more to it than that."

"More to it than that?" Simon was incredulous. "Honestly, Tieg. How often have you seen a woman with beetle shell hair and a face men would kill over?" *Exactly once.* "They must be related."

Fia was extraordinary for a multitude of reasons, but Tieg knew who Simon was referring to. Though the woman in question had also been keen to keep her differences hidden.

"Believe me. I've thought about it. I'm not sure how Brigid Johnston and Fia are tied, but you're likely right. There's something else though. I feel this energy—this buzz—when she's near me. I can't explain it."

Simon barked a laugh. "If you can't explain it, then you *are* in trouble. Do I need to explain the birds and the bees to you, my friend? That girl is a walking dream."

Tieg shot him a violent look. "That is not what I meant."

Simon held up his drink in a silent toast that had Tieg rolling his eyes. "Well, whatever it is, I hope you figure it out soon."

"I do too. My time in the city is short, and there is nothing I wouldn't do to destroy Owen Johnston. Whether I like it or not, Fia may just be the key to bringing him down."

Fia sat on the floor of the large reception room and sorted through another crate of books. It was the fourth carton she'd examined that morning. Simon wandered in on occasion to see if she could be persuaded into conversation, and each time he did, Tieg would materialize within moments to chase him away.

"I'm paying her to assist me with my books, not to entertain you, Simon."

"Yes, well, it's not as though this is my home or anything," Simon grumbled before leaving the room once again.

"I *can* focus on sorting and still maintain some conversation," Fia said.

Tieg didn't look at her as he read from the list. "I'm sure you can. Bring me the stack of folklore, please."

He had several empty cartons around him and was filling them with the sorted books by subject. He thought it would make the unpacking easier when they eventually got to Feyport.

Fia stood and stretched, twisting her back to release some tension before she scooped up the small stack of books Tieg had requested.

"Do you plan to read all of this yourself?" she asked as she handed them to him.

"I'd love to say yes, but I think that's a tad optimistic." He looked at the spines as he placed them in the crate. "I've read some of them already. Others I've skimmed. Some hold no interest for me, but I've had folks request them personally. Then there are those I've only heard about and can't wait to dive into." Fia didn't think she'd ever seen the man look so wistful, but that was the only word she could use to describe his face in the moment. "I've been searching for a few of them for years. Ever since I could walk to the shops on my own."

Fia wondered how on earth he could have known about exotic and rare books as a child but didn't dare to ask. Instead, she went with a safer question.

"How do you know if they're any good?"

He looked up at her with a half smile on his handsome face. It made him look younger then, more alive. *He loves this*, she thought.

"I don't. But what's good to me might not be to someone else and vice versa."

"Won't it be sad when you finally read them?" she asked.

"Sad? No. Why would you think so?" he looked up and studied her as she meandered in a small circle.

"Well, because then you'll have nothing left to look forward to. The anticipation will be gone. What if it isn't as great as you hoped it would be?"

"There's always going to be another, Fia. Always the next great read. As long as there is paper and ink, as long as people are willing to share their thoughts and fantasies, their knowledge and fears, there will be no shortage of great books to read." His tone was matter of fact and confident.

He stopped watching her and went back to the stack in front of him.

She thought about his words as she looked over his shoulder at the same stack. "If you were to recommend a book to me, which would it be?"

His face grew thoughtful.

"I'd recommend you start with the one you already possess."

Fia's eyes snapped to his.

"Did you think I'd forgotten you had it?" His tone wasn't teasing exactly, but it might have been close.

"No," she said softly, eyes cast down. "But I'd hoped you had. I don't want to sell it."

"I'm not asking you to *sell* it, Fia. I'm asking you to *read* it."

He must have deduced from her expression that day outside the bookseller's that while she did possess the book and value its importance to her, she hadn't read it yet. There was no way, however, for him to know why she hadn't.

"I've tried." During her sorting, Fia had left a pathway between the furniture and the stacks of books. She paced from the doors to the window to Tieg and his crates. Then she did the circuit around and back again. "The words are there and I can see them, but as soon as my eyes leave the page, they swirl and shift in my mind. The illustrations too. It's as if the book doesn't want to be read."

Tieg frowned at her words. "But you *can* read?

"Of course I can read," she snapped. "I wouldn't have asked for the recommendation if I couldn't read."

He put up his hands. "I didn't mean to suggest. . . Look I'm sorry. That came out wrong. I just don't understand. Is it in Latin or French or something?"

Fia sighed. "No, the words are just typical words and I can make them out at first glance, but then they dance about. I can't explain it any better than that."

"Would you be willing to let me look at it? I've heard stories about a book like yours, and I knew it was special that day in the street. Maybe I can help."

Fia twisted her fingers together as she walked back and forth. She ran a hand up the side of her neck and tugged at the hair falling loose near her face. She'd slipped her hat off that morning when she entered the study, when Simon had assured her the servants weren't to interrupt them. It was refreshing to be in the company of someone other than her brother who didn't mind her unusual appearance.

"I don't know. It's very precious to me. If something were to happen to it. . ."

"I understand," Tieg said. Gone was the wistful expression.

"I'm not sure you do. My parents died when I was very young. I remember them, but only in glimpses and glimmers. Oscar wasn't exactly a man, but he was old enough to come to the city. Not old enough however to care for a child. I went to live just outside the village, in a boarding school of sorts, that accepted a handful of orphans in addition to the students whose parents could pay. The lady there, Miss Magpie, was kind. So were some of the children. But not most. When Oscar was settled and I was old enough, I came to live with him.

"My point is, I have only a few memories of my parents, a dress that was my mother's and that book. Nothing else. Even though its meaning is lost on me, it *means* the world to me."

Tieg sat forward, elbows resting on his spread knees. "I understand," he repeated. "I'll not bother you about it again." He ran a hand through his hair and looked at the stack by his feet. With a grim nod, he handed a slim canvasbound book to Fia. The title was worn on the cover—*Folklore and the Fey*. "This is what I'd recommend."

A few days after Fia and Tieg's discussion of her book, Tieg informed Fia he had some business to attend to out of the city.

"Take a couple of days off; you deserve it," he said as he climbed into the wagon he'd hired for the journey.

She had been tempted to ask if she shouldn't come along and assist him but realized how that might come across not only to Tieg, but to any of their other acquaintances. And after Oscar's initial reaction to her moving, she doubted he would allow it at any rate. Instead, she accepted the week's wages Tieg handed her and planned on treating herself to some honey cakes and a quiet evening at home.

Snugging her cap down tight, Fia walked toward the confectionery. The city at twilight was one of her favorite things. She could feel the tension of the populace melting away along with the sun. The lamps flickered on and the foot traffic diminished. As she crossed the city center, and the park at its heart, the moisture from the grass kissed her skin and she delighted in the smell of the blooms on the trees.

At the sweet shop, she treated herself to a small parcel of honey cakes as well as a bag of caramel toffee. As an afterthought, she also purchased a small packet of peppermint drops for Claire. Hopefully they would help to settle her sister-in-law's pregnancy-induced dyspepsia and, perhaps in turn, her temper. It was a stretch, but Fia was willing to spare the pennies for even the faintest hope.

She was surprised to find Oscar and Claire out when she returned home. A pot of soup rested on the stove, so she helped herself to a bowl and left the peppermints and a few toffees on the table as an offering. She was going to head upstairs when the kitchen door banged open. Claire lumbered in, followed by Oscar, who staggered under the ungainly weight of a small cradle. Fia moved to help her brother and Claire immediately dropped into a vacated seat, moaning about her feet all the while.

Fia and Oscar lugged the cradle up the stairs and placed it in Fia's room, as it was soon to be the baby's nursery.

"Got it for a song," Oscar said when he stepped back.

Fia ran a hand over the smooth wood. It rocked gently under her touch. The headboard was beautifully carved in a pattern of birds taking flight from a single delicate branch of oak.

"On second thought, maybe we should move it into our room. In case you change your mind about the move to Feyport," her brother said. "Don't want you to feel like we're pushing you out."

She waved him off. "Don't be silly."

Oscar ran a hand through his hair. "You'll always be welcome, Fi."

Fia stood and wrapped an arm around her brother's shoulder, resting her chin against him. "I know."

"They'd be so proud of you." Oscar didn't need to elaborate further. Fia knew he meant their parents.

The tender moment was broken when Claire cleared her throat from the doorway.

Oscar took this as his cue and informed both women he was going to wash up and head downstairs to eat before the soup got cold.

"A moment, Fia," Claire said when Fia moved to follow her brother out.

Fia forced a smile. "Of course."

"I told Oscar I'd speak to you," Claire began. She hadn't come all the way into the room but stood just over the threshold, hands on the small of her back and eyes on the cradle.

"Oh?" Fia responded.

"Yes, and I heard what he told you just now about staying with us rather than moving to Feyport." Fia's eyes widened slightly. Was Claire going to ask her to stay as well? Perhaps to help with the care of the baby?

"Normally I'd support Oscar in any decision he'd make, but not this, Fia. *Not this*." Of course. She'd been a fool to hope Claire would want her any longer. "You are to take the position in Feyport. Go with Mr. Connolly. He doesn't seem to mind your . . . *peculiarities*. Start a new life *there*. Let us live a normal life *here*."

Fia couldn't think of a thing to say, so she simply nodded and willed the tears burning her eyes not to fall. At her silence, Claire finally looked at her. "I know you think I'm a terrible person, Fia. I'm not. The first time I met you, I was head over heels for Oscar. You know that. And because I loved him so much, I tried desperately to like you. Not just like you. I wanted to *love* you as much as I loved him. Well, I can't, Fia. I've tried and I just can't."

Fia couldn't find any words that would be suitable, so she remained silent. Claire turned to leave and Fia quietly closed the door behind her.

Only then did she let the tears fall.

SEVEN

Tieg had seen his fair share of tiny villages and small towns. They dotted the hills from the city to Feyport and beyond. Each and every one had its own personality. Some were quaint, others depressed. Some welcomed visitors with wide open arms, and some—buried under layers of fear and superstition—walled themselves in. He loved finding something unique in each place. For Feyport, that uniqueness wasn't a tangible thing. Not just the sea at its edge and the fearful respect of it. Not just the fields of barley and the smell of the distillery in the air. Not the people or the festivals, the shops or the church. It was a feeling he got when he was close to his home. A tingle of something special and unnamed. And of all the towns and villages he'd come across in his travels, he'd never felt anything close to it.

Not until he got off the road in Bodkin Green, that was. It was uncanny, the feeling. As much as he tried, he couldn't make sense of it. The small farm village of Bodkin Green didn't look, smell, or sound like the coastal town of Feyport. But he felt it just the same.

The hired wagon dropped him near a small square, with the understanding that the driver would retrieve him from the same spot in two days time.

The village had a small inn, a public house, a church. Several shops dotted the perimeter of the communal green square. He spotted a few sheep wandering along a fence line and heard the clatter of wagon wheels. The source of the sound was a run-down contraption approaching from the opposite direction. A well-fed cow, led by a rope tied to the wagon, walked behind it. Tieg waved in greeting and was pleased when the leathery man at the reins waved back.

Breathing in the fresh country air and the feeling of home, Tieg made his way to the inn. He wasn't entirely prepared for the wave of homesickness that struck him when he entered and was greeted by a middle-aged woman with apple cheeks and a flour-dusted apron.

"Checking in for the night?" The innkeeper was older than his sister by a good handful of years, but her warm smile and no nonsense efficiency made him think of Candice just the same.

He couldn't help but smile as he answered. "Two nights actually. If you've got them." In actuality, he had assumed they would have space but hadn't thought of what he might do if they didn't. Sleep under the stars, he supposed. He'd done it before and would certainly do it again if necessary, but he'd much rather be comfortable if possible. This quick trip might be challenging enough without a sore back to add to it.

As it happened, he was right not to worry. The inn was nearly empty, and he could take a room for as long as he liked. Tieg paid the woman for the space as well as dinner upfront and was rewarded with a tidy room complete with clean sheets and an enchanting view of the countryside and pastures below. After washing up, he ate a quick meal of cold ham on hearty bread and set off to begin conducting his business. He strolled around the small village and spoke with a few of the shop owners and a farmer or two, then returned to the inn and fell asleep with the window open and the blissful sound of country silence filling his ears.

The next morning he was up with the sun. The innkeeper pointed him in the right direction and assured Tieg he could make it to the boarding school in no time at all; he only needed to follow a small side road around the pasture and past a winding bend near the brook.

As he made his way up the packed earth lane, he took in the tiny stone cottages and expansive fields of early spring grass. He could hear the water bubbling merrily as he strolled and knew he must be approaching the brook the innkeeper had mentioned. He remembered Fia saying her childhood home had been near a brook, and he looked around as if expecting the farm to somehow make itself known to him. Nothing aside from large green pastures came into view as he ventured closer to the sound of water running.

The nearer he got to the hidden brook, the more the sound seemed to warp and change. What had once been the bubble and flow of water over stones soon became the sound of childlike laughter, at once vibrant and menacing.

A cloud passed over the sun and a chill went up Tieg's spine. He had the distinct impression of being watched. He couldn't see the brook from his point on the road, but what appeared to be a small stone bridge was coming into view. The water flowing through the fields must pass under it. Had the innkeeper mentioned a bridge? He couldn't recall.

The feeling of being watched grew thicker, and Tieg found himself stopping to look behind him. The wind ruffled the taller bits of grass and wild flowers, but otherwise he could detect no movement.

There'd been times like this back in Feyport when he would get the sense of something in the barley or lurking in the ocean waves. And while he'd never encountered any of the fey folk there, he was sure they existed. In fact, he and Glendon Johnston had spent countless days scouring every inch of the land surrounding the area in futile attempts to find them. Not long ago, there'd even been talk of a selkie among them for a time. His brother-in-law swore it was true. Tieg himself had seen the man in question a few times—once at the annual jubilee and then here and there with one of the local girls. Not being a close friend of hers, he'd never worked up the courage to ask her about it, but he desperately hoped it was true. The world needed more magic in it. His trip today was an effort to uncover another possible bit.

He got his feet moving again and eventually came to the small bridge. It was just wide enough for a modestly sized wagon to cross. Tieg dipped his head to see if anything lurked below. No sprites or nixies waited to pull him down. The sound of laughter still tickled his ears, but it was once again mixed with the burbling water.

Tieg shook his head at his own foolishness. From the top of the bridge, he could make out the bend in the road and the stone buildings of the school beyond. The sound of the laughter was coming from the dozen or so children playing in the expansive gardens surrounding the largest of the buildings.

Tieg made his way around the bend and to the front of the campus. A fair-sized two story building sat in the center. The slate roof was covered in moss and had a discolored metal gutter ringing it. A crooked weathervane sat perched above the chimney where a thin trickle of smoke was escaping.

Children ranging in age from toddlers to teens ran and played in the grass. Here and there, rings of flowers grew among the manicured lawn. Several shrubs had been trimmed into shapes—a toadstool, a frog, even a teapot.

The stone wall surrounding the property was low enough to see over but tall enough to keep the smallest children safely within its confines.

As he opened the gate, Tieg winced at a harsh painful squeal. A powder of rust came away with his hand. He smacked his hands together to rid the worst of the debris and walked up the cobbled path to the front door. He was stuck by the incongruous nature of the school, some parts lovingly tended and others in complete disrepair.

A small brass bell dangled at the entrance, and Tieg pulled the frayed rope attached to it. Several of the children looked up from their activities to study him.

A minute ticked by, then two, before he heard noise from the other side of the door. A girl of about fifteen swung the door wide and stood staring at him. She had wide set eyes and a space between her front teeth to match.

"Hello. My name is Tieg Connelly. I've come to speak with the headmistress."

The girl cocked her head to the side and studied him with a decidedly feline gaze. "Is she expecting you, sir?"

"Ah, no. No, she isn't. But I was hoping to steal a moment of her time."

"The headmistress is awfully busy, sir."

"I understand, but I've traveled quite a distance to get here. If she's not available today, perhaps I could call again tomorrow?" Tieg really didn't want to leave without speaking to the woman who ran the school. But short of barging in and demanding an audience, there really wasn't much he could do if she didn't have time to see him. He hoped he hadn't come all this way on a fool's errand.

The girl looked unsure but turned on her heel and tilted her head toward a small waiting area just inside the door.

Tieg nodded his thanks and sank into a worn brocade chair. Like the grounds outside, the interior of the main building was a mix of décor at various levels of upkeep. Large blooms of fresh flowers in beautiful arrangements sat on chipped and rickety tables. Gorgeous stained glass windows were half covered by thin but clean curtains. A gleaming brass clockface rested in a battered casing , the mechanism ticking loudly in time with the sound of children playing from outside. As Tieg's eyes drifted from place to place, they caught on not one or two, but five separate small dishes of what appeared to be cream scattered about the room, one on either side of the door and three others perched on windowsills. Perhaps the school had a collection of cats.

Tieg waited for approximately ten minutes before a harried woman popped through the door, tucked a stray strand of greying hair behind her ear, and introduced herself. "Sorry to keep you waiting, Mr. Connolly. I was just finishing up some things when Hazel let me know you were here. I'm Miss Magpie."

Tieg rose from his seat and dipped his head toward the headmistress. "It's a pleasure to meet you, Miss Magpie. I was hoping to take a moment of your time to see if you could help me with a mystery I'm trying to unravel."

"Not sure I can help, but I'll give it a try," the woman said. "If you'll follow me."

Tieg trailed the petite woman through a doorway leading to an open hall running the length of the building. Doors—mostly open—lined either side, and Tieg caught glimpses of what appeared to be a music room, a small library, and a classroom full of cramped oak and metal desks, as well as what might have been an solarium of sorts. To the left, he noted a large dining area with rows of long tables, surrounded by small chairs; to the right, he could hear sounds from a kitchen farther off in the distance.

Miss Magpie moved at a sharp clip, and even though Tieg's legs were almost twice as long, he found he had to hurry to keep pace with her. When they reached the far end of the hall, the small woman opened one of the few closed doors and stepped inside what appeared to be an office. She sat behind a rickety desk, and he took the chair opposite.

Watching her flit down the hall and now tidying a stack of unruly papers on the desk, Tieg realized how fitting the woman's name was. Her small frame and wispy hair certainly gave the impression of a bird. Her small dark eyes held an intelligence as they observed him over the laced knuckles she rested against her chin.

"So, what might I help you with?" she asked.

"It has to do with one of your former students," Tieg replied.

Miss Magpie stared at him for a moment and made a tsking noise. "I thought as much. Unless they are bringing me a child to enroll, it's the reason most find time to visit us here. But you should know, I don't generally give out information about my students, and certainly not to strangers."

"I understand and appreciate your position." Tieg spoke frankly. "It happens that this former student has come to be in my employ, and I'm concerned about her welfare."

She nodded at him to continue.

"Her name is Fia Walsh," Tieg said.

Miss Magpie continued to study him over fingers that had moved from laced to steepled, but still she remained silent.

"I'm certain you'd remember her," Tieg said. "She would be hard to forget what with the beetle shell hair."

Miss Magpie let out a long breath, her face holding a determination that Tieg respected.

"You see, Miss Walsh is helping me to build a library and accompanying gift shop of sorts. We're currently in the city, but I'm hoping to be on our way to Feyport within the week. It would help me to understand her background before expecting her to relocate to a small town she's never seen."

The headmistress nodded quietly but didn't immediately speak. After some time, she said, "I do know Fia. She was one of my favorite students. Last I knew she was moving with her brother to the city. It sounds like that's where you've met her. I'm not sure I can give you any more information than that. Perhaps you might consider discussing her background with her?" She raised her brows in a way that suggested he hadn't yet tried this tactic. "I'm certain the young woman I knew would be more than capable of knowing her own mind and making her own decisions."

He flushed a bit at the implied accusation. "Don't get me wrong. I agree wholeheartedly with you."

"Do you?" Clearly she didn't believe him at all.

"I do. But I am concerned she might not be aware of some aspects of her past." When the headmistress didn't speak, he continued, "She is indeed still in the city and living with her brother Oscar. I'm happy that she has agreed to come with me to Feyport. I think the settling there may be more favorable for her. I assure you, I have only her best interest in mind. The city can be . . . unkind at times. I know she'll miss Oscar. His wife Claire, perhaps less so. At any rate, I'm hoping to help her settle there and would love to make the transition as easy as possible. Is there nothing else you can tell me about her family?"

"Well, if you know she's with her brother, I don't suppose it could hurt to tell you a bit more. As far as I know, Fia came from a very happy family. Her parents doted on the pair of them. Everyone in the town knew it. When she was eight years old, a tragedy struck, and their parents were both killed. Oscar, being only a young man himself, couldn't take care of Fia in the city, but he was too old to live with me. He struck out on his own, and from what I understand has made a go of it there as a glassblower."

"You've been keeping tabs," Tieg said. "I've yet to visit his shop but have seen some of his work firsthand, and it's quite impressive."

"I get word every now and then." Miss Magpie stared out the window. "I'm glad he's doing well. He was a kind boy, and as I've said, Fia was always one of my favorites. She was a sweet girl and willing to help around the home. She's bright, and she did well in her lessons. But as I'm sure you can imagine, not all of the children were as accepting of her as I was. We do get the occasional soul in here who seems a bit off or a bit odd. I always do my best to protect them, but children can be mean just because they don't always know better. Or because they do know and relish in the teasing. Either way, Fia handled it all with a grace and loveliness I don't often see. She was the kind to try to make friends first and defend herself only if absolutely necessary."

Tieg thought of this, and it seemed to fit with the person he had come to know. Fia was always a ray of sunshine, even when he said something to offend her. When someone made a comment about her differences, she handled it beautifully even if she'd rather simply hide herself away. It was a trait to be admired.

He was lost in his thoughts when Miss Magpie spoke again. "So, Feyport, Mr. Connolly? You've lived there some time?"

"Yes." He cleared his throat. "It's my home. I was born there, and I suspect it's where I'll be buried."

"I've heard of it. By all accounts, it has a similar reputation as Bodkin Green." Her eye held a special sort of gleam. "That is why you wish Fia to move there?"

"I wish for her to go with me because I need help in my shop," he replied. "As you said, Fia is rather bright. She has a keen eye for the goods I'll be selling and the kind of temperament that suits the library I'm starting. But it does stand to reason that life might be a bit easier for her in Feyport than it is in the city."

"Is she still wearing the cap all the time?" she asked. "You know, I bought her a new one every year as she got older. Most days I could convince her to take it off for an hour or two, but the very next day, I'd find her with it tucked on tight again."

Tieg smiled at the kindness in the woman's eyes. "I've tried to get her to relinquish it from her head but have only managed to succeed on the rarest of occasions," he said. "Always, when she is out and about, her head is covered and she seems much more confident with that being the case."

"Some habits are hard to break. Particularly when they are born from bad experiences." The headmistress was likely well aware how childhood could shape a person.

"Do you think it odd she bears little resemblance to her brother?"

"Not particularly. Many children resemble one parent or another. Many more look like only themselves. It doesn't mean they aren't family."

"Did you know her parents well?"

"Not exceptionally well, but as I've mentioned, everyone in Bodkin Green knows everyone else to a certain extent." She studied him with her birdlike eyes.

"Miss Magpie, there is no delicate way to put this. Are you convinced that Fia was actually the Walshes' God-given child?"

"Oh," she mused. "I was wondering if that might be where this was going. I have no reason to suspect that she's not. However, it surprised most of the folks in town when Ed and Sheila Walsh had a second child. Oscar was quite a bit older and it didn't seem they would be blessed with any more babies. Then one day, Sheila came into town with that sweet bundle of joy. They treated her like a princess. No one could've loved that baby more than her parents did."

"I have another question for you." When she motioned with her hand for him to continue, he asked, "Have you ever met anyone with the same physical characteristics as Fia?"

"I've seen many things, Mr. Connelly," she said, "but the hair on that girl is something unique. I have some suspicions, but that's all I'll say on the matter."

Now it was Tieg's turn to nod. "One more thing, when I first met Fia she showed me a small, personal treasure."

"The book?"

"Yes, the book."

"I don't know what it is." She moved her hands and placed them flat on the desk in front of her. "All I know is it was one of the few possessions she brought with her from her home when she came to me. She said it was her mother's, and her parents always insisted she keep it safe."

Tieg was quiet for a moment. The pain of losing his own parents was still raw, and he ached to think of the tiny green-haired girl experiencing that sort of grief. "How did they die?"

"It was a tragic accident. They'd gone out on the water—where the brook empties into a small lake just south of here—for an afternoon. The boat they were in capsized. They drowned not ten feet from the bank. Thank the saints Oscar and Fia weren't with them that day. Then we might have lost all four."

Tieg, having gotten what he was after, thanked Miss Magpie for her kindness and promised to send word once they were settled in Feyport. He had no intention of telling Fia that he'd visited her old school, but he certainly couldn't share that information with the headmistress.

As they walked to the front of the small building, Miss Magpie stopped him. "Please do tell Fia she's always welcome here. If she needs a place to stay I've got a job for her. She can always help with the smaller children."

Tieg shook his head. "I'll pass on the information, but I'm hoping she finds her place with me."

EIGHT

Mr. Hastings held the bright persimmon and marigold globe up to a candle. Light bounced through it, dancing and shimmering around the shop. Fia couldn't contain the contented sigh that escaped her as rainbows filled her vision.

She hoped Tieg would find the myriad of glass trinkets to his liking, but when she turned to him for his response, she was surprised to find him watching her rather than the old glassblower.

"We can do them in a handful of colors. If there's something you were looking for in particular, it shouldn't be an issue," Mr. Hastings said.

Tieg's eyes stayed on Fia for a moment longer before he seemed to realize he was being addressed. "Oh, yes. Different colors. I think this one is fetching. Perhaps a few in the green glass would be good as well. "

"Of course. Green is all the rage now, isn't it? Now, this way. Walsh has been doing some wonderful glass animals—pigs and sparrows if I'm not mistaken. "

"Right." Tieg followed Oscar's mentor.

When he was just out of earshot, Fia turned to her brother. "He likes the beads you made as well. Not sure they'd do for his shop, but if you wanted to show him some, I think he'd buy them. "

"I was thinking paperweights. I've been making a few recently. It's a bookshop and library. I'd say they'd be useful."

Fia picked up a globe with a beautiful yellow starburst pattern dancing through its center. The surrounding glass was in layers and swirls. It was like nothing she'd ever seen before.

"Or bookends!" Fia nearly shouted as the thought came to her, a dazzling smile blooming across her face. "Why didn't I think of bookends earlier?"

Oscar smiled and nudged Fia with his shoulder. "You can't be expected to think of everything, Fi."

Fia's smile dimmed as she said quietly, "I've decided to go. To Feyport, I mean."

"Mmm." He nodded.

"I mean, it was always the plan really, but while Mr. Connolly was out on his business this week, it really hit me. It's what I want. To be helpful and useful. Sitting around making Claire uncomfortable isn't the life I want for myself, you know?"

This time instead of denying Claire felt anything but love for his sister, Oscar nodded and said, "I know."

Fia picked up another of the paperweights. It was a perfect apple-sized globe, one end flattened to rest firmly upon a desk—a brilliant violet and red flower blooming in its heart.

"These really are stunning. You have to send me something once a month so I can continue to marvel at my brother's talent." Her words might have been upbeat, but sorrow filled the spaces in between.

"When do you leave? "

"Day after tomorrow." She looked up under her lashes, her lips set in a straight line. "We have to make one more stop this afternoon, then spend the day tomorrow overseeing the rest of the shipments from Simon's. The train leaves early the following morning."

"Aww, Fi. I'm still all twisted up over this."

"It's the thing that needs to happen. We all know it. I'll be back for a visit at some point. And you can always bring the wee one up to see me whenever you like. As long as you don't tell Claire where you're going." She smiled, taking some of the edge off the words that felt too true.

Oscar wrapped his arms around her and squeezed. "I'll miss you."

Fia didn't have any words, so she allowed him to hug her until Tieg and Mr. Hastings returned. The old artisan hobbled along, chattering animatedly while Tieg followed behind, carrying a hefty crate brimming with glass of every color.

Following Tieg's previous interaction with the pompous poet, Fia was quite surprised when he informed her the man's residence was their last stop before leaving the city.

"I'm just confused is all," Fia explained when Tieg scowled at her. "You two definitely didn't seem to get on. I know he's an old acquaintance, and you mentioned dropping by, but I swear you were close to violence with him at the reading."

"You're not wrong," he said.

"Then why? I don't care to get his autograph in this"—she held up the thin volume of poetry and shook it—"drivel."

Tieg had procured the volume at some point and given it to Fia to bring along for the visit.

He made a chuffing noise but continued walking.

"Really, Mr. Connelly. Don't you trust me enough yet to let me in on whatever it is you're scheming?"

"Trust has nothing to do with it, *Miss Walsh*, and I am not scheming. I am curious about something more than anything."

"Curious?"

"Yes."

"And when your curiosity has been sated, will you tell me then?"

"I will."

"You promise?" she teased and was more than a little surprised when he smirked back and replied, "I promise."

Fia wasn't sure what she expected of the residence of Owen Johnston, but it certainly wasn't the open flat in which she stood. After reaching the address Tieg had for the poet and his family, the pair had climbed four flights of stairs to reach the door to the flat. Tieg rang a buzzer of sorts, and they were escorted in by a butler to a wide, open living space. The room was filled with light and a surprising array of artwork, plants, and musical instruments. It was as if a botanic garden had been crossed with a museum of art and decorated with the castoffs of a great composer. Windows lined three full walls, and the city view sprawled below.

Tieg stood in the center of it all, arms across his chest and a frown on his face. Meanwhile, Fia wandered from corner to corner, touching harps, cellos, and even an ebony piano polished to a high shine. She studied oil paintings and porcelain sculptures, exotic ferns and potted roses. Everywhere her gaze fell, riots of green, orange, and magenta filled her vision.

The butler returned from the side door he had exited moments before. "Mr. Johnston will be with you shortly. Please feel free to enjoy the space, but he has asked that you not touch the art. May I take your hat, miss? "

"No, thank you," Fia said.

"Very well." With those two words, he dropped his head and disappeared once again.

Fia continued her perusal of the beautiful room. She scrunched her nose as she looked at a painting hanging above the mantel. In it, a handsome stag galloped through the heather—flowers billowing over its hindquarters and transforming its legs into a serpentlike tail. "I realize I met him just the once, but he certainly didn't strike me as the type to want all of this," Fia whispered and held out her arms to encompass the room.

"I'll wager this is down to Mrs. Johnston and Glendon. He was always infatuated with magical tales and interesting folklore, and Mrs. Johnston would do just about anything to keep her son happy. They're good folks. I hope you have the opportunity to meet them while we're here." Tieg seemed far off as he spoke, and Fia was left wondering what exactly he suspected.

As if his thoughts could conjure them, the entry door swung open, and the most beautiful woman Fia had ever seen glided in. She was tall and thin, with large emerald eyes and creamy porcelain skin. She was smartly dressed in a bright cerulean skirt with a matching jacket and carried a deep indigo, beaded parasol that perfectly matched the silk scarf covering her head. How this woman came to be married to the rumpled poet Fia could not fathom.

The woman was accompanied by a young man about Fia's age. He, too, was tall and thin with a fair complexion and beautiful grey eyes. His disheveled hair was a deep midnight black, and when he saw Tieg, his face broke into a lopsided grin revealing a considerable overbite.

"Tieg Connolly! Is that you?" The young man dashed forward and took Tieg's hand in a firm handshake, using the other to affectionately clap Fia's employer on the shoulder.

"Ach, Glendon. Good to see you, mate." Fia was momentarily stunned when she noticed the bright a smile on Tieg's generally dour face.

Tieg stepped around Glendon and bestowed a similar smile on the stunning woman. "Mrs. Johnston, always a joy to see you. I hope you've been well." His words held an unspoken question, and the woman flicked her eyes to the side door before responding.

"Yes, Tieg. I'm quite well. Thank you for asking." Her returning smile was so dazzling, Fia nearly forgot her own name. She stood mutely by watching the entire exchange, not wanting to disrupt the reunion.

Tieg turned to her after a beat and gestured for her to join them. "Mrs. Johnston, Glendon. May I introduce my new friend and employee, Fia Walsh."

Fia was still processing the fact that he had called her a friend when Mrs. Johnston stepped forward. "Walsh, you say?" A subtle tremor in her voice, she stared wide-eyed at Fia.

She couldn't be certain, but she thought Tieg was watching them with a new level of interest.

"Yes, ma'am." She glanced at Tieg.

"It is a joy to meet you," the other woman said. "And where do you hail from, Miss Walsh?"

"I was born in Bodkin Green, but I've been in the city for several years now."

"Bodkin Green? Oh." Brigid Johnston's voice was little more than a whisper as she raised her hand as if to touch Fia on the cheek. She dropped it hesitantly when the door opened and Owen Johnston entered the room.

Their departure was swift. Glendon looked anxiously at his father, clearly wanting to speak reason to the man, but Owen's rage was a volatile, combustible thing and Tieg seemed to know it. He quickly made his apologies to Mrs. Johnston and encouraged Glendon to come visit in Feyport soon.

Fia felt somehow she was to blame for the older man's ire, but Tieg reassured her that the feud between them went back a good amount of time. Mrs. Johnston for her part seemed about to break into tears as she watched them go, and Fia realized the woman must have some real affection for Tieg Connolly despite her husband's wishes. It was all a bit confusing, and by the time they made their way to the street below, Fia was left with both a sense of relief that they wouldn't be seeing the Johnston family again anytime soon and suspicion that Tieg Connolly had gotten just the reaction he was hoping for.

NINE

The view from the train's window wasn't much of a view at all, but rather a moist blur of green and grey. Whether this effect was solely the result of the thick blanket of fog was debatable. The constant threat of tears in Fia's eyes might have been playing the tiniest part in obscuring her vision.

They were only an hour outside the city, and the goodbye with Oscar was still fresh. He'd held his emotions in check while they left the house—and a rather chipper Claire—in the early morning hours. Helping Fia hand her bags to the porter had been his undoing. He couldn't hide the redness in his eyes or the wobble in his chin as she embraced him then turned away and climbed the metal steps into the train carriage. She was careful not to let him see her fall apart. He needed her to be strong for the both of them.

As the train pulled out of the station, Tieg had asked how she was. Her quiet reply had him leaning forward and extending a crisp clean handkerchief. "I'm right here, if you'd like to talk."

She shook her head, and they rode on in silence.

The city bricks and chipping mortar gave way to patches of weeds and then more expansive green pastures.

Fia found herself hoping she hadn't made a terrible decision. Her mind told her this was the right thing to do, but her heart wasn't quite as sure. Over and over she thought about the many different ways this could go wrong. A tear overflowed her lashes, and she swiped angrily at her face.

"I'm going to stretch my legs. Can I get you anything while I'm up?" she asked her employer and the only person she would know in the tiny town they were traveling to.

Tieg looked up from the book in his lap and opened his mouth, but he drew his lips into a tight line and shook his head.

Fia pushed herself out of the seat and swayed with the motion of the train car. Placing a steadying hand on the seat back, she straightened her spine and headed toward the back of the car. Several travelers spared her a passing glance, but thankfully she didn't draw much attention.

As she approached the door to the next car, the noise from the rails intensified. The door opened in a rush of air, heavy with the smell of rain. Fia instinctively reached up to prevent her hat from slipping in the gust.

"Careful, miss." The train guard slid the door shut behind him. A man in his middle years, with a considerable belly and a kind face, he stepped aside to ensure she had enough room to pass. He'd been through the carriage once already—stopping to punch tickets and offer a welcoming smile. Fia had smiled back, even as her heart was cracking at the time. "It's a bit damp out there. Are you sure you'd like to cross just now? I might suggest the forward coach. The gap there is covered."

"I was hoping to get out for a breath of fresh air," she said.

"It's fresh for certain. Much better now that we've left the city behind. Still soggy though."

Fia smiled. "Soggy might be just what I need."

"All right then, miss. Take the next two cars back, then you'll find the end gate. There's a small platform there. It's quite a safe spot."

Fia thanked the guard and followed his instructions to the rear of the train. It was indeed wet, but the small overhang blocked a good bit of the rain. Fia held the rail with one hand and her cap with the other. She inhaled deeply, relishing the smell of saturated earth, grass, and adventure. As the car swayed gently, her mind settled for the first time in weeks or perhaps even years. The tension loosened minute by minute. She closed her eyes and inhaled one more time, letting the air out in a slow relaxing stream. When she opened her eyes again, the prickle of tears was gone, and she returned to the warmth of the carriage.

Tieg was staring out the window when she returned. Fia removed her damp jacket and folded it into the empty seat next to her.

"All right then?" he asked.

"Yes, Mr. Connolly. I do believe I am."

If the departure from the city had been full of sadness, the arrival in Feyport was the opposite.

The skies had cleared by the time the train pulled into the station. Compared to the hustling multi-track depot in the city, the Feyport station was almost nonexistent. With only one platform in each direction and a small copper-roofed ticket booth and accompanying shelter, it wasn't hard to spot Tieg's family.

He'd barely planted both feet on the platform before a sturdy woman, perhaps ten years his senior, had him wrapped in a tight embrace.

"Saints, Candice. You're likely to crush the soul from my body."

"Hardly. I'm sure it'd take more than the likes of me to do you in." She loosened her grip on him. "I'm just so pleased you've finally made it back. Penny's been after me nonstop about when you'd return. Now I'll finally get some peace."

Penny? Was that Tieg's girlfriend? The idea filled Fia with a sad sort of disappointment she didn't fully understand. He was only her employer after all and certainly entitled to have a love of his own. He was attractive and hardworking, and they had never discussed any of his possible attachments. She couldn't believe she'd never entertained the idea before, but it did make perfect sense.

"Ah. My favorite girl. I'm anxious to see her as well."

As the words left Tieg's lips, Fia's heart sank. The one person she knew in town and he'd likely be spending all his free time with his *favorite girl*. Rather than letting her feelings show, however, she did what she always did when she was uncomfortable or glum. She forced herself to smile.

"We'll see if you're still singing the same tune a week from now," a deep voice boomed. Fia turned toward a large man with a thick chestnut mustache and a slight thinning of his hair. He clapped a hand on Tieg's shoulder. "Good to see you, Tieg."

"You too, Ned. I imagine Niall's been entertaining her?"

"As much as he can. She's got enough energy to keep half the town entertained. And this must be our new tenant." The big man tipped his head toward Fia, the corners of his eyes crinkling as he smiled at her. "Candice has a room all set for ya."

"I certainly do. And aren't you a picture." She gave her brother a knowing look and wrapped Fia in an embrace to match the one she'd given Tieg.

Tieg sighed. "As I'm sure you've guessed, this is my sister Candice and her husband, Ned Bryan. They've got the inn I mentioned, and they're all too happy to have you stay there until you've decided otherwise."

Fia's smile wasn't forced as she was released from Candice's embrace. "Thank you for the hospitality."

Candice waved a hand. "Oh, no thanks necessary. It isn't much, and there'll be Penny and the cat to contend with, but we like it. Plus it's only a short walk to the main street and the space Tieg has for the business."

"We'll have everything you need, and if we don't, Candice here'll fetch me to get it," Ned added. "Now let's get your things."

It didn't take long for Fia, Tieg, and both the Bryans to collect the trunks and bags. Their things were loaded into a waiting wagon, and within minutes Fia was settled in next to Candice. As they pulled away from the station, she tilted her head and marveled at the clear expanse of sky. Not a cloud in sight.

Green fields, crisscrossed with grey stone walls, stretched from the hills in the east all the way to the road and beyond. She'd never been to the coast and had expected the ocean to be easily within view. The disappointment of not seeing it lasted only a short time. As they rounded a bend, she caught a glimpse of azure and then the view opened up and Fia's breath caught. She'd not expected it to be so . . . vast. Blue like she'd never seen filled her vision. Salt laced the air, and as she stared in wonder, she imagined she could taste the briny tang of it on her tongue.

The wagon bounced happily over the cobbles, and the staccato click mixed with the cry of swooping gulls.

"I had no idea," she breathed.

Tieg looked over his shoulder at her from the front bench.

"It's really quite something, isn't it?" Candice asked, and Fia could only nod in response. "Well, then. I think you'll like the room I've picked out for your stay."

It didn't take long before the horses veered off the road they'd been traveling, taking them on a gentle bend to the left. Great brambles dotted with small white flowers lined the road on both sides, and a dairy came into view, the cows in its pasture lowing in the distance.

Candice pointed to a huddle of buildings farther up the lane. "This road will take you up to the main street—the heart of Feyport. It's no more than a fifteen minute walk from the inn. Bakery, pub, the hall, and a few other shops are there. The school and the church too. Plus the property Tieg is renovating. Farther along is the road to the cliffs and then beyond that the Whiskey Road—where the distillery sits. I'll give you the grand tour tomorrow. After you've gotten a chance to rest a bit."

"That'd be wonderful. Thank you."

"That road there"—Candice nodded toward a slight dirt track—"will take you past the strand and straight down to the beach. You can also get to the water from townside, but I'll tell you not to venture down there alone. It isn't safe."

Fia thought it an odd warning. How unsafe could the picturesque beach be? But given her own loss at the hands of an unpredictable body of water, she didn't question it.

Ned pulled on the reins as they drew up to a modest building. The yard was a riot of colorful blooms, and the warm stone of the main building was offset by bright red shutters and a matching front door. A wooden sign jutting above the entry swayed in a gentle breeze. It read simply "Inn."

In one elegant motion, Tieg hopped from his perch on the front bench of the wagon and offered his hand first to Candice and then Fia. As Fia looked up at the welcoming spot which would serve as her home for the foreseeable future, the front door banged open and a rambunctious girl of perhaps seven years bounded down the steps and straight into Tieg's legs. She wrapped herself around the man, and he beamed down on her, the brightest smile Fia had ever seen on him lighting up his features. Close on the girl's heels was a young man who couldn't be any older than Fia herself—perhaps even a year or two younger. He had the same chestnut hair and pale blue eyes as Tieg, but even without speaking, the young man radiated joy and good humor.

Tieg looked down at the child. "Ah, and here's my favorite girl."

The girl held both of Tieg's hands, swinging them back and forth as she looked up at him. "What sorts of treasures did you bring me?"

"Now, Penny. Give your uncle some space," Candice chided, but Fia could see she had nothing but love for the child.

"Weeks I've been her closest companion, and just like that, I'm forgotten," the young man mused.

Ah. So this was Penny.

Whether Fia was embarrassed or relieved to see the mystery girl was Tieg's niece, she couldn't say.

"I've brought back loads of treasures. I'm sure we'll find one that suits you." Tieg dropped her hands, and she took off twirling down the walk in a whirlwind of honey brown braids and gingham skirts. She stopped long enough to briefly pet a multicolored cat who was lounging in a slat of sunshine on the porch.

The young man stepped forward, and Tieg gave him a brief yet heartfelt embrace. "Miss Walsh, let me introduce you to the youngest Connolly, my brother Niall. And that wee banshee is Penny. My niece."

Niall stepped forward, and in an over-the-top gesture took Fia's hand and placed a kiss on the back of it. "My pleasure, Miss Walsh."

She couldn't contain the smile that bubbled up. For all that he looked like Tieg, Fia could already tell Niall would be more than entertaining to be around. "Please. Call me Fia."

"Fia it is then!" He tipped an invisible cap to her and went about collecting some of her belongings from the wagon.

Tieg and Ned set to unloading the rest of Fia's things.

"You can take them on up to the yellow room," Candice said.

Tieg nodded at his sister, and he and the other two men disappeared into the inn.

Fia moved to the wagon and frowned when she realized her employer hadn't removed any of his own trunks or bags. "What of Mr. Connolly's things?" she asked Candice.

Tieg, having deposited his initial burden somewhere inside, bounded down the front steps and answered instead. "Those, Miss Walsh, will be going along home with me."

"Oh." She closed her mouth quickly and shook her head to clear it. "Silly of me. Of course they are."

Fia felt the faintest blush on her cheeks. Why had she thought he lived here as well? Obviously he wouldn't still be living with his family. He was an adult with his own business, and unlike Fia, he needn't worry about being on his own and the scandal it might cause.

"He isn't far. Just the other side of town," Candice said. "And unlike the city, the other side of Feyport is only a few minute's walk."

Fia smiled at her hostess, but it felt rather forced and tight.

"Let's show you inside, shall we?" Candice took Fia's elbow in one hand and wrapped the other around the young woman's shoulders in a half hug. They walked like that until reaching the top of the porch steps.

It would be false for Fia to say entering the inn felt like coming home, but it was welcoming and warm and the perfect mix between the cottage she'd spent her earliest years in and the school she'd lived in after her parents had died. The light was bright and flooded the space, sending dust motes dancing across her vision. The air held a heady mixture of cinnamon and apple, and Fia wondered what Candice had baked earlier in the day to impart such a heavenly scent to the home.

Fia's handbag bumped off her knees where it dangled from her hands in front of her. She turned slowly to take in everything the inn had to offer. Tieg scooted around her and headed toward the stairs, Ned just behind him grappling with a load of his own.

Candice pointed out the dining area and sitting rooms, then a side door into the kitchen. "You're always welcome to use what you like from the pantry, but don't feel as if you've got to do all of your own cooking. We always have plenty for the guests, and even though I'd like for you to feel at home here, you can take your meals with the visitors if you like."

She opened a door and held it wide for Fia to peek in at the expansive kitchen. It made Oscar and Claire's look like a cupboard by comparison. A fresh wave of the heavenly apple and cinnamon air wafted out, and Fia closed her eyes and sighed. It was simply divine.

"That'll be the bread I made this morning. We'll have some with our tea today, I think."

Exiting the dining room, Candice showed her the last door on the first floor. It led from the back of the house.

"This is my favorite bit." There was a gleam in Candice Bryan's eye as she led Fia out onto a large wraparound porch. It seemed to circle the entire back of the property.

Fia's breath caught. It was like nothing she'd ever seen before. Miles and miles of deepest cerulean waters filled her vision, the sky above them just a shade lighter and dotted with cottonpuff clouds. Despite the considerable distance to the actual shoreline, the breeze carried the sound of the waves clearly to her ears. Gulls circled and dove, their cries mingling with the waves to create a natural symphony. She could sway and dance to the bewitching tune for the rest of her life if she wasn't careful.

"Your room has the same view," a familiar voice said behind her. "And although the window isn't overly large, it opens wide enough to enjoy the breeze and to smell the sea."

Tieg stood, hands in pockets, staring out as if he was as enraptured with the view as Fia.

"It's . . . more than I could have imagined," Fia whispered quietly. "No wonder you don't care for the city."

Tieg nodded. "The stuff of dreams. Come on. Let's show you upstairs."

The room was simple but cheerful. Soft lemon paint covered the walls and pillows wrapped in a matching hue perched on the bed. A simple bureau with a washbasin, a small closet, and bookshelf finished the room. A lavatory down the hall contained a comfortable-looking claw foot tub in a separate attached room. "Just be sure to lock the door," Candice said. "We've unfortunately had more than one guest make the mistake of forgetting, and they paid for it with their modesty."

Back downstairs, Ned offered to take her coat and hat. Fia passed him the coat willingly but stiffened when he held out his hand for her cloche.

"It's all right, Miss Walsh. Ned is completely unshockable and Candice won't mind in the least. I can assure you." Tieg's voice was calm and quiet. No hint of exasperation or demand. Just . . . supportive.

Fia bit at her lower lip, eyes on her shoes.

"Whatever you are comfortable with," Ned said. "But I can tell you, we've no guests staying with us today and folk'll ring the bell if they show unannounced."

Fia looked up at the big man and pulled the hat off. Ned's good humor didn't fade or waver in the slightest as he accepted the cloche and hung it alongside her coat. As if they hadn't been interrupted at all, he continued to chatter on with Tieg about preparations that still needed to be made at the library.

Candice bustled out of the kitchen with the tea, and she too didn't blink or balk in the least. It was as if the girl occupying space in her sitting room had hair of a simple shade of blonde or brunette rather than iridescent green. Arranging everything, including the heavenly scented apple bread on the dining room table, she waved a hand at her husband and brother. Tieg pulled out a chair for Fia, and he and Ned dropped into chairs opposite her.

Penny, dragging a laughing Niall along with her, appeared in the doorway. After relinquishing her hold on the young man, the little girl bounced over to the open spot next to Fia.

"Did you wash?" her mother asked.

"Yes, Momma." She accepted a thick slice of the fruit and spice loaf and dropped a messy dollop of cream on top before taking a gigantic bite. As she chewed, she looked up at Fia. A large swallow later, she wiped her mouth and announced, "You have pretty hair."

Fia looked up in time to see Niall drop her a wink before taking a sip of his tea.

It was the only comment made by any of Tieg's family members. A large weight rolled off Fia's shoulders. Misty eyed, she sipped her tea and silently thanked the saints she had agreed to work for Tieg Connolly.

TEN

Apparently, the building Tieg had purchased for his library and business had been a barley storage house in another life. It was a simple but roomy space, essentially just a large square with four thick stone walls and a solid roof. Listening to Tieg speak about his plans, however, Fia could certainly envision it as so much more.

Tieg and Ned had already constructed rows of shelves along three of the walls, and as Fia stood next to the stacks of cartons and crates which had arrived, she began to feel a connection not only to the things she'd helped select, but to what the establishment might be in just a few more weeks.

Images of thick leather bindings and slim canvas ledgers, delicate glass globes and beautiful carved bookends danced in her head. She dropped down and opened one of the boxes.

"We'll have the counter here," he said, standing in the back, legs planted and motioning downward with his hands, one empty and the other holding a small hammer. Fia hadn't seen him without a tool of one kind or another since they'd been in Feyport. "The art and baubles will be purchased of course, so we'll need space for the register. The books though, I'm not sure about. Maybe a ledger to keep track of what gets borrowed out, or small paper slips?"

Fia pulled a few more books from the crate she was sitting next to on the floor. Checking the spines, she placed them to the side. "And if they'd like to buy the book outright?"

"You can help me set prices for most of them. But the rare ones will be lending only." He faced the back wall and the set of shelves there. "We'll keep those here. Behind the counter."

Fia squinted at where he was pointing. It made sense to keep those rare books separate. She hoped Tieg would tell her specifically which ones he intended so she didn't make a mistake and accidentally sell one he was particularly keen on keeping.

Weak afternoon light trickled in. The lighting in general wasn't spectacular in the space, but for the most part it shouldn't be an issue. What drifted in through the small windows high up on the walls could be augmented with lamps. Tieg also planned to have an outdoor reading area that could be used in fine weather.

"Can most of the folks here read then?" Fia asked as she dusted her hands and moved to stand. Tieg was there in an instant, extending his palm to grasp hers and assist her up from the floor. She had once again adopted the loose trousers and baggy sweater she'd been wearing the day she'd met Tieg. It made moving from the floor to a stepstool much more comfortable while she worked. When she told Tieg she would go back to dresses or skirts when the shop opened, he'd shrugged and told her to wear what she liked.

"Most. Yes." He nodded. "But not all. It's part of the reason I'm starting all of this."

"I think it's all really wonderful. There's so many things you could have done with your inheritance, Mr.

Connolly. Traveled. Bought land. Moved to the city. But you chose this."

She thought about the other men she'd encountered in her relatively protected life. Many of them would have done just those things. But Tieg was different in so many ways. She itched to ask what had happened to his parents but guessed he'd tell her if he wanted her to know. Neither Niall nor Candice spoke of them either, so it was either something very painful or very shameful. Judging by the siblings, she thought it likely the former.

"It wasn't much of a choice really. More of a calling I'd say."

"Regardless. It isn't just a shop. It's a gift really. For the people who live here," she said.

"In a way I suppose you're right." He looked as if he wanted to say more, but he shook his head slightly and busied himself hammering in a nail Fia wasn't entirely sure actually existed.

She had a hard time dragging her pale grey-green eyes from the man standing just a few feet from her, even though his back was to her. Eventually, she turned in a slow circle taking it all in once more. She sighed at the towering stack of boxes behind her.

"I suppose I should get back to work."

The following day was much the same. Fia rose early, ate a quick breakfast at the inn, and set off toward the library and curio shop.

She had gotten in the habit of leaving early in the morning in the hopes she wouldn't pass too many of the townspeople on the main street. It seemed, though, the hardworking of Feyport were up just as early as she was, and she began to see the same faces each day on her morning walk. Candice had been true to her word and had given Fia a tour of the town on her second day living at the inn. She introduced Fia to several people as they came upon them, and for the most part, everyone had been friendly and open. She smiled and waved to those she knew or to those who waved at her first, but she still wore her cap snuggly on her head anytime she left the security of the Bryans'. Delightedly she found she was warming toward the idea of eventually not needing it. What would it be like to walk around completely as she was? Not hiding. Not worried for herself or the impact rumors might have on Oscar and Claire.

The Bryans' easy acceptance of her and Fia's general nature combined to form something altogether unexpected. She was beginning to entertain the idea of meeting some people her own age. The opportunity hadn't really presented itself yet, but that might change. She'd only been there a handful of days, and both Niall and Tieg had assured her they would be happy to introduce her around. Each time she told them she was simply too busy. Lifting her chin and smiling to herself, she made a decision. Perhaps on the next day off she'd take one or both of them up on the offer.

Tieg was already hard at work when she entered the library.

"Morning, Miss Walsh." He had his hands full, installing a bracket over his head on one of the shelves but still managed to turn and greet her as she entered.

"Mr. Connolly." She smiled widely at him. "Let me help you with that."

She grabbed a wooden stool and carried it over next to him.

"That really isn't necessary."

Fia climbed up on the stool despite Tieg's words. She reached her hands next to his and grabbed the brass fixture, freeing up his hands.

Tieg quickly finished with the fastening, and Fia climbed down.

"Thank you. That was actually much easier with your help."

"I'm happy to assist. It is what you pay me for." She removed her coat and placed it on top of one of the crates. "I was thinking on my way here this morning."

"Should I be concerned?" he asked flatly.

"I should hope not." She chuckled. "Two things actually. First, would you mind introducing me to some of the young women in the town this weekend? I'd love to get to know a few more people."

His eyes widened slightly. He swallowed and answered, "Absolutely. In fact, I was going to suggest taking you with me this afternoon on one of my errands. I need to pop up to the distillery, and there's someone there I think you might like to meet. And this weekend, perhaps Niall and I can gather a few folks together for a picnic."

"That would be lovely. Both would be."

"And your second thought?" he asked.

"I was wondering if you'd thought of a name yet?"

Tieg had been wiping his hands on a rag but stopped, lips turning down a fraction. "No, I hadn't really thought of that."

"You've thought of everything else but not what to call the place?" Fia was incredulous.

"It looks that way." He returned to wiping his hands.

"Well. We need to call it something. Can't just say the library and shop. It's too much of a mouthful and people need to refer to it as something."

"Why not just Connolly's?"

"Not only is that boring, it's . . . I don't know. Not fitting."

"Not fitting?"

"Not at all. Hasn't anyone ever told you? Mr. Connolly, names hold power."

His eyes widened at her statement.

"It's something I learned from a very young age. If you want your shop to mean something to people, you've got to give it a name. A fitting name. Does that make any sense at all?"

"I've heard something like this before." He paused and looked a the ceiling, weighing what to say. "Not that long ago, Feyport had no name. It was just called *town*. Then one autumn things . . . changed. It was given a name and it stuck. Since that time, it feels as if Feyport has begun to . . . I don't know . . . blossom? So yes, Miss Walsh. It makes perfect sense. Perhaps you could help in coming up with a fitting moniker?"

Fia bit at her lower lip unable to contain the grin of excitement lighting her face. "If you insist."

ELEVEN

A few hours ticked by while Fia and Tieg worked in companionable silence. Niall and Ned arrived with another wagonload of boxes they'd fetched from the train station. Simon had been industriously instrumental in shipping things from the city. Ned brought along a cold lunch Candice had put together, and the four ate quickly before Ned had to return to the inn and Niall had to return to his friends.

"I swear. The lad is more social than any young man I've ever met," Fia mused.

"He's always been that way. Ever since we were kids. Not a soul in this town who doesn't like him. And the girls . . . forget it. I can't remember the last jubilee or festival we had when at least one young lady didn't leave in tears because he didn't have a chance to dance with her."

Fia retrieved her green leather book from her bag. On a whim, she'd brought it to work with her that morning. "I can believe it."

"Can you?" His gaze snapped up to her face, but he quickly looked away.

"I can. But don't worry yourself, Mr. Connolly, I've no intention of falling head over heels with my employer's brother."

"I didn't mean to imply—"

"Relax. I'm only teasing."

"So you do mean to fall for him?" His voice held a bitter edge.

"Not at all." Fia looked down at the book in her hand.

Tieg cleared his throat and asked, all bitterness gone from his voice, "Have you given up yet then, Miss Walsh?"

"Given up?"

"At a name. Have you given up finding this place a name?"

"I've given up on lots of things, but I can guarantee you, this won't be one of them."

He scoffed. "I find it extraordinarily hard to imagine you failing at anything, Fia. You just seem so . . . determined."

"That shows how little you know me, Mr. Connelly. Determined I may be, but there are many things even determination can't seem to overcome."

"So tell me then. What failures do you keep tucked away in secret?"

"Let's see." She counted on her fingers. "Reading this book for starters." She held up the book left to her by her mother. Tieg's brow furrowed. Fia either didn't notice the frown or chose to ignore it and continued counting on her other hand. "Then there's my inability to get Claire to *not* despise me. My lack of ability to make a decent piecrust. I can't swim, and I'm scared to learn. And perhaps most aggravating, my recent failure—one I've been trying to accomplish for the past several weeks—my inability to get you to smile."

Tieg's head snapped back, as if she'd physically struck him. "You've been trying to make me smile?"

"Yes. And failing miserably."

"I smile," he muttered.

"I've seen you smile exactly three times."

"It's got to be more than that. You probably just haven't been paying attention."

She lifted her hand and extended her index finger, counting once again. "First, you chuckled and smirked at the poetry reading. It doesn't really count as a smile as far as I'm concerned, but I'm going to give it to you just to be fair. Second, the day you introduced me to the Johnstons. You smiled at Glendon and then again at Mrs. Johnston, but because I gave you the smirk, I'm counting that as one. And number three. When we arrived last week, you hugged your sister and then smiled at Penny."

"Well, I—" He seemed uncomfortable. "I didn't realize it was such a rare thing, or that you would notice."

"Believe me, I've noticed." Tieg had a beautiful smile, and she ached—physically ached—not just to see it, but to be the one to trigger the reaction.

"I'll make an effort to smile more," he said quietly.

"Please do, Mr. Connolly."

"It might go a long way in achieving your goal if you'd stop calling me Mr. Connolly and just stick with Tieg."

Fia didn't hesitate. "I believe that's something I can do."

One corner of Tieg's mouth ticked up.

"Close, but not quite there yet, Tieg. Keep practicing."

Fia turned to place her precious book back in her satchel, no longer in the mood to try to decipher it. In so doing, she missed it as Tieg dipped his chin and hid the grin on his face.

A cloud had drifted over the sun and a faint misting sort of rain was falling as Tieg and Fia left the library and began the short walk up the road toward the distillery. It really was such a picturesque place, between the ocean and the barley-covered hills. Fia thought she might be happy to never leave Feyport.

Even the rain was different. Not cold and clinging, but light and refreshing. Rather than sending her for cover as it would in the city, Fia thought she could easily walk for hours in the fine mist.

As if reading her thoughts, Tieg said, "It's great now, but come November, the damp and the chill tend to get wearying."

"I'm no stranger to damp and chill."

"No, but the way the wind whips in off the sea can be wicked. It's days like this that make up for it, but in the dead of winter, you'll be happy for the fireplace at Candice and Ned's."

"You think I'll still be with them come winter?" Fia asked.

"I hope so," he replied.

"I'd like a place of my own at some point."

"It is nice to have a spot to call your own. To get away and just . . . be. I understand."

Fia had yet to see where her employer lived. Maybe one day, he'd show her his own place to 'just be.' She knew Niall didn't live with him. He'd mentioned renting a room with some other lads who worked at the dairy. There were three of them in total, she believed. He said it was a great bit of freedom but still afforded him the ability to save some of his own inheritance and work to keep the small pile growing until he could buy his own farm outright. Fia thought the idea of a small farm sounded like heaven. A heaven she'd lived in for the first years of her life.

She didn't want to make herself glum so asked, "Who are we going to meet?"

"I have some business to discuss with the owner, Rupert Camden. He was a close friend of my father's and is actually the man who introduced me to Simon Beck."

"Is Mr. Camden helping with the library?"

"Not directly no. It's business of a more personal matter."

When he didn't elaborate, Fia asked, "Then why bring me along?"

"It's not actually Rupert I wanted you to meet. It's the young woman who runs his shop."

"He has a shop at the distillery?"

"Funny enough he does. It's relatively new, but his business has been booming. The whiskey coming out of Feyport—Camden's Whiskey—is really sought after up and down the coast. He even ships to the city now. Anyway, he got the notion that since it's so popular, he could sell it right from a small shop on the premises to visitors and the like, rather than just to pubs and taverns."

"And what does that have to do with me?"

"I'm getting there." He ticked up one side of his mouth—a not quite smile.

"I appreciate the effort, but you'll have to do better," Fia said.

"Right. The young woman who runs the shop— Aylee Garrow—might be a good person for you to get to know."

Fia reached up and absently tugged on the edges of her cap.

Tieg stopped walking. "You said you might like to meet some of the folks who live here. People your own age. Aylee is the perfect place to start."

"Right." She nodded and forced a smile on her face. "I did say that."

"Fia." Tieg looked like he wanted to reach out, but he looked to the sky instead. "It hurts to see you so nervous."

It hurt him? Fia didn't know what to say.

"Aylee is the best sort of person. We went to school together, and her folks were also friends of my parents. They own the little mercantile on the main street. I don't know her well enough to say we're close, but I know what kind of person she is. She can help you get adjusted here, I think. It's a small town obviously, but the Garrows are well liked. Aylee and her sister Maeve in particular."

Fia chewed nervously on her lower lip.

"Do you remember when I told you the folks in Feyport had become a bit more accepting recently?"

She nodded.

"I believe Aylee and Maeve have had something to do with that. There were some things that happened here awhile back and well, it's just. . ." He looked like he was struggling how to put the words together. "I think Aylee might be able to help you feel like you belong here is all."

Fia got the distinct impression Tieg wasn't telling her the whole story, but then again, maybe it wasn't his story to tell. She desperately wanted to believe him, and thus far, he hadn't been wrong yet. Tieg hadn't judged her for her appearance and neither had any of those close to him. Simon, Ned, Candice, and Niall—even little Penny—all looked at her as if she were just another girl. It was so vastly different from anyone she'd accidentally encountered in the city who'd seen her without her head covered. Maybe this Aylee Garrow would also accept her. And really, how wonderful would that be? To have a young woman as a friend who would accept her? To be able to talk about life and love, her hopes and dreams? The very idea made her almost giddy.

"All right, Mr. Connolly." He raised a single eyebrow at her. "Tieg," she corrected. "Let's go meet this Aylee Garrow."

TWELVE

The sweet smell of aged oak and fermented barley perfumed the air. Fia didn't have a particular taste for whiskey in general, but she couldn't deny the scent of it being distilled, aged, and bottled was ridiculously pleasing.

The distillery was composed of a massive structure surrounded by a few smaller ones. As they approached the conglomeration of buildings, Fia could hear banging and looked toward what she initially took for a barn of sorts. Rather than farming equipment or livestock, she was surprised to see a thick-armed man banging strips of wood into large metal rings.

"That's the cooperage. It's where they make the barrels. Or repair them at least. Last I heard, Rupert was having a hard time finding someone skilled enough to keep up with the demands of his increased production."

"Can he not hire a few younger men and have them trained?" she asked.

"It's what I believe he should do, but Rupert says it's an artform, and I don't know enough about the process to argue with him."

"I see." Although Fia didn't see at all. She'd never been to a whiskey distillery and had no idea how any of it worked. She was more than surprised to find how gorgeous the grounds up there were, closer to a garden than a working factory.

Entering the largest building, the pair passed a small desk and rounded a corner into an open shop. A lovely young woman with bright copper red hair and a smattering of freckles stood at the far end, immersed in an animated discussion with an older gentleman sporting a thick sandy colored mustache. The woman was explaining how she'd chased a group of boys out after catching them trying to steal a bottle of whiskey. The pair made quick eye contact with Tieg and Fia, but the copper-headed beauty continued her story even as she waved them over.

"I'm telling you, Rupert, you'd swear I was a bog witch coming to steal their livers the way they scattered and ran when they knew they'd been caught. Never mind I've known them all since they were babes in their mother's arms."

The older man's lips twitched as he crossed his arms over his chest. "I suppose I should be speaking with their parents."

"Nah. I doubt they'll be trying anything like it again," she said.

"Well, if they do, just let me know." The man turned and smiled at Tieg. "Connolly! I wondered when you'd finally make it by to see me. Heard you've been back a week or more now." The older man's words held no malice. It was clear he and Tieg were on good terms.

"It's been a busy time, Rupert." He shook hands with the older man and nodded to the pretty young woman. "Hi there, Aylee. It seems you're doing well up here."

"I am." She looked thoughtful. "Though I'm still helping at the mercantile most mornings." She turned to Fia and smiled. "And who is this you've brought with you, Tieg?"

"This is Miss Fia Walsh. She's working with me on my venture." *With me.* Not *for me,* Fia noted.

"Fia, this is Aylee Garrow and Rupert Camden."

"It's a pleasure to meet you, Fia." Aylee continued to smile, but Fia could tell she was studying her just a bit.

Fia smiled and studied right back. "Likewise. Tieg had nothing but wonderful things to say about you both."

Rupert's grunt was full of skepticism, and for some reason it made Fia fight a laugh.

"Rupert, if you've got a minute to spare, there's something I'd like to discuss with you," Tieg said.

"Absolutely. I wouldn't want to ruin the good opinion Fia here seems to have of me already."

"Aylee, would you mind if Fia has a look around? I'd like for her to see what you've done with this place so she might get some ideas for ours."

Ours?

"I'd love nothing more. Always looking to show the place off. Oh, and Rupert? Maeve'll be stopping by in a bit. If you see Graham, could you give him a heads up?" Aylee asked.

The older man grunted even louder, this time with what felt like disdain rather than doubt. "I suppose. But those two will need to either work things out soon or save us all and call it quits. He's been near to useless on the floor out there for months."

He ushered Tieg out of the shop and into what appeared to be a long hallway leading toward the heart of the distillery.

"My sister Maeve and her husband are having some difficult times," Aylee offered Fia by way of explanation.

Fia only nodded, not wanting to seem as if she were overstepping.

"So, is there anything in particular you'd like to see?" Aylee asked Fia.

"Anything. All of it. I've never been to a distillery before, and I've never had a job like this. I'd like to be helpful to Mr. Connolly, so anything you can tell me that'll steer me in the right direction is welcome."

"Just what I wanted to hear!"

Aylee started by walking her out into the large main hall. "I can't really tell you much about how the whiskey is actually made. I know the basics, but that's it. The lads bring in the barley, dry it and roast it, then add water and yeast at some point." She pointed out large vats in the center space, but the women didn't get close enough for Fia to take in many details. "It gets distilled and put in barrels to age, and when Rupert and his top distiller think it's time, they take it out of the barrels and bottle it. I'm sure Graham or one of the other men can give you a better tour at some point. They aren't secretive about the process; I just haven't taken the time to learn."

The vast building was filled with giant pots, large metal constructs topped in copper peaks, and at least a dozen men doing a variety of jobs throughout.

"Once it's deemed ready and has been bottled, the bottles get packed into crates and shipped to various places. Or it stays here and I get to sell it. That and a few other things." Aylee led Fia back toward the shop where they had started.

Fia studied the space a little more closely. Wooden shelves were placed throughout. Most held tall cylindrical glass bottles filled with deep amber liquid and adorned with bright blue wax seals on top. Most had matching blue labels with *Camden Whiskey* printed boldly in black. She noted a few other labels mixed in—*Camden Special* printed on red labels and *Camden Batch* on white. Interspersed with the bottles of amber liquid sat a variety of small curved glasses, a few decanters, and even some small boxes of confections and crackers.

Aylee ran through how she kept track of the inventory and how she handled the sales. She showed Fia a few clever tricks for managing large totals and gave her pointers on how to stand her ground with a few of the more persistent customers. The time seemed to fly by, and before long the light in the building began to shift, signaling the coming evening. She couldn't be certain, but it seemed like the misting rain had let up.

"Enough people come here to buy whiskey that it makes it profitable?" Fia asked.

Aylee shrugged. "Some days are really bustling, but others—like today—it's slow."

"And you run it?"

"I do. Rupert offered me the position some months back. My family owns the mercantile in town, so he knew I could handle the sales."

"Are you and he. . .?" Fia didn't know how to ask outright what she suspected.

"Are we together?" Aylee laughed. "No. He's just a good friend."

"Oh. I didn't mean to pry." Fia blushed a little. It seemed so atypical for a young woman to work in not one place but two.

"Don't apologize. Stick around Feyport long enough, and I'm sure you'll hear the stories about me."

"Stories?"

Aylee sighed. "It's a long sordid tale." She lifted her eyebrows and pulled a dramatic face. "One day, when we have time to sit and chat at length, I'll tell you all about it. For now, suffice it to say, there was a time when Rupert thought to make me his wife. I didn't handle it well and there was someone—"

"Aylee," a melodic voice called from the front of the building.

"Ah, that'll be Maeve."

A stunning woman with long, rich auburn hair and skin like porcelain walked into the shop.

"Oh!" she said as she spotted Aylee and Fia. Then after a moment, she made a longer breathy "oohhh."

Her face transformed as she looked at Fia. It went from surprised to curious to excited in the span of two blinks. Fia reached up and found her hat still firmly in place. She didn't think the fringe of hair showing could be enough to raise suspicions, but anything was possible.

"Maeve." Aylee stepped forward and widened her eyes. Fia couldn't be sure, but she thought the younger woman shook her head. What she was trying to convey, Fia had no idea. "This is Fia Walsh. She's new to Feyport, and Tieg Connolly asked me to show her around a bit."

"That's right. You're staying at the Bryans? I thought I heard about that. Well, welcome to town, Fia," Maeve said, the light still in her eyes.

"Thanks. The Bryans have been wonderful."

"They are the best of people," Aylee said and cleared her throat. Maeve gave her sister a sympathetic look. There was some sort of history there, and Fia wondered if it was all part of the story Aylee said she'd share one day. "So, Fia. Have you met many others in town?"

"Not yet. Tieg mentioned a picnic on the beach in the next few days. Perhaps you could join us?" Fia asked hopefully.

Maeve replied, "We'd love to. Leave it to Niall to put together something. Although, there might be more young ladies there than you'd care for if word gets out." She chuffed a laugh.

"But, Fia," Aylee said before Maeve could add more. "I'm sure Candice and Ned have mentioned, but promise us you won't go down to the water by yourself. Not until you're more familiar with the area. You shouldn't be exactly fearful of the sea—we aren't. But it can be unsafe."

Fia was set to argue, but she saw the dark shadows in Aylee's eyes and the firm set of her lips. "You're right. They have mentioned it. I'll do my best to heed the warning."

The ladies were just finishing their cryptic conversation when Tieg and Rupert Camden returned.

"All set then?" Tieg asked.

Fia told him she was and gave Aylee and Maeve a warm smile, telling them she was looking forward to seeing them in a few days' time.

"I invited them to our picnic. I hope that's all right."

"It's perfect. Now let's get you home."

THIRTEEN

That night, after a wonderful meal of hot cottage pie—topped with the fluffiest buttery potatoes she had ever tasted—Fia sat on the edge of her bed staring out into the inky night sky and the even inkier sea below. Something about her interaction with Aylee and her sister earlier in the day both excited and worried her. The woman had seemed just as Tieg had suggested—welcoming and friendly. But Fia couldn't ignore the niggling feeling that they had sensed something about her and whatever it was had piqued their interest.

Unsettling as it was to think about, she could do nothing about it but wait and see. In the meantime, she felt she owed it to Tieg to give the library and curio shop her full attention. She hadn't read the book he'd lent her weeks ago and would need to return it soon to have it in the library at opening. Plus, she still needed to suggest a name to him. She knew the more she focused on the book she couldn't read, the harder it would be to focus on all the new opportunities she'd been given. Telling herself it was just for the time being, she took the green leather book out of her bag, wrapped it in a timeworn sweater, and placed it carefully under her mattress for safekeeping.

She grabbed the thinner canvas book, turned up the lamp a bit, and settled in against her pillows to read. Within minutes her lids grew heavy and she was yawning ferociously. She shut off the lamp, and just before she succumbed to the sweet bliss of sleep, it came to her. She hoped she would remember come the morning and then she drifted off completely.

Tieg was busy the next day and the day after. As much as Fia wanted to tell him her name for his new business, she simply didn't get the chance.

Things at the shop were coming together nicely, however. Thanks to Niall's help, the counter was finished, and Ned had delivered a set of sturdy wooden tables to display the soaps and lotions, art and trinkets. Fia had spent almost every waking hour unboxing, organizing, and arranging what she could while also staying out of Tieg's way. She'd filled a shelf with a tiny menagerie of glass pigs, chickens, and horses nestled alongside the bookends and glass paperweights. Oscar had also sent along half a dozen strings of delicately blown beads. These she hung from a wooden frame and placed it on the shop's counter to keep them safe.

The morning of their planned outing dawned clear and bright, and as they were on pace to have things ready for the opening, Fia didn't feel the least bit guilty about not spending the entire day indoors.

After dressing in a light cotton skirt and simple blouse, she grabbed a wide brimmed sun hat and pinned her hair up as best she could before heading to breakfast. She was surprised when she came down and found Candice waiting for her with a letter in hand.

"This came with the post yesterday. I meant to give it to you last night, but it slipped my mind."

Fia took the missive with a smile and sat at the table with a hot cup of tea and a warm slice of dense bread with honey. Opening it, she immediately recognized her brother's script.

Dearest Fi,

I write with the most joyful news. The baby has come! Not three days after your departure, Claire delivered a beautiful, healthy boy! I'm the proudest da there ever was. Can you believe it? We've named him Trevor after Claire's grandad. He's already a bit of a monster but also just perfect. I wish you were here to see him.

In other news, I've become so distracted, I fear my work at the shop isn't up to par. Mr. Hastings says to give it time, but I just don't have the focus right now to create things like I did not even a month ago. I'm sure it'll pass, but in the meantime, we have shipped a box of paperweights and a new set of bookends to your man Connolly. They should arrive not long after this post. Please do write and let me know how they are received.

Missing you terribly.

Oscar

Fia's heart was full to bursting. She always knew Oscar would be the world's most doting father, and this letter was all the proof she needed to know she was right. Little Trevor would be spoiled sweet in no time. She only hoped Claire would show the same level of affection to both the men in her life.

And she wished she could be there to see it with her own eyes. Maybe in time she'd work up the courage to visit.

As far as his lack of creative output, Fia barely thought it worth mentioning. Of course he was distracted. Who would expect a man thrown into fatherhood to divide his attention completely with his work? Oscar needed time to get into the new pattern of his life and he'd be back to his amazing artistic endeavors.

"Things are all right I hope." It was more of a question than a statement. Candice had sat down across from Fia as she'd read the letter.

"Wonderful in fact. My brother's wife Claire delivered the baby and all seem to be faring well."

"That is good news. Babies can be such a blessing." Candice stood and ran her hands down the front of her dress. "I've got to head into town. Have a grand time today, Fia. That brother of mine has been working you nonstop. You deserve a bit of a break."

Fia did plan on having a grand time. While she was still nervous, she was hopeful as well.

Niall arrived looking a bit rumpled but still dashing. He gaped at Fia's overly large hat.

"You can't mean to keep that thing on all day," he said, a horrified look on his face.

"I certainly can."

"It'll blow off at the first breeze."

She shrugged as she grabbed her sweater. "Then you'll just need to be a gentleman and chase it down for me."

"Ah, my dear Fia. You mistake me for someone else, I'm afraid."

He hooked his arm through hers and walked her out the back of the inn and to the steps off the side of the porch.

"Aren't we waiting here for Tieg?" Fia asked.

"No. He's got his hands full with the hampers of food. We're meeting him and the others," Niall explained as he escorted her down the steps. The lowest section of wood was a bit warped and bent slightly under their combined weight.

"And who might the others be?"

"Well, it's Aylee and Maeve. Tieg told me you met them the other day."

Fia agreed she had.

"Then Aylee's friend Dierdre and her husband Robbie. They just got hitched a couple of months back. Robbie and I go way back. He's a good lad. Doesn't say much but you'll like him. And I think that's it."

"None of Tieg's friends?"

"Tieg doesn't really have a wide circle. He's always kept a little to himself other than Glendon. Those two were inseparable until the Johnstons moved to the city. I tagged along with them as often as they'd let me. Glendon was full of this whimsical kind of energy. It's a wonder Tieg and he get on as well as they do actually." He glanced at her from the corner of his eye as they walked.

"Don't get me wrong, it's not that Tieg's unpleasant or anything. He's just always been the studious, dedicated, upstanding Connolly. He leaves all the fun to me."

Fia chuckled. Niall was the sunshine to Tieg's stormy skies. But the description of Glendon had her more than intrigued. He hadn't seemed whimsical when they'd met briefly in the city, but that had been under the worst kind of circumstance. His father had all but thrown them out. It might be he was just the sort of person she'd like to get to know.

FOURTEEN

The weather was splendid, the company quite delightful, and the setting nothing short of marvelous. Fia had never expected to feel such raw power from something so simple as water.

She'd meant it when she'd told Tieg she was scared to learn to swim, and seeing the surf pound against the sand and rocks did nothing to sway her from this stance. Neither did the repeated warnings she'd gotten from well-meaning folks to be mindful of the surf. But even cautious of the water as she was, she couldn't deny its mesmerizing draw. As long as she stayed firmly on the blanket, several dozen yards away from the water line, she could enjoy the rhythmic pounding in her ears and the fresh briny air in her nose.

Aylee and Maeve didn't seem to share her desire to stay a safe distance away from the sea's edge. No sooner had the sisters arrived with Aylee's dog Pepper and friend Dierdre—or Dee as she informed Fia she like to be called—and her husband Robbie than the sisters had their shoes off and were splashing along the foaming waterline, playing fetch with the shaggy black and white dog.

The sisters were easy to talk to, and Fia learned a good bit about the town comings and goings in the short time they sat near her while lunching. More than once, she thought she caught Maeve looking at her with a wistful or even hopeful expression, but each time she looked back, the auburn-haired beauty had turned to address someone else in the party.

As much as Fia found herself enjoying their company, however, it was Aylee's friend Dee who was the life and joy of the group. The curvy woman had stunning brunette curls and mirth in her every word and action. She laughed openly and showered her quiet and unassuming husband with more affection than Fia thought possible in such a short time.

"Care for another honey cake?" Niall asked.

"I'd say yes, but if I eat one more bite, I think I might rupture something," Fia replied.

Tieg had done well with the catering. He arrived with a large hamper loaded down with such an assortment of treats, Fia wondered where in such a small town all of it could have come from. There were cucumber sandwiches wrapped in waxed paper, cold roast chicken, containers of cool creamy soup, fresh fruit and cream tarts, jugs of cider, and the unbelievable honey cakes. When the entire party had assembled, they dove into the food as if they'd been starved for ages.

"Perhaps a walk on the beach will help you digest," Niall offered.

"Umm ... all right then." Fia eyed the water skeptically.

"You really should leave the hat, though. I refuse to chase it into the surf," Niall teased.

"If the hat stays, so do I."

A hand extended down to where she lounged on the blanket. "I have no issue with your hat. I'll walk you." Tieg scowled at his brother. Fia accepted his hand and dusted the sand off the back of her skirt.

"I was only joking," Niall called as Fia and Tieg strolled closer to the water's edge.

Fia made sure to stay several feet from the runup of waves, and Tieg managed to make her feel safe just by keeping himself between her and the vast expanse of water. Peals of laughter followed them as they strolled along, and Fia looked over her shoulder at the women dashing back and forth from the spray of waves to the dry sand, Pepper barking and giving chase all the while. Even Dierdre had kicked off her shoes and was frolicking with Aylee and Maeve. Robbie and Niall stayed put on the blanket, both reclining on their elbows to admire the sight.

"Thank you for this," Fia said as she walked.

"There's no need to thank me." Tieg continued to walk, hands shoved deep in his pockets and eyes on the rocks in the distance. "If this is to be your home—at least for the time being—I'd like for you to be comfortable. You need friends. Other than Niall, Candice, and me."

"Is that what we are? Friends?" Fia asked, a laugh in her voice.

"I'd like to think so."

"But you're my employer."

"Does that matter?"

"I don't—" She chewed her lower lip a moment and broke into a wide grin. "No. I don't suppose it does."

"Good. I didn't want to have to fire you," he said firmly.

"Tieg Connolly. Is that a joke? Are you actually joking with me?"

"I'm not the grump you like to believe me to be. It's just, when we met, I had a lot on my mind. I'm sorry if I came off as stiff." He studied the sand being shoved in front of his feet as they walked.

"I understand. You have big responsibilities. Niall mentioned how close you were with Glendon. That day—

I didn't realize. It must be difficult to have him so far away in the city."

"Yes, well, I'm hoping he and his mother decide to return to Feyport at some point."

"But not his father. Not Owen."

"What I wish for Owen, I'd rather not say in your company, Fia."

"Hmm. It sounds rather dark."

"It is."

They walked on for a bit longer before Fia stopped and her eyes widened. "Oh. Tieg. I completely forgot. I've got an idea for a name."

"You have? Let's hear it."

"Bindings and Baubles."

He was quiet a moment and Fia worried he hated the idea. It was a bit whimsical. Tieg Connelly was many things. Whimsical was not one of them.

"Oh." She groaned. "You loath it, don't you?"

"Not at all. It seems pretty brilliant actually."

"Really?"

"Really." Tieg turned to her and did the most astonishing thing. He smiled. A wide toothy luminescent smile. Fia felt her knees go weak. She blinked at him, all sense completely lost.

"Fia? Are you all right?" The smile vanished, replaced by concern.

She shook her head slightly and cleared her throat. "Fine. I'm fine." She felt heat racing up her cheeks and quickly began walking again.

The breeze coming in from the water was refreshing. It tickled her legs as her skirt fluttered in the breeze and cooled the heat from her cheeks. Fia tilted her head back and inhaled deeply. As she did so, the wind caught her sun hat and sent it skittering down the sand.

Niall's words about it flying into the sea had her chasing after it before Tieg even noticed what had happened. Running several yards ahead, she heard him call out to wait, but Fia's only thought was catching it so she wouldn't have to walk back to the inn without something covering her beetle shell hair.

The quicker she gave chase, the faster the wind seemed to carry the hat forward. Within just moments, it seemed it would be completely out of reach.

And then it just . . . stopped. It lay unmoving on the wet sand a dozen yards ahead and next to a massive rock outcropping. Breathing a sigh of relief, Fia slowed and made to grasp the offending thing. As she reached down, the sun went behind a cloud and the entire beach grew dim—twilight on a summer afternoon. The once sparkling sand was now ashen. The deep cerulean sky now a faint eggshell grey.

If the dimness of the light did not alarm her, the hushed and muted sound of the waves and seabirds did. She strained to hear her new friends and their joyful laughter. Strained to see the deep azure waters she knew to be just feet from where she stood. Even the tangy brine scent of the air was gone. It was as if Fia had stepped through a membrane into another reality—one lacking all vibrancy and vitality.

Fia spun around, the hat forgotten. Tieg should have been right behind her, but he was nowhere to be seen. Nor could she make out her other friends farther down the beach. Heart racing, she took several steps back the way she'd come before a silky smooth voice stopped her in her tracks.

"What's this now?"

Fia turned and saw a striking woman, accompanied by an equally striking man, sauntering toward her from the dry side of the beach.

"It looks to be a little girl lost, Mother," the man answered. He was tall and lithe with straight black hair hanging to his exposed collarbones and rich olive skin. His eyes were the darkest brown, so much so that Fia first took them to be all pupil. He had high cheekbones and full sensual lips. Dressed in a sleek charcoal tunic and fitted black trousers, he was, in short, beautiful.

Mother? Fia flicked her gaze to the man's companion. Surely she was no older than he was himself and just as stunning. She too had flawless olive skin, but her long flowing hair was more bronze than black. Her golden brown eyes matched the leather corset and boots she wore with crisp white riding pants.

"Not a little girl, Dub. Not this one. Can you not see it? Not sense it?" the woman asked. "She puts me in the mind of someone we used to know."

"Ah, perhaps just a little," the dark man mused. "But lost all the same. Lost not just from her friends, Mother. Also lost from herself."

"Yes, Dub," she crooned. "You are correct. Even in your darkness you illuminate."

Fia's feet seemed frozen to the sand. She wanted to run but didn't know how.

The pair stalked toward her slowly, parting in front of her so they could circle her from both sides. Her eyes grew wide as the man—Dub—leaned in and inhaled her scent. His nearness sent a shiver down her spine, and he chuckled in response.

The woman completed her own examination as she circled, tutting with what she saw.

"Lost indeed. And maybe soon to be lost even further." The leatherclad beauty cocked her head and narrowed her eyes as she stared at Fia. "I don't often offer that which might not be repaid, so listen closely, little lost one. Danger is coming for you in the guise of a man who cloaks his true self. He will bring ill to you. Fight him with all that you are."

The woman turned as if to leave, extending her hand to the beautiful dark man.

"Wait," Fia stammered, although she wanted nothing more than to be rid of their presence. "Who are you? Why tell me this?"

"I tell you so that one day you might repay my generosity." the woman answered.

"Are you a witch?"

The woman chuckled. "Oh, dear one. I am not *a* witch. I am *The* witch."

"And he is your son?"

"One of three. Should you meet the others, Dother and Dain, pray they are in generous spirit as well."

The witch turned her back and they walked away. Dub looked over his shoulder, a dazzling yet ravenous smile on his face.

Fia blinked and the sun returned all in the space of a heartbeat. With the noonday light came the crash of the waves, the bark of a dog and the frantic calls from Tieg. Fia stumbled and fell to her knees as the world came crashing into her from all sides.

FIFTEEN

"You say the witch called the man Dub?" Maeve asked as they sat around the table at the inn. Fia didn't like the worry etched on her brow. Fia had forgotten all about the hat after her encounter on the beach, and now she wasn't certain if Aylee, Maeve, and Dee were worried about the story she told or by the color of her hair. At least the small lumps of horn were still easily covered by her thick waves.

"That's what she called him, though I've never heard a name like that before." Fia squeezed her eyes shut and rubbed the bridge of her nose. Tieg sat next to her, hands on his knees, looking almost ill. "Nor the others. Her other sons, I mean. Dother and Dain?"

"Darkness, Evil, Violence." Maeve whispered the words.

"I'm sorry?" Fia didn't understand.

"Dub—Darkness. Dother—Evil. And Dain—Violence," Maeve explained. Maybe it wasn't her hair color after all that had them troubled.

Aylee looked sympathetically at Fia. "My sister is a wealth of knowledge when it comes to the fey and their folklore."

"It's not folklore, Aylee. You of all people should know that by now," Maeve chided her sister.

Aylee nodded. "Of course I know, Maeve. But Fia may need a bit of time to adjust to how interesting things here in Feyport can be."

"Do you mean to say those people were fey?" Fia could hardly believe it. She'd come there hoping it might be true but not really believing it could be.

"It seems that way," Aylee answered.

Tieg reached over and placed a hand on Fia's knee. The touch was warm and reassuring.

"And you all have experience with fey? Is that right?"

"Some of us more than others." Dierdre raised her eyebrows and shot a saucy look Aylee's direction, reenforcing Fia's desire to hear the young woman's story.

"This is why my hair doesn't bother you. Why you've all been so accepting." Fia thought about it and nearly jumped out of her seat, Tieg's hand on her knee all but forgotten. She paced around the table. "You don't think . . . I mean. Look, I'm not fey if that's what you're thinking."

"Oh, Fia. No." Aylee stood. "None of us assumed that. Although if you were, it'd make not a difference to any of us."

"I think we are all missing the point," Niall said. "Whoever she was, witch or no, she was either threatening Fia or warning her."

"Not a threat," Maeve said. "If she meant to harm Fia, she easily could have done so today. Tieg you said Fia just vanished from your sight?"

"She ran off ahead, and it was as if this stygian darkness rolled in off the sea. Fog but thicker. Blacker.

The closer I got, the more it receded. I've never seen anything like it and I hope never to see it again."

"So a warning then." Niall tapped his fingers on his chin. "Someone cloaked? What could it mean? Fia hardly knows a soul in Feyport save us, and I don't think we fit the bill."

Fia ceased her pacing and dropped back into her seat. Tieg didn't replace his hand on her knee, but she noticed him clenching and unclenching his fist where it rested on his own. "Well, as I see it, it was a beautiful day up until that point. I can't tell you all how wonderful it was. I have work to do and so does Tieg. I refuse to sit around worrying about something I can't control just because some frightful woman declares it."

Tieg looked at her, one side of his mouth dipping down. Before he could voice anything, Fia continued, "I promise to be careful. I'll keep a watchful eye. Believe it or not, I've spent my life being careful of who I was around, and I'm very wary of my surroundings." She said this lightly. All in the room could certainly appreciate how she'd needed to keep her guard up in the past. This wasn't really any different.

"I don't know you well, Fia," Aylee said. "But I think that's fair. We are all here if you need us. If you can't find me up at Camden's, pop by the mercantile. And Maeve is up on the same row of homes as Tieg—the little place with the hydrangeas growing rampant."

Maeve huffed at the description of her cottage.

"I'll be sure to check in on you too," Niall offered with a wink, and Fia laughed in response.

Tieg was the only one who seemed less inclined to just let Fia act as if nothing had happened. Whether this was because he'd brought her to Feyport or had been the one to lose sight of her on the beach, or for another reason entirely, she couldn't say. But in the end, it didn't matter his reasons. She was an adult, and she had both a life to live and a job to do.

"I appreciate all of your concern, and I hope to see you next week at the opening, but for now, I think I'll retire to my room and try to get a good night's rest. Thank you all again for such a lovely outing."

Fia smiled at them and disappeared up the stairs before anyone had the chance to change her mind or see the smile slip from her lips.

The sun hadn't yet set when Fia fled the company of the well-meaning people downstairs. She just couldn't keep up the bright and cheerful exterior when faced with not only the dreadful experience on the beach, but also with the idea that had descended on her while they were talking.

She made a quick stop in the washroom to rinse the sand from her skin and splash some cool water on her face and the back of her neck. She immediately locked her door and shed the clothing from the day. Slipping on her favorite soft white night dress, she crossed to the small mirror. She ran her fingers through the tousled ends of her bobbed hair and studied how the light sent a rainbow of color through it. Against the pale skin of her neck and bare shoulders, the effect was quite striking. And unnatural.

These people believed in the fey. Not only did they believe, they lived in a town recently named Feyport. How much more did she need to know? And here she was with her deepest green iridescent hair and what might possibly be horns budding from her scalp. If that didn't yell fey, what did? She'd spent her life knowing she was different, but just how different she'd never fathomed.

On more than one occasion, she'd felt certain her old headmistress, Miss Magpie, was on the verge of disclosing some long-buried secret to her, but it never happened, and her parents had died when she was so very young, they certainly could no longer answer the questions she was plagued with. Oscar never acted as if he were concerned, but Claire? Oh, Claire certainly suspected something.

Now Tieg and his family—even his friends—seemed to know what she might be. Aylee might have acted as if they didn't suspect, but surely that was just to ease Fia's mind. She wanted answers, but there was no way she'd been able to stay in the dining room with all those wonderful accepting people and let them watch as she broke down and then attempted to put herself back together. Some emotional moments were best lived behind closed doors and away from prying eyes.

Fia paced back and forth near the window, wondering how best to proceed. She needed answers. And where did one get answers when they didn't know where else to turn? They got them from books.

Fia stopped her pacing and snatched the thin canvas book she'd been flipping through the previous days. It was a fantastic mix of snippets and tales about everything from kelpies and selkies to banshees and sprites. Perhaps it had something to point her in the right direction.

As she sat on the bed and flipped open the cover, a knock sounded at the door.

She let out a long breath, really not in the mood to chat with anyone. Not even Candice and her wonderfully baked snacks would be able to sooth her jumbled up thoughts and ragged emotions.

"Fia?" the warm familiar voice asked. *Not Candice then.* "Can I have a moment?"

Did she really want to speak with Tieg tonight? She didn't know. But she had never been a coward, and that wasn't going to change just because she'd had an overwhelming day. Crossing the room, she unlocked the door without really thinking.

Tieg's eyes widened as the door opened. Color dashed up his cheeks before he dropped his eyes to his toes. "I . . . I thought you might . . . never mind. I'll see you tomorrow." He stammered the words and was turning to leave when Fia realized what had him in such a state.

"Surely you've seen a woman's shoulders before, Tieg Connolly."

"Of course I have," he grumbled.

"Mine are no different, I'd wager."

"Of that, I'm not so sure."

"Come in. I can pull on a sweater if you'd rather."

"No." The word was quick and a bit forceful. He grimaced. "No. It's all right. I'll only be a moment. Just wanted to check to see if you were well. That was all a bit much, I'm sure."

She stepped to the side and extended her arm, welcoming him farther into the room. He obliged, hands in his pockets and glancing around. He spotted the book she'd been about to dive into and jutted his chin toward it.

"Finally giving it a go?"

"I've been looking at it in bits and pieces, but I figured it might make for some decent reading tonight."

"Let me know what you think of it. You sure you're good?" He cocked his head, deliberately looking at her face and nowhere else.

She shrugged. "No. Not sure at all. But I will be."

"I think you will be too. See you in the morning then?"

"Bright and early." She smiled sadly at him, and he nodded.

After Tieg left, she got comfortable. She flipped through the book until something caught her eye. It had to be more than mere coincidence. Fia's heart rate picked up. With wide eyes, she began to read.

For longer than the good people of our isle can remember, a witch has roamed our fair lands. A warrior of old, set to conquer, Carman has traveled the countryside and city alike with her terrible and ruthless sons Dub, Dother, and Dain. Where they travel, darkness and despair follow. Carman has brought blight to the crops of our fields and darkness to the hearts of man. Although absent from sight for over a century, the memory of her presence brings a chill to even the bravest soul. Beware the witch and her sons.

Below the words, a faded, partial color illustration of a regal woman dressed in leather warrior garb and three dashing men—one with hair of raven, one crowned in spun snow, and a third with hair of fire and eyes to match—took up the remainder of the page. If Fia squinted just so and tilted her head, she could make out the resemblance between the sketch and two of the four people it was meant to depict. Fia went on to read about the famines and strife the family had been accused of causing. The very idea of the pair she'd encountered that afternoon being this witch and her son—the embodiment of darkness—was nearly too much to take.

She flipped to the next page and read an entertaining tale of an imp and its mistress, then a chilling account of something called Dullahan—the Headless Horseman—and finally the description of the pooka, which sounded both enchanting and terrifying all at once.

A deep yawn racked her body, and Fia stretched her arms high above her head, deciding it might be time to finally attempt some sleep.

She took one last look at the book in her lap, planning to close the cover, when a small entry caught her eye. It too was accompanied by a simple illustration and a brief two-page description. Never in her wildest nightmares would Fia have thought such a simple thing as an entry in a folklore book could cause her such acute terror. She read the passage through. Then read it again. After a third time, she knew she'd get little sleep, but she closed the book and shut out the light just the same.

SIXTEEN

The day of the opening arrived. Fia and Tieg had gone to great lengths to plan everything to be just so. The shelves were organized and the books straight. The art and glassware were polished, the soaps and lotions displayed. Tieg had ordered small cookies from the bakery, and Fia planned keep a pot of warm tea brewing on the simple stove for the guests. The exterior tables were arranged with chairs the night before, and Niall had even gone so far as to drape long lengths of red bunting along the exterior walls and over the windows.

The one thing they could not plan for, however, was the weather.

Just after the sun rose, grey clouds rolled in and a heavy spring rain began to fall. It came in great dowsing bucketfuls, so thick Fia could barely see more than ten yards ahead as she trudged from the inn to Bindings and Baubles. She had the presence of mind to dress in her heaviest boots and had thrown her snug wool coat and cap on over her cream sweater. Even so, she was beyond soggy by the time she arrived.

As she approached from the road, she noted a small wooden pen erected on the side of the building. It ran from the stone wall all the way toward the thick hedge traversing the back of the property. It hadn't been there the day before, and Fia wondered why Tieg had gone to the effort of putting it up the morning they were to open. And in the rain no less.

Tieg met her at the door, his mouth set in a grim line. "I've got the wood burner going at least," he said by way of greeting.

"I'm sure it'll let up soon and the place will be swamped." Fia sounded more optimistic than she felt. If they hadn't already papered the town with announcements about the opening, she would have suggested putting it off for the day.

"Swamped is likely"—Tieg nodded toward the door where a puddle had begun to form just over the threshold—"but not in the way you mean."

"I'm so sorry, Tieg. I know you wanted the day to be a success."

"Aye. But no use moaning over it now. We may need to eat an entire tray of shortbread ourselves though. Can't be letting them go stale."

"That sounds like a challenge." Fia smiled at him.

"I have something for you," Tieg said as she settled into one of the reading chairs.

"For me? Really?"

"Really. It's just a token of my appreciation for all the hard work you've put in around here."

Fia smiled at her employer. "It's actually been quite a bit of fun. But I'll still accept a gift if you've gone to the trouble of getting me something." She expected a new bottle of perfume or a small bar of soap. What she most certainly did not expect was the small wriggling animal Tieg scooped out of a sack he'd had hidden behind the counter.

Fia's mouth formed an "O" and then she was grinning from ear to ear.

"You've gotten me a hedgehog?" She extended her hands and took the tiny bristling creature, careful to avoid the spines on it's back. "Tieg. You got me an actual live hedgehog."

"I didn't actually get him. He just showed up in my garden a few days ago, and well, I remembered how fond you were of the one in the city shop, so I figured. . ." He shrugged. "He'll need to stay in the yard at night when the weather permits. I don't want to risk having him eat any of the texts. And Candice certainly won't allow him at the inn, though I'm sure Penny would be thrilled to sneak him in on your account." He stopped and watched Fia as she cuddled the tiny animal.

"Of course. He'll like to burrow in the hedge anyway. But inside when we're here? Are you sure?" She beamed at him. It might have been the most wonderful gift she'd ever received.

"I don't think it'll be a problem. Do you like him, Fia?"

"Like him? I absolutely adore him, Tieg. Thank you so much."

A smile of pure relief washed over Tieg's face. "Well then, what will you call him?"

"He looks like an Arther to me. What do you think?"

"I think Arther suits him quite well."

As everything within the library and curio shop was already arranged, the pair didn't have much to occupy them as the rains continued to pour down outside. If it hadn't been for the disappointment of the ruined opening, it would have been a wonderful morning. They sat in companionable quiet, eating cookies and reading by the woodburner. Arthur snuffled around in between them and explored as if he owned the shop himself.

"I meant to return the book you loaned me today. I finished it last night but didn't want to risk it getting wet on the way here." Her tone was steady, despite the worry the book had brought her. She'd read it cover to cover more than once since the dreadful day on the beach, and she was no closer to understanding what it meant.

Tieg looked up from his own reading. "How did you find it?" he asked carefully.

Fia wondered if he knew what was hidden in its pages—if he'd chosen to give it to her hoping she might glean a meaning from it—but dismissed the idea as a reflection of her own solicitous thoughts.

"Enlightening."

He pursed his lips. "You should keep it."

"I don't know that it's necessary. And you've already given me one gift today." She snuggled the tiny hedgehog and placed it back in her lap. "At this rate, I'll be in debt to you for all eternity. But maybe you can put it on the back shelf?" She knew he would understand what she meant. The back shelf books were those to be kept on the premises. They could be read by anyone but weren't to leave the building.

"I'd say that's fair. And I didn't give you the hedge— I mean Arthur—so you'd be in debt to me."

Despite all the questions Fia wanted to ask, they didn't discuss the book further.

Several hours after the rains began, they let up and the sun shone down in bright ribbons through the cloud breaks. A few birds began making noise outside, and Fia stood to stretch and peek out the door.

The small town was coming to life, and she noticed more people out on the cobbles and headed their way.

Aylee and her friend Dee were the first to arrive. Then Mr. Camden, Aylee's parents, several of the men from the dairy, and Jenny the shop assistant from the bakery down the road. Within a couple of hours, it seemed half of Feyport had stopped in to check things out or purchase a small item.

Fia had grown familiar with many of the faces of Feyport's residents although she'd had conversations with only a select few. That day, she talked to more people in one afternoon than she had in the weeks leading up to it. For the most part, the people were friendly. She didn't feel out of place, and only a few gave her odd looks or questioning stares. As it had been such poor weather, not many questioned her choice to leave her hat on indoors. Candice and Penny stopped in, and Penny left with a new book of beautifully illustrated animals. She'd asked for a handblown cat to accompany it, but Candice squashed the idea straight away.

Fia was so busy helping customers, she didn't notice exactly when Tieg's mood transitioned from dour to content. She only knew at one point in the afternoon she looked up to find him talking animatedly with Ned and gesturing to a nearly empty shelf which had been full only hours before. It seemed they would need to restock sooner than expected. Oscar's fanciful glasswork—the tiny animals especially—was a particularly big hit with the townspeople. She couldn't wait to write him and let him know.

Arthur had gone into hiding as soon as the shop became crowded, but every now and again Fia would hear a child exclaim or a lady tut when they caught sight of the small fury thing.

The books too were welcomed by those who stopped in. A few were purchased, but many more were sent out on loan, and over time, Fia's back became tight from all of the back and forth, bending and stooping.

The last few visitors had left, and Tieg decided it was time to close up for the day.

"That went so much better than I expected." He had a strange look on his face—half content and half disbelieving. "I just hope it wasn't all novelty and we go another week without seeing a patron."

As the place was empty, Fia felt comfortable removing her cloche and setting it on the counter. She ran her hands through her slightly sweat dampened locks and inwardly cringed at how she must look. "Once word spreads, I wouldn't be surprised if you don't have folks from all up and down the coast coming to visit."

"I do love your optimism, Fia."

Fia blushed and quirked her mouth to the side. "Well-"

She was cut off by the sound of the door opening. Fia's head turned in tandem with Tieg's as they looked toward the front of the shop. Tieg's eyebrows rose nearly to his hairline. "Glendon! What on earth?"

The tall slender man had a laugh on his face as he stepped into the shop with his mother.

"Mrs. Johnston. I'm so pleased to see you both here." Tieg stepped forward and looked around the pair, no doubt checking to see if Owen Johnston had accompanied them.

The beautiful woman glanced around quickly before her eyes fell on Fia and remained there. Fia smiled back, a little unsure. Mrs. Johnston was dressed in a simple yet lovely sapphire dress and a matching turban decorated with a beautiful jeweled butterfly broach at its center. The colors set off her complexion wonderfully, and Fia once again thought what a stunning woman she was. Why she was married to Owen Johnston, Fia would never understand.

Mrs. Johnston released a long breath, a calm expression falling over her face. She tore her gaze from

Fia and turned to Tieg. "You've done a lovely job. It's simply enchanting."

"Fia did most of it." His tone was matter of fact.

"That's hardly true," Fia argued. "You had the space in order long before I arrived. Niall and Ned certainly put in their fair share as well."

"Yes. But you brought it to life. Arranging and organizing. I shudder to think how it'd all look if left to just Niall and me."

"Well, whoever is responsible"—Brigid Johnston gave Fia a knowing look—"should be proud."

Glendon was making a slow circuit of the place, picking up trinkets and studying spines. "I've got to hand it to you, Tieg. When you first told me your plans, I thought you'd gone and lost it. But this is really something. It rivals some of the swankier places in the city. Hope these country folk know what they've got here."

"They seemed to love it," Fia said. She'd moved behind the counter and was busy tidying the stacks of ledgers and papers that had gotten a bit out of hand during the afternoon rush. Her eyes fell to her cloche, and she grabbed it with the intention of snugging it back on.

"Please," Brigid said quietly. "Leave it off. Your hair is . . . the most beautiful thing I've seen in some time."

Tieg's brow furrowed but smoothed out quickly. He cleared his throat. "Let's hope business keeps up," he said.

Glendon smiled and slung his arm around his friend. "Haven't lost that optimistic attitude of yours then?"

Brigid Johnston smiled at her son and Tieg. "I'm sure it will continue to be an unmitigated success." The front door banged open, and the smile fell from Mrs. Johnston's face. Fia thought she might have flinched a bit as the form of her husband filled the entry.

"I thought I might find you here." Owen sneered as he looked around before focusing on his wife and son. "Seems you enjoy making me trail after you again and again."

"It was no secret we were coming here, Da. I told you, I wanted to be here for Tieg's big day."

"All I ask is that you give me the courtesy of notifying me when you won't be around," he leveled at his wife. "Particularly when you know I'm to be working."

Tieg scoffed. "Is that what you call it? Working?"

"You'd know nothing about it." Owen spat the words without looking at Tieg.

"I'd wager I know more than you think I do."

Owen Johnston's head snapped toward Tieg, and in the process his eyes scanned over Fia. Something cold flashed there, and Fia took a step back. Tieg crossed the short distance from where he'd been standing with Glendon and positioned himself directly in front of the counter where Fia was working, arms crossed and legs set in an firm stance.

"I'll be asking you to leave now." Tieg's tone was frosty but firm.

"Not without my wife. If Glendon chooses to stay and entertain himself, fine, but Brigid is coming with me."

"You know I'll not be leaving Ma with you alone." Glendon's face was set in a grim expression, and Fia could see the pain and frustration there. "It's amazing, Tieg. Truly. Congratulations."

Tieg nodded, and although Fia couldn't read his expression from where she stood at his back, she imagined it matched his friend's.

Brigid looked at her husband. "Why don't you wait outside, Owen. I'll be along in a moment."

When the poet made no move to leave, she sighed and tilted her head. "For star's sake. There is nowhere for me to go. I'll only be a moment. I'd like to look at the glasswork, and I don't believe Mr. Connolly would like you in his establishment any longer." Something in her posture and the tone of her voice spoke of a warning to the man. Fia couldn't understand it. By all accounts Owen Johnston controlled his wife and, through her, his son in a way that made Fia feel sick with anger. Seeing Brigid stand up to him, she wondered what kind of strange relationship they actually had.

She knew many people lived in unhappy and sometimes even violent unions, but in just the short time she'd been acquainted with the Johnstons, their marriage had made her more than sad or uncomfortable. It made her want to wish ill on the man, and that wasn't like her at all.

Owen looked as if he would argue but then thought better of it. "I'll be outside. I'd appreciate it if you don't keep me waiting for long."

As soon as the door shut behind him, Glendon and Tieg both released the tension they'd been holding. Even Mrs. Johnston relaxed a fraction. "I'm sorry for the unpleasantness." The woman spoke in their general direction, but Fia got the impression the words were more for her benefit than Tieg's.

"Can you not just leave the man?" Tieg asked.

It was Glendon who answered, sorrow in his voice. "You know how well that went the last time."

Tieg's face hardened even further. "Yeah, mate. I do."

"While I would love nothing more than to return full time to Feyport, the idea now would be exceedingly unwise." Mrs. Johnston looked at Fia as she said the words, and Tieg's face softened in understanding.

"When do you return to the city?" Fia asked.

"I'd love to stay in town for a few more days, but Owen doesn't like it here. Too many bad memories he says."

"Bad memories of his own making," Glendon added and shot Tieg an apologetic look.

"His life choices started long before the accident, Glendon. You know that," Tieg said. Fia was utterly confused by the conversation and promised herself she'd ask Tieg what they were discussing after the Johnstons left.

"Yes," Mrs. Johnston said. "Yes, they did. But there were some beautiful things that came to be because of those choices. And for that, I'd not trade a thing." She looked from Glendon to Fia and then back again. "We really should be getting on now. Thank you, Tieg. I hope we see you again soon. And Fia. . ."

Emotion choked the woman's voice, and she turned to leave before she said what was on the tip of her tongue. Glendon smiled at Fia and then shook Tieg's hand briefly before he followed his mother out the door.

SEVENTEEN

"It was the worst day of my life."

Tieg sat on the back porch of the inn, staring straight out at the sea in the distance. The chair he was in creaked and moaned with each rock as he pushed himself back and forth with one foot. The other was crossed over his knee. Fia, in the chair adjacent, sipped at the mug of spiced cider in her hands, not wanting to interrupt him.

After the Johnstons had left, Tieg had insisted on walking Fia back to the inn, despite the fact he'd need to retrace his route all the way back past Bindings and Baubles to get to his own home on the far side of town. Candice had been so pleased to see him, she'd insisted he stay for a celebratory dinner in honor of the opening and wouldn't let either of them help with the tidying up after. Not quite ready for bed despite the long and tiring day, Fia had suggested they sit outside for a few minutes.

Tieg obliged without any argument. She'd meant to ask about the tense conversation with Brigid and Glendon but never got the chance. He started talking almost as soon as they sat.

"Glendon and I grew up together. The Johnstons moved here from the city when he and I were toddlers. We lived on the far north edge of town, just past the distillery. My parents had a good-sized piece of land that they rented out to barley farmers. It had been in my mother's family, but they had no interest in farming it themselves. My da was a teacher. The Johnstons moved into a cottage just down the road from us, and my mother would watch Glendon on the days Owen needed the house quiet. Seems like he always needed the house quiet, because Glendon was at ours more than he was home.

"Candice helped my ma, and Glendon and I would drag Niall about with us when we'd be causing trouble. It was a good childhood."

Fia remained quiet as Tieg paused, never taking his eyes from the sea.

"As we got older, Glendon would drag me about more and more. When we weren't in school or he wasn't away with his father traveling, he was forever devising these trips out into the hills or down by the strand. Faerie hunts he'd called them. He was always looking for something we could never find. I used to think it was all just a daffy bit of fun, but as we became teens, I started to wonder if he believed in all the fey. He'd never admit to it, but there was this look in his eye like he wanted the will-o-the-wisps to snatch him away or to discover one day he was a changeling swapped for some imaginary slight his mother had made to the queen of the faeries. He'd occasionally tell me he felt like a part of himself was either missing or not meant for a dull town like ours and wished he could return to the fairfolk. I didn't understand it, but I didn't need to. He was as much my brother as Niall, I suppose. And the funny thing is, after a time, I started to think he was right. I started reading up on the old folklore, and there were whisperings in town that felt too real to be just old nanny tales. It's when I started collecting the books."

Still Fia didn't speak, but her previous conversation with Niall about Tieg and Glendon came back to her. *Glendon was full of this whimsical kind of energy. It was a wonder Tieg and he got on as well as they did.*

"It was clear he wasn't happy at home, but none of us realized just how bad it was until he and Brigid turned up at the house one night. She was frantic. Said she'd discovered something about Owen and he was in a quite a state that she'd discovered it. She was sure he would do something terrible. When my ma asked what she'd found, she refused to say. She wouldn't even tell Glendon. But it must have been something bad, Fia. She looked frightened, but more than that, she looked . . . enraged."

He stopped and took a long drink from his mug. After setting it back on the table, he moved to the railing and bent forward, resting his forearms on the white painted wood.

"My folks—being the kind of people they were—offered to let both Glendon and Brigid stay with us. She was thankful but told my mother it would be only for the one night. She was taking Glendon away with her at the coming sunrise.

"My parents didn't think it was a wise thing to do, but Brigid insisted. She said she knew where she needed to go and alluded to finding something she'd been missing for years. Glendon, having always claimed he was missing something, was eager to go even though she wouldn't tell him where or for what purpose. He was old enough to lead his own life by this point, but he insisted his mother needed him and he her for the time being."

Fia finally broke her silence. "How long ago was this?"

"It'll be three years this August." Tieg pressed his lips into a firm line as he continued to stare at the sea.

Glendon had said earlier things hadn't gone well the last time they tried to run. Something disastrous must have occurred that night.

Fia rose and walked to where Tieg stood at the railing. She placed her hand on his shoulder. "What happened, Tieg? Were they not able to leave?"

"They did. Just as Brigid said they would, they were up before the sun the next day and on the road to saints know where. Owen soon realized they'd left him, and he showed up at our door within an hour or two of them leaving. Because Brigid hadn't told my folks where they were going, they couldn't answer his questions, but the reality is, even if they did know, they wouldn't have told him.

"Owen Johnston was not well liked in town, by my family or any other. People saw how he treated his wife and son. Her like property and him as if he didn't exist.

"My ma told me to take Niall outside before things got ugly. Candice was already married and living here with Ned. Thank the saints." His voice trailed off, and Fia knew he was lost in a dark memory. She almost asked him to stop talking. She didn't want to know what came next. Didn't want to hear what she suspected. But she kept silent. If he was willing to say it, she was willing to hear it.

"Niall and I were down by the cliffs when I first saw the smoke. I thought it was just one of the farmers burning off their crops, but then something in me just clicked. It was coming from the direction of home and I knew—I knew it was our house." He took a deep shuddering breath. "By the time anyone arrived to help, the entire front porch and the roof were ablaze. Folks did what they could, but it was too late. My parents never made it out."

He didn't say the words but the meaning was clear. Owen Johnston arrived at their home and by the time he'd left, Tieg's parents we dead.

"He killed them? Owen Johnston killed your parents?"

"No one could ever prove anything. Despite him being the last person to see them alive, the council said there was no way to prove he had anything to do with it. There was an old oil lamp on the porch, and it was a bit windy that day. But I know. I saw his face before I took Niall to the cliffs. He was livid."

"Glendon and Brigid?" Fia asked, a small tremor in her voice.

"He must have known where they were heading. Glendon wrote me a couple of months later and said he'd found them not two days after they'd stayed with us. Drug them off to the city and hasn't been back since. Glendon was rather vague in his letters. He sent a stiff sort of condolence on behalf of Owen and Brigid, but I know Glendon too well. He was as destroyed by the events as me."

A soft caressing breeze blew up from the waters in the distance. Fia wasn't sure it could bring any comfort to Tieg, but it helped to soothe her as it blew through the short curls around her ears.

"Niall and I moved in here with Ned and Candice for a time as we settled what we could. The house was a complete loss, and we had it torn down. I wouldn't have moved back there even if it could be salvaged. We sold off the land, and Niall and I both got jobs at the dairy until I had enough saved to buy the space for Bindings and the rent on my own place. I think it's what my da, having been a teacher, would have wanted." He continued to stare out at the water. "So we've got that in common. I was old enough to not be an orphan, but it's a gaping hole just the same."

"I don't know what to say, Tieg. I'm so sorry." Fia was fighting tears as she too studied the depthless darkness of the sea beyond them. "They sound like wonderful people."

"They were. And you don't need to say anything. Just-"

"Just?" she whispered.

Without looking at her, he laced his fingers through hers. "Just stay out here with me a little longer. Let's enjoy the view of the sea."

EIGHTEEN

Much to the surprise of both Tieg and Fia, the excitement surrounding the opening of Bindings and Baubles did not wane over the days following its opening. Although it wasn't quite as busy as it had been on the first day, those who hadn't visited initially trickled in and several citizens of Feyport stopped in almost daily. The sales were good and the library loans were better.

Tieg kept a list of the items he thought would need to be restocked soon and asked many visitors if there were additional items they would like for him to make available. Fia was surprised at a few. Inks and fountain pens, stationery and scented candles were a few of the more popular ideas. Tieg took the list to Aylee's father, Devon Garrow, to ask if supplying these things would in any way hamper the man's business at the mercantile. Devon assured him it would not and seemed relieved that someone else might be able to supply some of the finer things his shop couldn't.

Tieg was in decent spirits, but Fia could still see the reserve in him that never fully lifted. She thought most if that was down simply to his personality, but she wondered how heavy the appearance of Owen Johnston sat with him. Not that they'd seen any of the Johnston family again. As far as Fia knew, they'd been in town only a day or two before heading back to the city.

After nearly three weeks, Fia became accustomed to life in the gorgeous seaside town. She woke each day happy to go to work, came home each night pleasantly tired, and got to know more and more of the town's citizens. She still hid her hair and the small knobby bumps adorning her scalp under a cap most days. Thankfully, the tiny horns seemed to have stopped growing for the time being. She was almost beginning to think she might go without the hat eventually.

One Friday afternoon, Tieg told her he needed to head to the city for a few days. It was necessary for him to visit a few artisans and place more orders for goods to be sold. He'd also received word from the hedgehog-loving bookseller that she had received a copy of one of the rare manuscripts he'd been seeking. He planned to inspect it and with any luck return with it in three days' time.

"I should be back by Tuesday. Take the next two days off. There's no need to have the shop open for the weekend, but if you can handle it alone on Monday, I'd appreciate it if you'd open up." Tieg was busy jotting notes in a small leatherbound journal he'd taken to keeping over the past weeks. He looked up when she didn't immediately answer.

"You don't need me to go with you?"

"I'll be fine I think. And so will you. Niall says you can join him tomorrow at the pub with his friends if you like. Otherwise, just take the time to relax. Stay at the inn or have tea with your friends." The tone of his voice didn't completely convince Fia he believed his own words, but she certainly wouldn't allow herself to become a burden to the man who was kind enough to employ her.

Your friends. Tieg clearly meant Aylee, Maeve, and Dee. While Fia hadn't given the young women that designation herself yet, she supposed it fit. She'd seen them often in her time in Feyport, and they did the sorts of things friends did together. They'd gone picking wild flowers more than once and had shared picnics on the beach.

Fia had asked if they might take her to the cliffs one day, and Aylee had nearly broken down at the idea. Fia had felt terrible but hadn't understood what upset the beautiful woman. By all accounts the cliffs were the most scenic of places near Feyport.

Dee and Maeve had both been there as they sat near the strand watching birds go by and throwing a stick to Aylee's dog Pepper. It was then, with the help of her sister and best friend, that Aylee finally told Fia about the tragic events of one autumn past. She'd befriended a stranger who had been more magical than anyone she'd ever met. There was some unpleasantness with an old suitor and things had ended in heartbreak for Aylee. While she wouldn't go into specifics, it soon became clear to Fia that Aylee had fallen in love with the quirky stranger, and while her life now was more complicated for it, she had a hopeful gleam in her eye when she spoke of her future. Fia couldn't exactly discern if the man was somehow still around, despite the sense of tragedy in the tale. Aylee didn't elaborate, and Fia felt it was too rude to ask. Perhaps as they got closer, she'd get the whole story.

Fia told Tieg she would indeed make plans with Niall. His uplifting presence would help take her mind off the darker things that still troubled her. She hadn't forgotten either the witch's warning nor the troubling entry she'd found in the fey and folklore book. And she still wanted to see the view from the cliffs, so she planned to have Niall take her there rather than the noisy cramped pub as he was likely to try to persuade her.

Tieg was satisfied with her plan

The air was thick with the sound of night-loving insects and soft whispering winds. In the far distance, Fia could still hear the waves crashing on the shore, but it was more background noise than anything.

Candice had outdone herself with dinner, and Fia feared she might have made a fool of herself with the size of the helping she'd devoured, but between the creamy vegetable soup and the warm buttered bread and small pork medallions, there was no help for it. At least the only other guest at the inn was an older man traveling from the north on his way to the city, and he seemed inclined to keep to himself rather than comment on her portions.

After an equally generous helping of trifle and a warm cup of tea, Fia had run upstairs to retrieve her mother's leatherbound book and a small lantern to bring out on the back porch. It was such a beautiful night, Fia thought it a shame to waste it indoors.

She opened to the first full color plate, and the image there swam before her eyes. One moment it was a lush garden scene, the next a portrait of an exquisite woman with long flowing hair which bled into the foliage of the background. She had luminous skin shimmering in the sun. From the crown of her head, two impressive antlers grew. The artistry was unlike anything Fia had ever seen. How had the illustrator been able to capture such detail and light within the fragile paper, she couldn't guess. Fia blinked, and the panel shifted, revealing a naked young man at the woman's feet—a look of utter devastation on his face. For the first time in her life, Fia thought she could make out the words written below the illustration. *Let man fear the Leanan Sidhe. Her gifts are not without price.*

Her heart raced as Fia turned the page. Words tumbled and swirled before her. She picked up on snippets only to have them dance away before she could piece it all together, but this was more than she'd ever gotten from the inked pages before. Artist and desire. Deceit and death. Muse and magic. She read them and forced her mind to latch on even as the book seemed determined to keep its secrets from her. After several long minutes, her eyes began to strain and her head to pound. She shut the green leather cover and leaned her head back, closing her eyes against the night and her own frustration.

The back door of the inn shut softly, and Fia open her eyes and found Tieg standing over her, a concerned look on his face.

Her brow furrowed in response. "I thought you were leaving?" He dropped down into the chair next to her.

"I am. First train in the morning. I just wanted to see you before I left." The shadow of concern didn't leave his face. "Are you good, Fia? You look a bit pale."

Struggling with the book must have pulled something from her. She smiled, hoping to relieve a bit of his unease. "Just tired, I suppose. And you just saw me not two hours ago."

"True. I did. You're tired? Is your employer working you too hard?" he asked in a mock serious tone.

She chuckled. "Not at all. I quite enjoy my position, thank you."

"Do you really?" Fia didn't know if his expression was hopeful exactly, but it was certainly something akin to it.

It would have been easy to give him a teasing quick reply, but for some reason she felt it necessary to fully explain. She thought for a moment before saying slowly, "I do. More than I ever thought I would. It's not just the books and the work, though. I feel like I belong—both at the shop and in Feyport."

"And here I thought you were just in it to get your hands on all those fancy lotions I keep ordering from the city."

"I won't pretend the soaps and oils aren't a fantastic perk." She smiled but then her face stilled again and her voice took on a serious tone. "Being here"—she spread her hands wide, encompassing the porch and inn, but also the still night sky and the dark waves below—"I can see myself staying forever. That isn't a feeling I've had in a really long time. If ever." She chewed on her bottom lip. "That probably sounds ridiculous to you. I've only been here for a handful of weeks, but it just feels . . . I don't know. Like home?" She could feel some of the color return to her cheeks.

"Surely you felt at home in the city. With Oscar," he said solemnly.

"Oscar tried. But Claire . . . well. You only got a brief taste of her. She . . . doesn't like me very much."

Tieg's brow furrowed even further, the corners of his lips turning down into the deepest scowl she'd seen yet on his handsome face. "I wish I'd met you sooner then."

"You met me at exactly the right time. If it had been any sooner, I'm not sure I would have accepted your offer to come here. I hadn't reached the point yet where I knew I needed a change."

"Well then, I'm glad I met you when I did. I still can't believe I took you for a lad, though. What an idiot I was." He sighed and ran a hand through his hair.

Fia laughed again. "Just meant my disguise was working as I planned." She sat quietly for another moment, staring out at the inky blackness where she knew the sea moved to meet the land. "I am well and truly happy you brought me here, Tieg. I even seem to be getting a bit closer to understanding this." She held up the leather-covered book.

"I can't tell you how happy it makes me to hear those words from you, Fia."

"You really want me to read this book, don't you?"

He looked momentarily confused then seemed to realize she was teasing him. "I would love for you to read the book, dear Fia, but I am much more interested in your general well-being. I'm happy that you are happy." He stood and grabbed one of her hands, pulling her to her feet. As she stared up into his wonderfully familiar face, she saw a longing there she couldn't deny. Her body answered it with a tightness in her chest. Tieg reached up and grasped a loose curl near her cheek and rubbed it between his fingers. "When I get back, I'd like—" He frowned, searching for the words.

She knew she should be concerned with his hand so close to the budding horns she hadn't yet worked up the courage to show him. For some reason, it didn't seem important. If he felt them, so be it.

One side of Fia's mouth curved upward. "You'd like?"

His voice was quiet and husky. "I'd like to—" He ran his tongue over his lower lip and cleared his throat.

Now she was smiling at him fully. Fia had extremely limited experience with men. But she had read a lot of books and had heard other young women in the cafés in the city. She had a feeling she might know what it was he wanted, but she certainly wasn't going to make it easy for him.

"Fia?"

"Yes."

"Would you mind if I kissed you?"

"I thought you'd never ask." She stretched up on her toes and placed her lips softly against his. He seemed momentarily taken aback by her movement, but then he was cupping her face, holding her still as he deepened the connection with her. Fia closed her eyes and lost herself to the sensation of Tieg's mouth on hers. He tasted like peppermint and sage. As he brushed his thumbs along her cheekbones, the feeling of belonging slammed into Fia even stronger than before.

She wrapped her arms around his waist and savored the feel of his strong muscles beneath her palms. When Tieg moaned, she thought she might fall apart right there on the porch of the inn. Tieg deepened the kiss, and Fia answered with just as much hunger. Breathless, Tieg finally pulled back, and the expression on his face brought more joy to Fia than she ever thought possible.

"That, Mr. Connolly, is a proper smile."

NINETEEN

"Don't take this the wrong way, Fia," Niall said as he looked over at her from his spot opposite on the blanket, "you're normally a doll and all, but what in the name of the saints has gotten into you this morning? That ridiculous smile hasn't left your face since we've been here." He looked at her, and his own smile fell from his face in such a comical way, Fia had a brief moment when she thought he might be choking. "Oh no. You aren't taking a special liking to me, are you?"

"A special liking?" Fia practically barked at him as the laughter mixed with her words. "No, Niall. I like you just the same as I always have."

Relief washed over his features. "Thank the stars for that. I'd like to have at least one fetching young woman in Feyport I can just be myself with and not feel like I'm at risk of an eminent engagement."

Fia raised an eyebrow at him, and he explained, "They are all so serious about it. One wink or a turn around the dance floor at the jubilee and the next thing I know, they think we're courting. I'm only eighteen for the love of it. I'm still in my prime. Certainly nowhere near reading to settle in for a family."

Fia was near to bursting with laughter as she looked at him with as much seriousness as she could muster. "Rest assured, your bachelorhood is safe with me."

The pair had walked from the inn, past the strand, and to the far side of town where a long winding path led through the sea grass and up to a set of bluffs overlooking the teal and cobalt waters below. The cliff face sat atop a nearly sheer wall stretching far below to the white crashing waves. It was quite possibly one of the most stunning things Fia had ever seen.

The sun beat down on them, but the breeze from the water cooled the perspiration from Fia's brow. She wore the same floppy sun hat she'd had on the day she'd met the woman calling herself a witch. During one of her early morning walks on the beach, Aylee had retrieved it from where it had nestled among the rocks and delivered it back to Fia at the inn. Niall had already threatened once to snatch it from her head and send it sailing to where only the peregrines or kelpies could reach it.

Fia had simply laughed him off, knowing he would do no such thing.

"Then who *are* you all goo-goo about?" he asked.

"Who says I'm goo-goo about anyone?"

"I do. Were you not just listening to me? I am a very astute observer, and if you aren't feeling the pitter pattering about someone, I'll eat my hat. Or yours for that matter. When are you going to stop wearing that thing everywhere we go?"

"My hat is no concern of yours, Niall Connolly." She laughed. "And neither is my love life."

"Oh come on, Fia. I know everyone in town. I can give you the inside edge on whoever the mystery man is. Although, I can't imagine who you'd have had time to get to know what with all the work you've been doing with Tieg at Bindings and Baubles." His face went momentarily blank just before he sprang to his feet. "It's Tieg, isn't it? Tieg? You're goo-goo over Tieg?"

Fia sat up straighter and grabbed a handful of the tall windswept grass growing all around them. She pulled the seed heads from the blades and scattered them to the wind. "I told you. I'm not goo-goo. Stop using that word."

"Okay. You aren't goo-goo. But it is Tieg, isn't it?"

"Maybe." She squinched her face up and looked at him with one eye mostly closed. "Is that a bad thing?"

"Well, no. But Tieg," he said wonderingly. "I just never thought the grumpy bastard would land someone like you."

"What do you mean like me?"

"Like you." He waved a hand at her. "I don't know. Gorgeous, funny and . . . happy."

Fia beamed at him. "You think I'm gorgeous?"

He scoffed. "Of course I do, Fia. As does every other man in Feyport with a pulse."

She decided not to dive into that topic much deeper. Niall was just being himself—kind and jovial. "Why shouldn't Tieg be with someone who's happy?"

"I never said he shouldn't. I simply said I never thought he would. Our parents' death was hard. It *is* hard. I mean, you can certainly relate. But Tieg took it the hardest. He really believes it wasn't an accident, and he might be right, but he can't let it go. Almost like he blames himself or something. I don't know." He plucked a handful of grass where it grew waist high on his side of the blanket and watched as it drifted away in the breeze. "This last month or two is the first I've seen him more like the old Tieg."

He shook his head as if to clear it. "Come to think of it, I don't know why I didn't see it before. You've made a big impact on him, I think."

"He's made a big impact on me too."

"Good. You both deserve a little happiness, I'd wager." He bent to collect up the blanket, tugging it even as Fia sat on one end. The motion scooted her slightly down the incline, and she gasped out a laugh. "Now if you've had enough nature, I could really use a pint."

They made it to the bottom of the pathway—Niall sharing his plans to remain a bachelor, traveling and enjoying the company of whom he chose when he chose it for the entirety of his life—when hoofbeats interrupted their conversation.

Niall stopped and looked up the road away from town. "Wonder who this could be."

The roan horse and rider barreled down upon them, and Fia screamed as the rider's black leather boot connected with the side of Niall's head. He went down like a sack of hay, blood leaking from his hairline to mar his still face.

In the next moment, a hand reached down and latched under Fia's arm. With a grunt of effort, the rider hoisted her onto the horse across the front of the saddle. She kicked and struggled to no avail. The awkward position and speed of the running stallion made it nearly impossible to maneuver herself. Her hat fell from her head and was trampled along the cobbles as her body bounced against the animal's shoulder.

After several agonizing minutes, the rider slowed in front of a moderately sized whitewashed stone cottage. His breathing was heavy and wet over Fia's head. Taking the horse around the back, he dismounted and led it to a small stable, all the while keeping a firm grasp on Fia's wrists, holding her in place. Once the stable door was closed, the rider yanked Fia from the saddle and unceremoniously dumped her on the ground in a relatively clean pile of hay.

From her position on the ground, she finally realized who her captor was. Owen Johnston hadn't seemed fit enough to ride a horse quite so well, much less possess the strength to bodily lift Fia from the ground, but apparently whatever desperate madness pushed him to the act had also sustained his effort.

"What on earth have you done?" Fia yelled. "Niall—"

"Quiet. If you know what is good for you," he panted the words, "you'll keep your mouth shut."

"I'll scream my bloody head off before I do anything you tell me." She jumped to her feet and ran toward the door.

Owen reached out and slapped her hard across the face. Tears sprang to Fia's eyes at both the unexpected act of brutality and the pain searing across her cheek.

"I have no qualms about making the next blow hard enough to incapacitate you as I've done with young Connolly."

Fia backed away, eyes darting from the door to Owen and back again. She could make a run for it but knew her chances at success would be better if she waited for him to be distracted.

"Now, Fia Walsh. Listen to me. This doesn't have to be any uglier than it already is. Give me your hands." Fia hesitated as she noted the length of cord dangling from Owen's belt. "I said give me your hands."

He stalked toward her, and Fia shrank back until her shoulder connected with the wall to the closest pen. Owen reached out and snatched her left hand, expertly looping one end of the cord around her wrist, then wove the loose end around her other hand, yanking the rough material so tightly, it pinched her skin. He used the painful tether to lead her into the back corner of the stable where he tied it to a heavy metal loop in the wall. Fia realized with some horror he intended to keep her captive, but for what purpose and how long she couldn't fathom.

Once she was restrained, he used his sleeve and wiped perspiration from his ruddy face.

"What is it you want from me?" Her voice wobbled as she looked at his face. She expected to find a mask of anger or lunacy, but worse, Owen showed an expression of haughty indifference, as if this entire adventure were no more than a simple nuisance to him. A nuisance that left him sweaty and breathless.

"At the moment, what I would like is for you to remain quiet. I've no wish to gag you, but I'll do as I must."

"You hardly know me, Mr. Johnston, but you can't truly expect that I'll stay silent simply because you wish it."

"I know you well enough." He looked around as if searching for something. Fia could tell the moment he made his decision. "So be it."

Owen grabbed a handkerchief from his jacket pocket and stretched it lengthwise, stepping behind her and pulling the cloth around her face. He tied it snuggly and used one hand to pinch her cheeks until she opened her mouth, causing the fabric to slip in. She bit down, but it was no use. He snugged the gag, and she could no longer speak.

Fia stood trembling as he looked her up and down.

"I don't suppose you've got the book on you." He said the words more to himself than to her, but Fia felt she should still reply. The man was after all, at least according to Tieg, a possible murderer. She shook her head.

"I thought not. No matter. I can deal with that later."

Was this all about her book? Fia couldn't imagine it to be true. She knew it was valuable, but to go to these lengths to procure it seemed a stretch.

"I'll be back before dusk. You may want to rest while you can. We've a good distance to travel tonight." He slipped out and shut the stable door. She heard the wooden cross beam thunk into place as her tears began to fall.

TWENTY

If Tieg lived to be a hundred, he would never be able to repay Rupert Camden. The train simply wasn't fast enough and neither were the coaches. But due to some divine providence, Rupert happened to be in the city in the petrol-powered truck he used at the distillery.

Tieg was once again staying with Simon Beck, and Rupert had arrived for tea just before the housekeeper delivered Niall's telegram into Tieg's hands. He'd read it over several times, his brain unable or unwilling to make sense of the missive, before looking up into the silently waiting faces of his friends. One look and Rupert seemed to understand something was terribly amiss, and within minutes the two men were taking their leave from Simon and speeding up the road back toward Feyport.

Simon assured Tieg he'd send word back to Niall and Candice that their brother was making for home with haste and would go directly to the inn. Rupert, for his part, remained a stalwart and composed driver, taking them at breakneck speed along the country roads. He stopped once when sheep barred the thoroughfare and once to refill his tank. Despite the grave situation, he was calm. Tieg on the other hand was a bundle of dark thoughts and vicious plans. Not generally prone to violence, Tieg vowed to himself, should any harm come to Fia, he would hunt down the person responsible and enjoy making him suffer.

The journey which had taken Tieg the better part of the previous day via train was returned in a little over four hours in Camden's truck. Night had settled over Feyport when the men arrived outside the inn in a shower of gravel and dust.

Candice was out the door and racing toward Teig before he'd shut the door of Rupert's vehicle. "Ah, Tieg, it's a nightmare."

"Tell me."

"Niall can give you a better account—he was there. But he's taken a good blow to the head. I've been telling him to rest, but he won't hear of it. Ned's got half the town out looking already."

"Slow down, Candice. I still don't understand. The telegram said she'd been taken but not by whom or to where."

Camden had come around the truck and stood with arms crossed waiting for the tale as well.

"Come inside, the both of you," Candice said. "We'll tell you what we can, but it's not much."

Tieg noted how tired his sister looked. She wasn't one to lose her head in an emergency, but that didn't mean the strain wasn't there. Candice and Ned had taken a liking to Fia from the moment they'd welcomed the lithe and joyful young woman into their home. Once again he thought of all the ugly things he'd do to the person responsible, and he had an inkling Ned might be right there alongside him as he did.

Tieg didn't want to waste time, but Candice was already moving toward the front porch. As she swung the door open, Teig could hear the buzz of activity within. If half the town was out with Ned looking for Fia, the other half appeared to be in Candice Bryan's sitting room.

"Tieg," Niall squawked the moment his brother entered. Teig's frown deepened several degrees as he took in the blossoming black and eggplant bruise accompanying the large goose egg at Niall's left temple. "Saints and sinners, Tieg. I feel like a right bastard."

"Tell me what happened," Tieg demanded.

"We were having a grand time out on the cliffs. Just sitting and chatting. Enjoying the view. It was getting on to lunch time, and we decided to head to the pub and grab a bite. Just at the base of the paths, as we were coming toward the edge of the road, I caught sight of a bloke on a horse coming hell for breakfast right at us. I didn't even have time to push Fia out of the way. The crazy bastard kicked me square in the temple, and when I came to, the rider and Fia were both gone. Not a hair of either of them around.

"I knew Fia would never leave me in the road like that, so I got up and hurried back as quick as I could, but the pounding in my head made it a slight bit slower than it should have gone. Anyway, I reached the main street and popped into the Garrows' place. Aylee's da helped me to get back to the inn, and he and Ned took off to see if they could figure what had happened." He ran a hand over his head and winced.

"And you didn't catch a glimpse of the rider? See who it was?" Rupert asked.

"He was coming so fast and wearing a riding cap pulled low over his brow. All I know for certain is he was riding a roan and seemed about average build. That's it."

Tieg sighed. "You were close to town. No one else was at the cliffs or could have seen the rider or which way they went?"

"No, Tieg. I'm sorry." Niall groaned and tilted his head back. "I just can't for the life of me think who would want to do something like this. All I can come up with is that warning she got weeks ago on the beach."

Tieg himself had been racking his brain to think who would have wished ill on Niall enough to deliver such a blow and could also mean to snatch Fia away. He'd feared it was some rough sort passing through town. If that were the case, it was no telling which way they would have gone or what exactly could be happening to Fia at that very moment while he sat there doing nothing. Niall's mention of the witch brought the entire situation into clarity.

"Goddam bastard." Tieg growled more than said the words. "I'll kill him."

Candice's eyebrows rose into her hairline. "What is it you know?"

Danger is coming for you in the guise of a man who cloaks his true self. He will bring ill to you. Fight him with all that you are.

Cloaks his true self.

"It has to be," Tieg said more to himself than anyone else.

"Has to be who?" Niall asked, losing patience.

"Owen Johnston." Tieg spat the man's name between his teeth.

"I don't understand. Owen isn't even in Feyport any longer. The three of them took off back to the city weeks ago. What makes you suspect him?" Candice asked.

"I've got my reasons."

Niall raised his eyebrows and spread his arms in a we're waiting expression.

Tieg shook his head. "Let's find Fia first, and if I'm right, I'll explain it all then. She should hear it before anyone."

Candice continued to look dubious, but bless Tieg's brother. Niall was already heading for the door. "What are you waiting for, Tieg? Let's go."

TWENTY-ONE

Judging by the shadows engulfing the stable, evening had fallen.

Fia's hands were riddled with pins and needles from the awkward way they were tied, and she wondered how much longer she'd be stuck in the uncomfortable position. She'd initially tried to wiggle her hands free from their bindings but eventually had given up and instead attempted to rest. Sitting against the short wall, hands resting first on one shoulder than the other, she wasn't sure which she feared more, Owen Johnston's return or the idea that she might be abandoned altogether.

As it turned out, the poet kept his word, and as dusk settled, the door opened with a squeal and the flickering light of a lamp's flame bounced in.

He didn't speak to her at first but rather busied himself checking the horse's saddle and bags. When everything was to his liking, he turned and addressed her.

"You need to listen to me and listen well. We will be traveling as quick as possible but we'll be taking the less traveled paths south. Because time is of some import, I'll have you in the saddle with me. If you value your life, you'll keep quiet and not struggle. ." He yanked the gag from her mouth. "I have no qualms about dragging you if necessary, but I'd rather it not come to that."

"Where are you taking me?" she asked.

"South."

That could be anywhere.

"Back to the city?"

"South. That's all you need know." He reached up and unfasted the rope from its hook. He gave it a small yank, and Fia rose wearily to her feet. She desperately wanted to not get on the horse with Owen Johnston but didn't see any other choice. She didn't doubt him when he threatened to drag her along. "Have you ridden much?"

She shook her head.

"I imagine you'll be quite sore come morning then." He grabbed the horse's reins in one hand and tugged Fia along with his other. "I'd have hired a wagon if I thought one could be trusted in this damned town."

They walked outside, and Owen pointed to a small step. "Use that to seat yourself in the saddle."

Fia's legs were wobbly as she did as he instructed. It took her two attempts to haul herself into the right position. Her heart was thundering in her chest. If she left here with Johnston, she didn't know what might happen. She had no idea what he could possibly want with her and was fairly certain no one knew who was responsible for her disappearance. Particularly if Niall was unable to recount the ordeal.

Niall. Tears threatened at the very thought of the joyful young man. Not knowing how he was faring was even worse than not knowing her own fate. And with Tieg gone into the city, she wasn't certain who would be out looking for her. She scanned the nearby area, hoping to see some clue to tell her where exactly they were or to catch some sign of a rescue party.

Her captor extinguished his lamp, robbing Fia of even the smallest hope. It was not yet the pitch of darkest night, but her vision was limited to the small area around them. She could still hear the ocean in the distance and smell the sweet lingering aroma of the distillery, so they must be near town. She knew, however, he wouldn't be fool enough to travel through the center of Feyport. It might be dark, but people would still be out and about.

She heard Johnston fasten the unlit lamp somewhere behind her. The horse shifted on its feet, and a moment later, the bulk of Owen Johnston settled behind her. He reached around her and held the reins. With a brief flick, the horse began to move.

Fia had been right. The pathway they took wove over small trails and paths, skirting the outside of town. The moon rose over the hills to the east and from its light, she could make out low stone walls, fields, and pastures. They passed several small outbuildings, but anytime a home or dwelling came into view, the poet seemed to find a path to skirt it.

After an hour in the saddle, back straight lest she touch the man abducting her, Fia's body began to ache. It started where her backside met the leather saddle and traveled down her thighs and up her spine. Fia's dismay grew. She'd kept silent so far, but the farther away from Feyport they got, the more anxiety began to eat away at her.

Unable to keep her questions in any longer, she finally whispered, "Why are you doing this?"

The poet was quiet so long, Fia was sure he wouldn't answer. When he finally did, his words made little sense. "Brigid is gone, and I have grown accustomed to her presence."

Fia's mind swirled. She knew Brigid to be unhappy in her marriage, and both Tieg and Glendon seemed more than willing to help her escape the man, but why in all the isles Owen Johnston should think Fia could make some sort of replacement was beyond her.

"You can't mean for me to be your wife?" Her stomach roiled at the thought.

"Don't be disgusting." The acid in his tone was both confusing and somehow reassuring, but before she could ponder what he meant further, the night around them grew even darker. An inky veil dropped from the trees and blotted out the moon and stars. It creeped from the ground and crawled up the horse's legs until Fia felt as if she were swimming in a river created from the night itself. The shadows were enough to make her spine tingle and her heart skip, but the sense of foreboding that danced on the edges of the darkness made her head throb and her soul cringe.

That dark fringe whispered to her. It sang in quiet tones of blood and vengeance. Hate and violence. Seated atop the poet's horse, she wanted nothing more than to turn in her seat and claw the throat from his body with her bare hands. To gouge his eyes and to laugh at his pain.

Fia blinked and the thoughts flitted away like cobwebs in the wind, but still she could feel them waiting to claim her again. The darkness and violence continued to surround her, but they no longer consumed her.

Darkness and Violence. The witch's sons. She didn't know how she knew, but it was clear to Fia. They were no longer alone on the road.

"Stop the horse," she said.

Owen's voice was full of haughty spite as he replied, "I think not, and unless you wish to lose your tongue, you'll keep it still."

"Perhaps it's you who should be separated from your tongue," a smooth male voice came from the shadows. Fia thought she might recognize the deep timbre but couldn't be certain. "Or an equally valuable body part."

Fia's heart raced even as she squinted into the darkness trying to make out the owner of the voice. Two figures materialized in the gloam as the horse and its riders neared them. Fia had been right about the voice's owner. The handsome visage of Dub stood before them, but she was surprised when his companion wasn't the striking woman who claimed to be his mother. At his side stood another eerily handsome man.

He was taller even than Darkness. Where Dub was strength and steal, all dark hair, eyes, and shadows, this second man was still as water, frigidity personified. Hair the color of salt, skin the hue of ice and eyes to match—a blue so pale they were nearly entirely white save for the pupils. But even in his pale monotone, he was achingly beautiful.

Fia looked from one to the other. Owen stiffened behind her, and when he spoke, his voice had lost any trace of superiority and was nothing but a quaver in the night. "You've no business here. Let us pass."

The pale stranger cocked his head and stared past Fia to the man seated behind her. "All is our business." Fia hadn't expected such a melodic voice from the tall stranger. "Particularly when violence seasons the night."

"There's been no violence here." Owen's voice was barely more than a whisper.

"Keep your lies in your head. Violence speaks to me. And right now it tells me all in your heart." The white-haired man took a step forward as he rolled his head on his shoulders. "Such delicious violence."

Owen made to turn the horse around, but before he could so much as flick the reins, Dub was there, ripping them from his hands. Owen jerked back and nearly toppled from the saddle. Dub took no notice but held out his hand to Fia. "Come. It seems you've failed to heed the warning so generously given."

Fia hesitated. While she knew she should be happy to escape Owen Johnston and whatever he had planned for her, the idea of willingly accepting Darkness's hand was just as unpalatable.

He added, "Fear not, little lost one. Dain and I have no reason to cause you ill. Mother will be most unpleased should anything befall you before she's collected her favor."

With a trembling hand, Fia accepted his and allowed the tall dark man to help her down from the horse. She looked warily toward Dain. Was Dother—Evil—also lurking about in the shadows? If he was, she had no wish to meet him.

Dub led her away from the horse, and she watched with some trepidation as Dain continued to circle around the poet and his mount. Surely he wouldn't kill the man outright. He had no cause. The predatory look in his eye, however, argued against that notion. Perhaps there was indeed some history between the witch's sons and the poet. Fia was learning anything was possible. It sounded as if Owen Johnston had unleashed his temper on more than one poor soul in the past.

"Come now, little sister. This night is done with you." Fia walked back the way she'd come, Dub at her side. She glanced back over her shoulder at the sound of the horse's whinny. "Let your mind be still. Dain likes his fun, but he'll not harm the man too severely. That one's fate lies in another's hands."

He led her farther back along the road. The night remained unnaturally dark, and Fia stumbled along next to him in silence. After what felt like an eternity, she made out the distant lights of Feyport. It was then she realized the darkness had subsided and she could see the moon and stars high overhead. She turned to tell Dub she could continue on alone, but he was already gone.

Fia blew out a long breath and quickened her pace. She could hear voices up ahead and saw torch beams bouncing along the path not two hundred yards before her. As she raced toward the lights and the men carrying them, she recognized the hulking silhouette of Ned Bryan. They must be out searching for her.

"Here," she called. "I'm here." The voices in the distance grew louder and more animated.

"Fia! Fia, thank the stars!" Rapid footsteps pounded toward her, and she sobbed with relief as Tieg ran to her and crushed her to his chest. Ned was several paces behind him huffing as he came up the slight incline. "Saints and sinners, Fia. Are you injured?"

"No. No, I'm fine, Tieg." She drew in the scent of him and wanted nothing more than to stay buried in his chest, but then she thought of Niall. "Oh saints, Tieg. Niall? Is he all right?"

"Yes. Worried sick and likely to have a wicked headache by the morning, but well enough." He rubbed his hands down her back and took a step backward, dipping his head to look at her face. She thought he might kiss her again, but Ned arrived, huffing slightly, and the moment was broken.

"What the devil happened, Fia? Niall couldn't say who it was that hit him, but Tieg here has his suspicions."

"I'll wager your suspicions are correct," she said to Tieg. "It was that odious man, Owen Johnston. He came on us as we were leaving the cliffs. He knocked poor Niall to the ground and dragged me off with him. He held me somewhere outside of town until nightfall. We were headed south. But I've no idea where."

"The man no longer deserves to walk this earth," Tieg bit out. "Did he hurt you?"

Fia, never one to condone violent behavior, felt a little flutter in her chest at his words.

"No, Tieg. I told you I'm unscathed. Physically at least. And I understand how you feel about the man, but I'm not certain you'll have the chance to take your vengeance on him."

His brow furrowed.

"I'll explain it all, but perhaps on the way back to the inn?" Fia was beyond tired, and she wanted nothing more than to wrap herself in a warm blanket and sip a cup of hot cider. She needed to see that Niall was well for herself and to let the last twelve hours float away from her.

"Of course," Ned said. "We'll need to let the others know you've been found as well."

"The others?"

"The better part of Feyport has been out on the hunt for ya. We started looking as soon as Niall told us what happened. Then a bit ago, Tieg, Niall, and Rupert Camden found the lot of us and we split up into sets of two. The others are to meet us back in town soon for an update," Ned explained.

For some reason this simple statement brought tears to Fia's eyes. Never in her life had so many people cared about her and accepted her like the people of Feyport did. The thought that she had nearly been dragged away from it all was unthinkable. But just as concerning was the idea that she had garnered the attention of not only Owen Johnston and his desire for her, her book, or both, but also the attention of Carman and her sons. What would it mean for those she cared about when the witch, Darkness, Violence, and Evil came to collect what they thought was due?

She'd need to worry about that later.

It took the trio nearly an hour to traverse the paths and tracks from the countryside back into the town proper and over to the inn. During that time, Fia told Ned and Tieg all which had transpired since she'd enjoyed her afternoon on the cliffs. Several times, Tieg made noises that indicated she was confirming something he already believed, but he never interrupted or interjected his thoughts.

By the time they reached the center of town, most of the others had returned. Niall was waiting with Aylee's father and flew to her side the moment she approached with her escorts. She hugged him back just as fiercely and winced when she saw the dark stain tracing down his temple.

He shrugged her off with a comment about the ladies fancying a man with scars, but the relief was plain on his face. After all were assured that the culprit was gone and likely not to return in the near future, the other townspeople drifted off to their homes, while Fia, Ned, and the Connolly brothers made their way to the inn.

"You'll both be fools if you think Candice won't make you stay the night," Ned told them as they walked.

Neither brother seemed too put out by the idea.

TWENTY-TWO

Mentally, physically, and emotionally, Fia was worn and weary. Fatigue permeated her very core and demanded rest. And yet, sleep would not come.

They'd made it back to the inn in the small hours of the morning and had then spent many more minutes convincing Candice they were all truly well.

Fia had gotten the sense from Tieg's sister she was expecting him to tell her a longer story than the one Fia gave about her time in the stable and on the road, but Tieg seemed reluctant to share whatever it was he was guarding.

They'd huddled at the table sipping warm mugs of tea dosed with brandy and nibbling on bread with creamy soft cheese. Only when Candice was convinced Fia's belly was full did she agree to let them all retire to their assigned rooms. As the inn had several visitors, Niall and Tieg would be sharing but neither seemed to mind.

It was only after she'd changed into her nightshirt and detangled her short curls that Fia noticed the small envelope waiting for her on her pillow.

She'd been thrilled when she opened it to find another missive from Oscar, but her joy faded as she read the words he'd penned to her.

Dearest Fi,

I'm please to know things are going well for you up in Feyport. From what I understand, the little venture you are a part of is doing quite well.

I wish I could say the same for my own creative tasks. It seems as though whatever bit of ingenuity I once possessed has fled from my being. I'm still a capable glass smith, but everything I produce seems to be lacking. I can still make a decent vase or standard lampshade, but even those are common and uninspired.

Both old Hastings and Claire tell me not to worry. They blame parenthood and distraction and claim my gift will return once I'm more settled in my new role. Mr. Hastings did let it slip in passing that he believes I might be taking your loss harder than I let on, and part of me believes it might be true. I miss your smile and happy attitude. Perhaps a trip up north is warranted sooner rather than later?

Trevor is growing so much already, and I would love for you to meet him. You and he are kindred spirits I'd wager. I've not much experience with babies, but he does seem to bring smiles to all around.

Well, enough of my woes. Please write back and tell me how you truly are.

Your loving brother,

Oscar

She read the letter through twice, worry for her brother piling on top of everything else. Niall had been injured. She'd spent the better part of the day fearing for herself. Tieg had been brought back from his business trip early and was clearly keeping something from them all. Her mother's green leather book seemed to be more than just valuable to her. And she'd drawn the attention of some truly unsavory characters in the witch and her sons. Now it seemed as if Oscar was struggling with his livelihood and had not only Claire to worry over, but tiny Trevor as well.

She lay down and turned out the lamp in an attempt to calm her mind, but just as she was close to succumbing to some much needed sleep, a door closed across the hall and all she could think of was Tieg being just a short distance away. True he was bunking with his brother and she had much bigger concerns to mull over, but knowing he was sharing the same roof was sending bubbles of excitement dancing in her stomach.

Tossing from her side to her stomach for the dozenth time, she finally gave up and threw her legs out of the bed. Crossing the room, she opened the window and inhaled the cool humid air. The light outside was already changing, and Fia knew dawn wasn't far off. She rubbed at the tension in her neck and returned to her bed, snuggling down under the quilts. The sound of the ocean was just the lullaby she'd hoped it would be. Within minutes, her mind had settled and Fia finally plunged into a deep and dreamless sleep.

By the time Fia rose the next day, the inn was quiet save for Penny running up and down the stairs chasing her cat. Candice informed her the most recent lodgers were out for the day and both Niall and Tieg had been up and off to work a handful of hours earlier, Niall with a slight but manageable headache and Tieg with a slight but manageable scowl.

While Fia felt some shame in sleeping longer than the Connollys, she didn't feel it was completely unwarranted. She took her time eating a late breakfast of hard cooked eggs and soft buttered toast and went back upstairs to ready herself for work. On a lark, she grabbed both the letter Oscar had sent and her green leather book. She was determined now more that ever to read it and learn what mystery it was holding back from her.

She was trotting down the front steps when Ned joined her. "I'm to be your escort today." He smiled and extended his elbow to her.

"That really isn't necessary." She smiled but accepted his elbow just the same.

"Tell that to Candice."

"Your wife means well."

"Aye. That she does."

They walked past the thick hedges of flowering blackberry thickets, their tiny white flowers alight with honeybees, and down past the dairy. It was the same route Fia took every morning, but generally at a much earlier hour. Fia was surprised to see how vibrant the colors around her were now that the early morning fog had burned off and the sun cast its golden rays straight down onto the land.

As they made their way up to the main street of town, Ned smiled and waved at every single person they passed. He stopped and chatted with more than a few and even took the time to pop into the Garrows' shop to drop off an order for some basic supplies the inn was in need of. Fia was pleased to see that while she garnered the occasional shrewd or mistrustful glance, most of the townspeople were just as pleased to see her as they were Ned. A few asked about her misadventure the day before. Once or twice she had the feeling it was just a bit of gossip some were after, but several others seemed genuinely concerned for her safety.

Devon Garrow informed her that the town council had been made aware of the incident and anyone who spotted Owen Johnston was to notify a council leader. The idea made her feel a bit safer than she had the night before, but she still wondered if Ned would be on guard duty for the foreseeable future.

The walk to Bindings and Baubles took twice the time it typically did, but when Fia made it to work, she was in a decidedly better mood than she had been when she'd woken.

Tieg was sorting through a crate full of pressed powder and finely milled soap when Fia arrived. Ned accompanied her inside, and Tieg brushed him off when he said he'd be back to collect her at closing.

"No need, Ned. Tell Candice I'll walk Fia home tonight." He kept his eyes firmly on her, even as he spoke to his brother-in-law.

Ned tipped an invisible cap to the pair of them and went about his business.

Once the big man was gone, Tieg approached her and placed a hand on her cheek, his face a mask of concern. Fia could feel the slight tremor in his fingers and smiled reassuringly at him. "I'm fine, Tieg. Really."

"You got a decent rest then?"

"It was a bit of a challenge to fall asleep, but yes. I'm perfectly peachy now."

The concern was still etched on his handsome brow. "I was so worried, Fia."

"I know, Tieg. But it's over. He's gone and I'm safe."

Tieg blew out a long breath, removed the hat from Fia's head, and tipped his forehead so it was touching hers.

"I'm sorry your trip was ruined. I know you wanted to get a look at that rare book."

Not letting go of her, he said, "The book can wait."

"Do you plan to travel to the city again soon then?"

He lifted his brow from hers and placed a kiss where it had previously rested. "I'm not sure my constitution can handle the strain. You have a tendency to welcome the most unsavory of adventures." Fia knew he meant it to be joking, but the words stung just the same. She did seem to get into more trouble here than she had in the city or even in Bodkin Green. The last thing she wanted was to attract more unwelcome attention on the people here she was coming to care for.

Trying for a light tone, she teased, "Then I suppose you'll just have to allow me to accompany you next time."

"I think I might," he agreed.

Thoughts of the city brought Oscar to mind. As Fia retrieved the letter he'd written her, she also pulled her green leather book from her satchel and set it on the counter. She showed Oscar's note to Tieg. "I don't think you should plan on any tiny glass animals or beautiful beads in the near future."

Arthur waddled over, and Fia bent to scratch his nose as Tieg read the letter.

Her employer wore an unreadable expression. "Hmm. I suppose not." He handed back the letter and ran a hand through his hair.

She quirked an eyebrow at him. "It seems to me there might be something on your mind, Tieg."

"There is actually. I wanted to discuss your future here at the shop." He looked uncomfortable.

Fia's stomach dropped. "I can work more hours if you like. Help out with more of the ordering." She was quick to offer anything he needed.

"You already do more than enough, Fia. I . . . I just don't know how to say this."

Fia could feel her lips trembling, and she fought to keep the smile on her face. It was clear he wasn't happy with her work or else he wouldn't be so nervous. "Just say it, Mr. Connolly." Her voice was soft but serious.

His eyes snapped up at her tone. "I don't want you to feel like you owe me anything because I'm your employer. It makes me uncomfortable having you working for me when I want something else entirely, and I have no idea what to do about it."

"Oh." She could no longer maintain the semblance of a smile. "I see."

"I don't think you do." He grabbed her hands and begged her with his eyes to understand what he was trying to say.

"Should I pack my things and head back to the city then?" She thought her heart might actually shatter if he said yes.

"No." The word came from his mouth with such force, she flinched back before he softened his tone. "No, Fia. Look. I'm getting this all wrong. You know what? Never mind. We can discuss things another time, when I'm more myself."

"So I still have a job."

"Of course. I meant what I said before. You'll always have a place here with us."

Her smile returned. Big and bright as the noonday sun. It was what she wanted. To have a place. She was still confused about what he'd been trying to tell her, but she would worry over it later. Between Oscar's letter and the stress of the previous day, she wanted nothing more than a quiet afternoon.

Once again Tieg seemed to read her mood. "Things here have been fairly slow, and I expect they'll stay that way for the remainder of the day. You should relax for a bit. Perhaps read a book?" He nodded to her mother's tome.

"I wish you'd just tell me what it is you think I'll find in these pages."

"I have no idea what you'll find. But something tells me whatever it is will be important to you."

"But you suspect something."

He set his lips in a firm line and nodded. "I do. I've suspected something for quite some time now. But it's a tad on the outlandish side and if I'm wrong . . . it could hurt someone I care about. So I'd rather see if you can help me solve the mystery first."

"And the answer to the mystery is in my mother's book?" She ran her hand over the smooth, timeworn leather.

"It might be, yes."

"Does it have to do with Owen Johnston or is he just a greedy scoundrel who wants to cash in on the book's value?"

"Again, Fia, I'm not sure. But I believe he has a part to play in all this."

Fia sighed and shrugged. "All right then. I'll give it another go."

She dropped down into a relatively comfortable chair and cracked the leather cover open. Once again the images in the book swam and danced as her eyes tried to bring them into focus. She grunted in frustration and tilted her neck back, eyes shut tight, and took a few centering breaths, then looked down at the open pages once more. The words came and went as if they were scrawled in the sand of a windswept beach. She looked at one of the color plates and caught sight of a beautiful woman with long flowing hair the color of pine forests and cold water seaweed. She blinked and the image faded back into a swirling mosaic of color and shadow. She snapped the book shut and stood up, pacing back and forth across the empty shop.

Tieg grabbed her hand and entwined his fingers with hers, leading her back to her chair.

"It isn't working, Tieg. I don't think I'll ever be able to read it." Frustration brought the uncomfortable sting of tears to her eyes. "The other book, the one you lent me? It had an entry that scared me. Badly."

"What do you mean it scared you?"

"There was a passage. About women who are described. . . Well , it sounds as if they look like me."

"And that scares you?" His voice was gentle but prodding.

She nodded, the tears no longer just threatening.

"All right, Fia. It will all be all right." He rubbed his hands down her arms.

"They didn't sound like good women, Tieg. What if this says the same thing?"

"Then we will get through it. Together. Yeah?" He dipped his head, forcing her to look him in the eye. "This book will not beat you, Fia. Of that I'm certain."

"Why don't you see if you can read it?" She held it out to him in a beseeching gesture.

"That wasn't written for eyes such as mine, Fia." He walked behind her and rubbed the back of her neck gently then trailed his hands over her shoulders and down her arms in a soothing gentle massage. Fia opened the book once again and placed it in her lap, allowing his hands to work the tension out of her body as her eyes and mind focused on the words.

This time, the writing held fast and she was able to read the first few pages without stopping. After several minutes of strain, the words tried to run from her, but her mind caught them and coaxed them into submission. As she turned another page, Tieg placed a kiss on the crown of her head and walked away. She missed the comfort he provided but not enough to give up on the amazing leather-encased codex before her.

She read of fey magic and hidden talents. Of strength and weakness. Of time and longing. She read of lovers lost and lovers gained. Of beauty of mind and beauty of the flesh and finally of the beauty of eternal sleep after a life of endless sorrow.

She read of the leanan sidhe and the gift of creativity they bestowed upon those in their thrall. They were muses in the purest sense of the word. Fey humans who could wield powerful magic, handed down from mother to daughter in a pure line of unending beauty and ingenuity—never gifted to male children and often so powerful it could bring cleverness and imagination to even the dullest of artists or artisans. So strong was the gift, it had to be closely guarded lest the wrong sort of vile men get greedy for its use.

The book moved from a history of sorts to an instruction book of how to guard and utilize the magic of the muse. It instructed the reader on how to diffuse the power to many people, bringing entire groups a measure of beauty in the arts. It also informed how to ensure the magic was passed from mother to daughter and mentioned how with each mortal the muse shared her gift, her antlers would grow.

At this bit, Fia's hand rose and rubbed the solid lump over her left ear.

She wasn't sure how long she read. She skipped over the colorful illustrations at the center of the book, preferring to continue with the text for as long as she was able. She would return to the art when she was done reading. Her eyes were growing weary, and her head was hurting from concentrating on the words. She'd made it nearly to the end when she read a passage that sent a shiver down her spine.

Beware the dangers of allowing a sole human mortal full access to the magic of the leanan sidhe. Once drunk on the cleverness and inspiration the muse may share, it is often difficult to relinquish the gifts. Men having been gifted the muse's power may never know life without it and, in fits of melancholia at its abscess, will end their lives rather than live in the desolation of absent creativity.

As Fia turned to the color plates, her breath caught in her throat. The first set of images depicted a beautiful woman with deepest green hair. From the top of her head, a set of antlers rose majestically. Rather than making her look odd or bestial, they added to her singular beauty. The same woman was depicted in scenes surrounded by nature, one in a glen covered in wild flowers, one near a stream, and one with a man half transformed into a bear.

In the next images, the woman sat with an ordinary man. Around him easels were decorated with works of art. In the next plate, the woman sat at a piano bench as the man next to her threw back his head in rapture at the music he was playing. In the third image, the woman sat next to another man, his hair tousled and his face manic, as he vigorously scribbled ink onto one of dozens of papers around him.

From these images the plates took a decidedly darker turn. The green-haired beauty was walking away from a man who was groveling at her feet, clawing at her gossamer gown as if he could catch her and keep her with him. In the next image, the woman was happily resting in a forest surrounded by tiny sprites and elfin creatures, a wild merriment on her face. In the last and perhaps most disturbing image, the same manic author was seen dangling from a tree—a thick noose around his neck and scattered blank pages surrounding him.

Fia closed the book and drew in a ragged breath.

She had read the entirety of the green leather volume and had understood every word and every image. She wasn't sure how long she'd been enraptured by the book in her hands, but it must have been hours at least. The light from the shop's windows had faded, and Tieg stood behind the counter tidying things up. At the sound of her closing the book, he looked up, a mixture of concern and curiosity on his handsome face.

"Is this me? Is this who I am?" She held the book out to him.

"I don't know."

"But it has to be, right? This is why you don't want me working here anymore. I'm the same as the monster in these pages." It all made perfect sense. Just hours earlier he'd been trying to gently tell her he no longer wished to employ her in the shop. He couldn't find the words himself and had wanted her to read the book so she could put all the pieces together on her own.

He rushed to her side. "You could never be a monster, Fia. Never."

"No? Look at me, Tieg." She pulled her hair back from the budding antlers. "These weren't here two years ago."

His eyes widened before he quickly schooled his expression.

"It doesn't mean you are a monster. Fia, you are the most beautiful, selfless, wonderfully joyful woman I have ever met. I don't know exactly what that book revealed to you, but I am telling you, you are no monster."

"This book suggests otherwise."

He seemed frantic. "What does it say, Fia? What did it tell you?"

"It's a book about the leanan sidhe. The fey muses."

He closed his eyes and nodded, a look of acceptance and confirmation written in the lines of his face.

"You already knew, didn't you? You've suspected something. All this time."

"I suspected there might be more to you than you knew. I wanted you to discover who you are. That's all. Remember what Aylee and Maeve said before? The fey are *human*, Fia. They are just humans with the gift of certain magics. Even if what I suspected is correct, you aren't a monster."

Her lips turned down, and she fought the pain in her chest as she shook her head. "Humans can be the most monstrous creatures of all."

"But that isn't *you*." Tieg's voice was loud as it reverberated off the stone walls of the small building, and she flinched at his sudden outburst.

"Up until a few months ago, I was just Fia. A girl who'd lost her parents and lived with her brother in the city. It was simple. Now . . . I don't really know who I am."

He stepped forward to embrace her, and she stepped out of his reach. For a split second, Fia saw real anguish in his eyes, but then he tightened his lips and set his jaw.

"I only wanted to help you."

"How does this help me? Knowing what I am does me no good." The words left her in a rush.

"Not *what* you are, Fia. *Who* you are."

"And who is that? Am I still the same girl from the same family?"

She stopped and her breath caught. *Was* she the same girl from the same family? The book made it sound as if the gift of magic was passed from mother to daughter, and as far as Fia could recall, her mother had shown no such talents. Men weren't flocking from all over Bodkin Green to become better painters or musicians. But it wasn't her mother's lack of fey magic Fia's mind turned to. She could sort through what her mother might or might not have been later. Instead, her mind jumped to the only artistic person she'd ever had much contact with.

Oscar. Oh. Oscar.

Oscar who until recently had been the city's best glass artisan. *Had* been. Her heart broke wide open. His work was suffering recently. Maybe it wasn't parenthood at all causing his recent trouble. It did seem to coincide with Fia's departure.

She stifled a sob. Her brother was suffering, and she could be the one responsible. She wished more than ever her parents were still alive so she could get some real answers.

"I don't want to destroy men's lives, Tieg." Her voice was barely a whisper. She looked at him through the tears filling her eyes.

"What do you mean destroy men's lives?"

"I need to go."

"Fia, wait." She was already grabbing her bag and shoving the book into it. He stood between her and the door, hands outstretched begging her to stop.

"I need to think, Tieg. I need to go."

She shouldered past him and out into the narrow lane in front of the one-time barley storage. Dusk was creeping in and the smell of wet grass and night-blooming flowers perfumed the air.

People were still out and about. Lamps were being lit all up and down the town and many were keen to enjoy the warm spring air. Laughter floated on the breeze from the direction of the pub. As the lane gave way to the wider cobblestones of the main street, Fia put her head down. The last thing she wanted was for some well-meaning soul to approach and strike up a conversation. She didn't want to explain the tears leaving salty tracks on her cheeks or the way her breath hitched each time she thought of the secret she carried inside her.

Her first impulse was to jump on a train back to the city as quickly as possible. If what she suspected was true and she could in some way help Oscar through this decline in his creative occupation, she wanted to do just that. Perhaps if she was careful, he wouldn't become too reliant on her being around. After that, she could speak with Tieg about the rest of it. His business wasn't necessarily an artistic one, so perhaps it would be safe for her here. The book made it sound like as long as she didn't focus on one person in particular, things might be safe for those around her. She just didn't know. And what was worse, she didn't know who to ask.

Ultimately it was too late to catch the last train back to the city, but she wasn't ready to face Candice or Ned either. She'd been told countless times the beach could be dangerous, and after her last visit to the cliffs with Niall, she had no desire to wander there either. For a town the size of Feyport, it shouldn't be too difficult to find a quiet spot to sit and think.

As she passed the Garrows' mercantile, then the bakery and town hall, her eyes caught on a small church and its surrounding churchyard. In the dimming light, it appeared quiet and peaceful. She ducked through the gate and wandered past the warm glow of yellow light spilling from the church's tiny windows.

Along one side, a small stone bench sat nestled in the shadow of the building. She sat and looked out at the headstones dotting the grass. Many were old and crumbled, but closer to the wall, several were decidedly newer. Fia wondered which one bore the name Connolly and if Tieg, Niall, and Candice visited this spot often.

Thinking of Tieg's parents brought her mind back to her own parents. Why hadn't her mother shown any signs of possessing magic? She'd left Fia the book on the muses and therefore must have been one herself, but Fia had no recollection of anything magical. She had been young when they died, but she would have thought Oscar would be aware of something and he certainly would have shared it with her. None of it made any sense.

She stayed in the churchyard for a good long time, turning things over and over in her mind. Music from the pub drifted toward her. It was comforting in its own way—knowing people were near but not expecting anything from her. She should be getting back to the inn soon. The last thing she wanted was to make Ned and Candice worry over her yet again. As her eyes drifted over the gravestones one last time, they picked up on a slight twinkling among the trees and shrubs. The twinkling coalesced into several pearly white balls of light. The orbs bounced and danced like bubbles in the night. Fia could hear the sounds of childlike laughter from the direction of the lights.

She grew uneasy as they floated closer. Without knowing why, she felt she needed to move before they got too near.

Jumping up, Fia hurried to the churchyard gate and out into the street, tinkling laughter chasing her every step of the way. She looked over her shoulder expecting to see the menacing orbs directly behind her.

The churchyard stood vacant. No lights. No threatening specters. Not so much as a glowworm.

Fia exhaled and chuckled at her own foolishness. It must have been a trick of the lamps. As she shook her head and turned back to the street, she ran smack into the solid wall of Ned Bryan's chest.

"Saints, Fia. I've looked all over town for ya. Tieg didn't know where you'd run off to and Candice was fit to filet him. Thought it was best to see if I could track you down. Save him a bit of heartache."

Fia felt a wave of guilt wash over her. "I'm so sorry, Ned. I had a bit of a shock. I wasn't thinking."

"No harm done, but the roast'll be getting cold. We should hustle on home."

Not knowing what else to do, Fia accepted his arm and threw one last glimpse over her shoulder. She knew what she needed to do. With any luck, the train would be on time and she would be back in the city by the following afternoon.

TWENTY-THREE

The train was not on time.

In fact, Fia was frustrated to learn it wouldn't be running at all until the following day.

She'd woken and slipped out of the inn while the sky was still dark, hoping to board the first train which typically left just before dawn. When she'd approached the booth to buy her ticket back to the city, the kindly old man—who happened to be a regular at Bindings and Baubles—informed her a mud slide an hour south had buried the rails. Crews were working on it, but it would be hours before it was clear enough to travel and that was if there wasn't any other significant damage.

It brought to mind the last time she'd tried to run away without telling her family where she was going. It wasn't fair then and it wasn't fair now. Not that the Bryans were her family but still. Tieg was her employer and recently he had become something more. And Niall. Aylee and Maeve. They were her friends, but they *weren't* her family. Were they?

She'd been stopped the last time too.

Perhaps it was a sign. Or perhaps just ill-favored timing. Either way, Fia realized she was acting like a coward. Slipping away without a word would only hurt the people she'd come to care about. She was confused and angry. Frustrated and scared. But that didn't give her the right to be selfish as well.

Lifting her chin and adding a bounce to her step, she decided to make the most of the delay. As quickly as she could, she returned to the inn and snuck upstairs to stow her bag before heading to work.

Tieg deserved to hear her plan himself and if Fia was right about him, he'd probably offer to go with her to the city. She wasn't sure she wanted or needed that, but she did need to explain.

The sun still hadn't risen, and Fia had an hour or more before Tieg would be at the shop. Candice, always an early riser, was humming to herself in the kitchen when Fia came back down the stairs. A heavenly aroma was drifting out into the sitting room—a drool-inducing mix of warm baked bread and savory sausage. Not wanting to be in the way, Fia grabbed a mug of tea and slipped out onto the back porch.

Hoping to collect her thoughts on how to approach Tieg with her plan to return and assist Oscar while still hoping to have a job to come back to, she sank onto the bench swing and watched as the sky lightened in the first blush of dawn.

As if Tieg had been summoned by her thoughts, his voice called from around the front of the house. "Fia. Fia, is that you back there?"

She wasn't entirely sure she wanted to have this conversation at the moment. In fact, she'd hoped to put it off until the tea in her mug had warmed her spirits. Unfortunately, she couldn't think of a suitable way to escape without the entire inn knowing what was happening.

"I'm on the porch, Tieg. Come around." She tried to keep her voice low so as not to wake any of the inn's other guests.

Tieg seemed to have no such qualms. "Fia!" he shouted. "Come around to the side of the building. The gate is stuck."

Fia frowned. Why was he making such a racket? He easily could have come through the front door and straight out the back.

"Fia. Please. I need you to come open the gate." His tone was rising in a very un-Tieg like frustration.

Huffing, she stood and placed her mug on the small side table. Walking the length of the inn's rear porch, she jogged down the side steps and around the corner to the heavily shaded walkway. Trees overgrew the path on that side of the inn, and large flowering shrubs crowded against the gate. As Fia stepped closer, she slowed. Tieg had definitely said to come to the gate, but as she approached the iron fencing, she couldn't see him anywhere.

It wasn't like Tieg to play tricks on her. Niall maybe, but not Tieg.

Uneasiness grew in her chest. It wasn't like him to grow annoyed over such a small thing as having to wait, and it certainly wasn't like him to hide from her in some silly game. "Tieg?" she whispered. "Tieg. Where'd you go?"

The bushes to the left rustled, and Fia was more than a little surprised to see a boy of about five step out of the shadows and into her path.

"Fia. There you are." Tieg's voice came from the child's impish mouth. When she startled back, a wicked grin came over the boy's face, and Fia noted the rows of small pointy teeth. With utter clarity, she realized this was not only very much not Tieg, it wasn't a child either.

She'd been ticked by a pooka. And so, *so* easily.

"Oh, Fia." Tieg's voice crooned at her. "Have I offended you? My sincerest apologies."

The thing giggled as she took another horrified step backward, not understanding what the creature could possibly want with her.

"Enough of that now, Piplash," an alluring voice admonished.

Fia realized it wasn't the pooka at all who wanted anything from her, but the witch Carman. Again Fia was struck by the woman's apparent youth and beauty. She'd understood many of the fey to be fair to look upon, but with her richly hued skin and burnished metal hair, Carman was unlike any woman Fia had seen before.

The tiny trickster groused at the witch, clearly unhappy that his fun was so short lived.

"Off with you now. The sun approaches and you'd do well to be home before the light of day catches you out."

The creature wearing the boy's face and Tieg's voice, bowed to the witch and blew a kiss to Fia before he scampered off to heavens knew where, the shrubs quivering as he passed through the leaves.

Fia was at once relieved at its departure and mortified to think she now stood alone with the witch. "You really should be more cautious, lovey. It might have been someone who wished you ill standing here. I'd have thought you'd learned that lesson well by now."

"I thought—" Fia caught herself. It really didn't matter what she thought. The witch was right. She needed to be more cautious. Tieg never would have called to her in such a way. He'd simply have marched through the front door of the inn.

Carman tilted her head and raised her brow.

"What is it you want from me?" Fia asked.

"Why, to collect my favor."

"Your favor?"

"Yes. It's rather soon I know. Sometimes it's years before I collect, but as it happens, something's come up and there is a need for you to repay my kindness."

Fia frowned. "But your kindness wasn't asked for and it did nothing to help me even if it had been." Her voice was full of disgruntled confusion.

"Careful now, little lost thing. You don't want to risk my ire."

That was true enough. Fia had spent the past several days worrying over the interest the witch and her sons had shown in her. The worry had been well placed. The idea of having Dub or Dain after her was bad enough, but if the witch saw fit, she could call on her third son Dother—Evil. That was one fey Fia certainly didn't want the pleasure of meeting.

"What is the repayment?" She dreaded the answer but needed to know.

"It's a simple task really. I need for you to bring back to me one who was taken many years ago."

"Who?"

"A dear friend."

Fia's brow furrowed. For some reason, the idea of Carman having someone she thought of as a friend was unsettling.

The witch must have read the thought written on Fia's face. "Is that so hard to believe?"

"No," Fia stammered. "I just . . . well, if you can't bring this friend back, how do you suppose I'll be able to manage it?"

"I believe she would do anything you ask of her, if she is able."

The cryptic words confused Fia, but then again, everything the witch said confused Fia.

"Who is this friend and how am I to find her?"

"Travel to the place of your beginning. Look for the one who shares both your gift and your curse. Tell her I've missed her and that all is safe for her to return."

The place of her beginning. Fia was growing weary of all the riddles and half-concealed answers. She had begun in a small town few had ever bothered with.

"Do you mean Bodkin Green? Your friend will be there?"

The witch nodded. Fia had just made up her mind to stop running away and now the witch was asking her to leave Feyport and return to her childhood home in exchange for a warning that had done her no good in the first place.

"But I can't just leave."

"Take the young man with you. He seems eager for you to find yourself. I suspect he may even wish to help."

Clearly the witch meant Tieg. After all, it was his voice her little creature had used to lure Fia into this conversation in the first place.

"And if I do as you ask, you'll leave me and my friends be?"

The witch nodded, a greedy glint in her eye that Fia didn't trust.

"What if I go and I can't find her or she won't return to Feyport with me?"

"I doubt that will be a problem, but if it's reassurance you need, this I will give. If you locate my friend and she willfully refuses you, our debt is still paid."

"Why can't she simply return on her own? Why do you need me to fetch her?"

The witch turned to go, and Fia caught a glimpse of the shadow of a man farther up the walk. She couldn't see him clearly but shuddered at the flash of orange hair blowing about his face in the breeze. Dother. The brother Fia feared the most. When she was almost to the man, the witch called over her shoulder, "You ask too many questions little one." Both figures melted into the shadows.

Fia stood on the walkway for several more minutes, trying to control the trembling that had overtaken her. As the misty morning light washed over her, she finally made herself move.

As poorly as their last conversation had gone, and despite Fia's trepidation about her future, it seemed speaking with Tieg was now more important than ever.

TWENTY-FOUR

Convincing Tieg to accompany Fia to Bodkin Green wasn't really convincing at all. She'd simply gone in to work, explained her encounter with the witch, and said she didn't know how long she would be away. Tieg had looked at her steadily and openly asked, "When do we leave?"

As far as Bindings and Baubles went, Maeve Garrow seemed thrilled with the prospect of keeping an eye on things while they were gone. It would get her out of the house and let her focus on something other than her own troubles. Niall too was more than happy to pitch in and volunteered to check with Maeve each afternoon after he was done at the dairy to make sure she didn't need anything. Once Fia was able to throw a few belongings in her bag, the pair were off.

As the train was still down, they made use of a small wagon Rupert Camden was able to loan them. By Tieg's estimation, the trip would take four days each direction. The weather was good and the travel was easy. Tieg knew which towns had decent inns, and they had no trouble procuring rooms along the route.

More than once Fia could feel the pull of Tieg's eyes on her, and she felt fluttering in her chest each time it happened. She didn't bring up her previous plan to return to the city, and he didn't mention her leaving his employ. The truce they had was brittle, and Fia hated the idea that their easy camaraderie was broken, but selfishly she thought if she avoided the topic, he wouldn't be apt to discuss it either. She didn't know what she would do when he finally told her she no longer had a job at the tiny library and shop, but she would cross that bridge when this errand was done.

Maybe showing him the sprouting antlers had been an enormous folly.

The worst part was how Tieg had returned to the dour, scowling man he'd been when they first met. Fia longed to see him smile again but didn't know how to bring it about. She was terrified of hurting him as the book suggested she might.

It was their third day on the road. The cart was swaying along the uneven lane when Tieg's voice broke the monotony. "What are you thinking about?"

"I'd rather not say. Why?"

"You have that little divot between your brows that means you're troubled."

Her eyes slid to the side toward him and her frown deepened. "You can tell when I'm troubled?"

"I can tell lots of things, but yes. Troubled is easy. You almost always have a smile on your face, even if it isn't a genuine one."

"You can sense when a smile is disingenuous?" She wasn't so much skeptical as surprised.

"With you? Of course I can." He sighed and shook his head a fraction as if surprised he needed to elaborate. "You have a dozen different smiles for just as many occasions. There's your normal everyday resting smile. One when you're trying hard not to laugh at something ridiculous I've said. You've got one in particular when you smell baked goods and another when you're imagining trying all of the new scented soaps we've received. But you also have a little half smile you use when you're confused but don't want to ask something and another you put on when you're sad but don't want to talk. A smile doesn't mean you're happy, even if you'd like to make it so.

"On the rare occasion, it slips, I know you're really upset. So what is it that's troubling you, Fia?"

"Again, I'd rather not say." He'd noticed all of it. Every expression. Her attempts to hide behind her smile had been fruitless. At least where Tieg was concerned. How was Fia supposed to tell him she was torn between begging to keep her job at the risk of hurting him unintentionally and running away to the city in an effort to help not only him but also Oscar? Running should be the right thing to do, but it felt so wrong to her. Saying any of this would give him the opportunity to make the decision for her, and he'd already told her he no longer wished to employ her.

"I understand." His shoulders stiffened and he held the reins in a white-knuckled grip.

After several long minutes of silence between them, he said, "I didn't grow up believing in the fey."

It was an odd conversation starter, but Fia didn't mind. It was a welcome change of subject.

"Back when I was small, town was different. The people were friendly and welcoming for the most part, but superstitions were thick in the air and outsiders weren't so welcome. Glendon always believed, and I suppose it softened me to the idea."

Fia thought that odd. She'd been welcome enough in the quaint seaside town, and she thought the people wonderful. Sure she got the odd glance and caught the occasional whisper when folks thought she couldn't hear, but it was nothing compared to the city.

"You know Aylee and Maeve are full of information about the fey and with good reason. Not long ago, a stranger washed up in town. He became close with Aylee Garrow."

"Yes. She told me a bit about it."

He nodded. "I didn't get a chance to know Cailean—that was the fellow Aylee helped out—well, but Ned did. What happened to him was terrible. And after, things changed. We—the town I mean—changed. You'll still find a crusty old curmudgeon or uptight biddy who likes things just so, but for the most part, we have embraced the magic. We've come to know the fey are just people with a particular skill or ability."

He fell quiet. Fia wasn't sure how exactly she was meant to respond.

"Do you catch what I'm saying, Fia?"

She opened her mouth but shook her head. "No. I don't think I do."

He sighed. "All the stories and all the folklore out there make it sound like being fey is a bad thing. Like possessing the magic makes you wicked or evil. It doesn't, Fia. The fey are just people. Human people who have been gifted a tiny bit of the trove of magic in the world. And just like people, some can choose to use it unwisely or in a villainous way. Those are the stories that got recorded in books or handed down by folks who were harmed or angry or just plain jealous. And I suppose the fey did themselves a disservice all those years ago by going into hiding rather than letting the world know them for who they are. But that doesn't mean every person who possesses some of the fey magic is wicked or evil.

"You are a person, Fia. A wonderful human who up until recently didn't even know you had this magic. You are *still* that same wonderful person. You have the same heart, the same soul. You are still *you*. No matter if your hair is green or blonde, if you have antlers or can shift into some magical beast, if you could sing me to my death with your voice or flit about as a tiny sprite. You will always be you."

A single tear trailed down Fia's cheek as she listened to Tieg. Absently she swiped at it as she stared straight ahead.

"So whatever nonsense you're thinking about yourself right now, it isn't true. You said the other day you didn't want to destroy any man's life. The only men's lives you could destroy are the ones whose hearts you might break."

Fia was at a complete loss for words. She itched to lean over and brush her lips against his, but despite his beautiful speech, fear of reprisal kept her from moving.

She knew they were still another hour or so from stopping for the night. The sun was sinking, but not yet set and the sky was a lovely shade of periwinkle touched with peach. Trees rose up on both sides of the road and tall bunches of wildflowers dotted the underbrush.

She heard the buzzing of insects and occasionally had to slap a pesky midge from the exposed skin on her neck or hands, but otherwise the area was perfect in its ordinariness. There were no fey creatures calling her name, no beautiful witches asking for favors to be repaid, no alluringly dangerous fey men to send her pulse racing. The only thing out of the ordinary, she supposed, was her. She was fey, but she was also just a young woman enjoying the scenery surrounding her.

Tieg, as of yet, had not seemed to suffer in her presence. Neither had Ned or Niall, Rupert Camden or any other man from Feyport. True, she hadn't met many artists or artisans, but surely there were some about in the small town.

She still needed to reach out to Oscar and ensure he was able to continue his glassblowing work, but after that? She didn't quite know. Tieg had at least seemed to think she might be able to keep her gift in check. If only he'd let her stay on at the shop, she'd be more confident.

She knew she should say something but refused to broach the subject and ruin the perfectly decent mood. So she said something else entirely.

"I don't remember much about my parents. I was quite young when they died." She chewed absently on her lower lip. "I believe I mentioned that to you before?"

"You did."

"My father was hardworking, and my mother was the most gentle woman. I remember tending the garden together. Pulling weeds and picking fruit. I recall chasing Oscar endlessly around the yard and playing with a pair of kittens. One grey with a white chest, the other grey from toes to tail."

"And were they as much fun as Arthur?"

She chuckled. "No one is as much fun as Arthur."

He clicked the reins as a slight bend came in the lane. The horses nickered in response.

"But most importantly, I remember my father singing."

Tieg turned his head, and the compassion in his clear pale eyes was impossible to miss.

Fia cleared her throat. "His voice was . . . terrible."

This clearly was not what Tieg had been expecting her to say, and his brow rose in surprise. Fia barked a laugh. "I mean really and truly horrible. It never stopped him from humming and belting out ridiculous tunes though."

She laughed at the memory of her and Oscar running around inside the house, hands over their ears trying to escape the off-tune, cracking bray. It didn't take long for

Tieg to join in the laughter with her. It was a melody all its own, his laugh, and Fia found herself wishing to hear it each and every day for the rest of her natural life.

"My point being, if I am to believe this book is correct"—she patted her satchel where the green leather volume traveled next to her—"and I am indeed a muse, one would suppose my mother was as well."

Tieg nodded in agreement.

"But if my mother was a leanan sidhe, how could my father not posses a single drop of musical ability? Or any other artistic ability for that matter? Wouldn't she have brought out something in him?"

"Maybe. But, Fia, I've been around you for weeks and have yet to develop any artistic merits. Unless you count the colorful language I spout while cleaning up hedgehog droppings. I've become a master there." Despite his joking words, his tone was forced and he wouldn't look at her as he answered. Once again, Fia was left with the feeling he knew more than he was letting on.

"Let's just get this trip to Bodkin Green sorted," she said with a levity she didn't feel. "Maybe once we do, things will become a bit more clear."

"I think it's a wise play. There is still something I need to talk to you—"

"Oh look," Fia cut him off. His scowl only deepened. "There's a public house just ahead. I'd love a good hot bowl of something tasty, wouldn't you?"

"Sure, Fia. Soup would be grand."

TWENTY-FIVE

The schoolyard hadn't changed much at all since Fia last set eyes on it. Some of the children had grown and been replaced by others with different names but similar mannerisms. The trees were just as tall and lush, the grass just as green. The stone wall and rickety weathervane were both still in need of repair. Rings of flowers still sprouted in the most unlikely of spots. The only discernible difference was the shrub which had been trimmed in the shape of a squirrel was now inexplicably carved down into a toadstool. It was a shame. The squirrel had always been her favorite.

When they reached the door, Tieg went to ring the bell, but Fia didn't bother to stop. She simply bounded up the steps and through the front door as if she still lived in residence.

They hadn't made it five feet inside when they were greeted in the entry by a fair-haired young woman. In a blink, she broke into a laughing, gap-toothed smile and rushed forward, throwing her arms around Fia.

"Oh, Mabel! Look at you!" Fia gushed. "When I left you were just a little thing, and now you're all grown."

"Fia. I've missed you! And your hair is out! I'm so happy you've got your hair out. I spend hours sometimes in the garden looking for beetles just so I can remember the exact shade of your hair."

Fia brushed absently at her chin-length wavy locks. "Yes, well. I've become a bit more accustomed to folks seeing it of late."

"In the city? How is it? Does the air really smell stale there? Are the scones really as dry and crusty as everyone says they are? Do you go dancing every night? Have you met any dashing young men?"

Fia laughed and quirked her lips to the side. "It's fine, though I haven't been there in the past several months. Yes, the air is acrid some days but fine on others. Yes, the scones leave quite a bit to be desired. Nothing like the baking here. No dancing. And umm. . ." She looked sideways at Tieg, a fierce blush coloring her cheeks. "Maybe."

Tieg had the good grace to look at his shoes and pretend he didn't know what she was on about.

Mable looked where Fia's gaze had drifted. "You? What are you doing back here, sir?"

This time, Tieg was unable to ignore the conversation and his unease was quite on display. "I . . . uh, well." He grimaced.

Fia's brow scrunched down. "Back here? Have you visited Bodkin Green before then, Tieg?"

He blew out a long breath. "I have been, yes. This young lady was kind enough to allow me to speak with the headmistress once before. It's, well. I should explain."

"Yes, you should. But maybe not just now. I'm really anxious to see my old headmistress." Turning to the teen, she asked, "Is Miss Magpie about somewhere?"

"She's in her office. But I ought to warn you, Fia, there's been some strange goings on in recent days. She may not be all too jovial this morning."

"Nothing too serious I hope."

"I don't rightly know. I'm not privy to her private conversations, but I'll tell you this. She had visitors a few days back. A beautiful woman and the most handsome young man." Mabel rolled her eyes heavenward and sighed dramatically.

A chill ran down Fia's spine. Had Carman and one of her sons visited the small boarding school? It didn't seem to make any sense. If they had, surely the witch wouldn't have sent Fia on this particular errand.

"I don't mean to be pushy—Mabel, is it?" Tieg said. When the girl nodded, he continued. "Would you be able to tell Fia here what the lady and young man looked like?"

"Oh, sure. He was just the most splendid thing. Probably close to your own age, Fia. Tall and thin, just like you are, in fact. But with the darkest jet hair and the most adorable overbite. A wonderful smile. Not that he smiled at me, of course. I could just tell by the way he assisted the lady. I do believe he was her son."

"And the woman?" Fia asked. "Did she look old enough to be his mother?"

"I suppose she looked well for her age, but yes, I think so."

Fia relaxed a bit. Carman had appeared to be as youthful as her sons, and she'd certainly not noticed anything *adorable* about Dub. Still, she needed to be sure. "What of her hair and complexion? Was she bronze haired with sunkissed skin?"

Mable frowned. "No, not particularly. Her skin was just as creamy smooth as yours and, well, as for her hair, I can't really say. She wore this beautiful embroidered scarf wrapped in the most exotic way. I don't think I noticed a single strand poking out."

Fia's and Tieg's sighs of relief were released almost in tandem.

"You don't suppose it was Brigid and Glendon, do you?" she asked Tieg.

"I suspect that is exactly who it was. You should speak with Miss Magpie. I'll wait out here if you like."

"Oh no, Mr. Connolly. You've come this far and apparently you've already been introduced to the headmistress. You are coming with me."

Fia had known Miss Temperance Magpie for the better part of a decade as she'd grown up in the boarding school. Not once in all those years did she feel as if the woman was deliberately keeping something from her.

The day Fia sat in her office with Tieg, however, Fia knew something was amiss. After a joyful and watery eyed reunion when the pair had been led to the headmistress's office, the slight and practical woman bade them sit and offered them tea. It was after the initial pleasantries that Fia began to feel like Miss Magpie—though happy to see Fia alive and well—would prefer to have them off and gone from the grounds sooner rather than later.

It might have been the way the normally harried yet pleasant woman looked just over Fia's shoulder rather than at her as Fia explained the past few months of her life, or it might have been the way she worried at the little hairs escaping the tight bun on the back of her neck. It could also have been in the way she snapped at Mabel when the girl lingered in the doorway or the way she looked fretfully at Tieg when Fia informed her he was trying to assist with her task.

It might have been all of the little things or none of them. Fia wasn't quite certain.

"Is there something troubling you, headmistress?" Fia would rather have it out in the open if it were the case.

"Why would you ask?"

"It's only Mabel mentioned there'd been some trouble lately but didn't say what. And ever since we've arrived, I feel as though my presence here may be a burden."

"That girl talks more than she ought."

"She means well. We were close before I left. I think she was just excited to see me."

"Believe me, I know. The child moped for months."

"At any rate, I don't intend to stay long, if that's what worries you. We've rooms at the inn, so there's no need to go about having a spot in the dormitory prepared. I'm in town to look for someone and thought to stop in and say hello. We'll be on our way shortly."

The older woman pursed her lips and set her shoulders. "I'll not have you leaving here on bad terms, Fia. You were always one of my favorites. I don't mean to be elusive. Really. It just so happens there has been some trouble lately. And while it might relate to you, it certainly wasn't *caused* by you. I've just come under a bit of a shock really, and I'm still trying to see how best to proceed."

"Did it have to do with Brigid Johnston?" Tieg asked.

The tiny steel-haired woman narrowed her eyes at him. "Yes. In fact it did." She turned her attention back to Fia. "She had some outlandish things to say, and well, I'd rather not share them with you until I can be certain they are in fact true."

"Outlandish in what way?" Fia prodded.

"I don't want to cause you more heartache, Fia. You've been through enough."

"Can you at least tell us where they might be staying?" Tieg asked. "They're old friends of mine, and I'd love to chat with them. Perhaps Fia could even hear this outlandish story for herself. Then you wouldn't be in any sort of awkward position."

"Friends of yours? I see. I suppose you failed to mention that connection when last we spoke."

"At the time I didn't feel the connection was worthy of note."

"But you do now?"

Fia had grown exasperated. "Would either of you care to share what it is you're both referring to?"

"My apologies, Fia. Perhaps it is best if you seek out Brigid and her son for yourself. Interestingly enough, word in the village is they might be staying at your parents' old farm."

"I didn't realize Oscar was letting it out."

Miss Magpie chose to ignore the question. "I suggest you go and speak with the woman and her son. It was good to see you, Fia. You're always welcome, as you know, but I'm afraid today I've got much to do. If you'll excuse me."

Feeling decidedly dismissed, Fia said goodbye to Mabel and led Tieg to where she'd spent the first seven years of her life.

TWENTY-SIX

Fia's family home lay in a state of moderate disrepair.

After her parents had died and Oscar had set off for the city, apparently the people of Bodkin Green felt it best to leave the place be. After all, Oscar still owned the land and the small farmhouse in the center of it. He could have sold it but had chosen not to. He'd mentioned it to Fia once—telling her he'd hoped to one day retire there after he'd saved enough money from his job at the glassblower. Unfortunately, he didn't have the funds to pay a caretaker, so the thatched roof had holes and the ground was untamed.

As they approached, memories came flooding back. Tiny Fia running through the grass, her hair streaming out behind her in a green-black tangle, her dress dirty and her feet dirtier. Oscar teaching her to skip stones in the pond at the far end of the fields. Her father showing her how to best milk a cow to get the sweetest cream. Her mother— plain russet hair and freckled skin—baking bread and mending socks.

And then there were the darker memories. A man arriving to tell Oscar the news. Their parents were dead. Perished in a freak accident. Him trying to comfort her while barely able to keep himself in check. The day they'd said goodbye to their parents in the small churchyard service, Fia still not entirely grasping that they were gone. Then saying goodbye again as Oscar left her at the boarding school—a promise on his lips to send for her as soon as he was able.

"I couldn't even look at the ruins of our home after the fire," Tieg said, as if sensing where her thoughts had strayed. "I thought all of the good memories would be turned to ash and cinder, but they weren't. It took time for me to dig them up out of the wreckage in my mind, but eventually I found them."

Fia nodded. "Mine aren't gone; they're just worn and thin. I was so young when it all happened. It's actually good to be here. To see it. To help the memories become crisper and brighter."

The door stood ajar on the front of the house and a thunking came from around the side. It was rhythmic and measured, broken occasionally by brief moments of silence. As they grew nearer, Fia realized it was the sound of wood being chopped. Sure enough, Glendon Johnston appeared from the side yard, long lean arms laden with a small pile of spit logs and black hair falling into his bright green eyes.

Despite his burden and the thin sheen of sweat covering his face, he smiled broadly at the sight of them. Dropping the logs on the front porch, he dusted his hands on his trousers and met them in the yard.

"We go years without seeing one another, Tieg, and now you've popped up three times in as many months. And always with this lovely lass in tow."

"To be fair, Glendon, it was you who popped up in Feyport the last time." One corner of Tieg's mouth ticked up.

"True." Glendon winked at Fia.

If there had been the beginning of merriment in Tieg's expression, it winked out as quickly as it came. "Is your mother here too?"

Glendon nodded, also much more somber.

"Has he found you yet?" There was no need to elaborate on who 'he' was.

"No, but I'm sure it won't be long."

"How'd you do it? Get away, I mean."

"Surprisingly it wasn't all that difficult. He's been distracted lately. When we left Feyport the last time, I could tell something was plaguing him. Ma's been ready to claw his eyes out before, but recently I wouldn't be surprised if she slit his throat in the night. He must have been feeling it too. I don't know." Glendon glanced toward the door as if expecting his mother to take issue with his words.

"Anyway, the day after we got back to the city, he went out for a game of cards and came back off his ass and smelling like a gin mill. Passed out drunk on the sofa. Ma took one look, grabbed her bag, and we were off into the night. Came right here—for some reason I still have yet to comprehend—and we've been here since."

"Glendon," Brigid's voice called from inside the small home. "Who are you—"

The tall lithe woman stepped out onto the porch, pulling a golden and teal shawl around her shoulders. She had a matching piece of fabric wrapped around her head. At the sight of Tieg and Fia, Brigid's face stilled. She looked around the yard as if expecting someone to be lurking about then rushed out and threw her arms around a very startled Fia. When Brigid pulled back, she was simultaneously laughing and wiping tears from her cheeks.

"You're here. Right here. In Bodkin Green." She turned to Tieg and wrapped him in a ferocious hug. "Tieg Connolly. Why on earth? I mean . . . how?"

Fia looked uncertainly from Brigid to Tieg and then at Glendon. The tall dark-haired man wore a bemused expression. "Don't look to me, Fia. I'm as confused as you are."

Tieg cleared his throat. "Perhaps we'd better go inside."

The group followed his advice, and soon they were seated around a worn but sturdy pine table, mismatched mugs of warm tea in each of their hands. Apparently someone had taken the time to shoo away the cobwebs and dust that must have accumulated over the years.

Tieg looked between Fia and Glendon, pursed his lips, and shook his head. "I don't know how I didn't see it before," he muttered quietly.

Fia was uneasy. While she desperately wanted to understand what was happening, a small voice in the back of her mind told her she would not like what she was about to learn. The voice whispered for her to run. To simply get up from the table and leave. She could head to the city, find Oscar and beg Claire to let her stay. She was filled with the certainty that whatever it was Tieg had been keeping from her would alter her for the rest of her life. She'd had too many shocks already. One person was not meant to take in all she had in the past few months and remain the same. Unchanged. Unmarred.

She was pulled from her foreboding by Brigid's voice. "How long have you known, Tieg?"

"Only just now, I suppose. But I've suspected for some time. Although, to be fair, my suspicions had nothing to do with our appearance in Bodkin Green. It's just a happy coincidence the witch sent us to the place you happen to be residing."

"The witch? You don't mean Carman, do you?" Brigid asked.

"The very same," he acknowledged.

"Well, if Carman sent you here, then it's no coincidence at all." Brigid let out a long breath and smiled, almost to herself. "I received word a few weeks back that if I should need a place to stay, this cottage was known to be empty. She has her spies everywhere."

"It's you?" Fia asked in surprise. "You're the witch's long lost friend?"

"Carman and I go back quite some time, yes. She has a way of sticking her nose in where it doesn't belong, I'm afraid." Though the words were scathing, Brigid said them with fondness. "I'll not say I'm sorry she sent you, but I do apologize for everything else, dear Fia."

"I don't understand what you're talking about."

Brigid smiled sadly. "No, I don't suppose you would."

"She's not the only one," Glendon added with a good amount of exasperation.

"I really don't know how I didn't see it," Tieg repeated as he looked between Glendon and Fia once again.

"See what?" Fia was moving beyond frustration and into anger. It wasn't an emotion she felt often, but when she did, she had a difficult time controlling her temper. She would burn brightly and quickly then peter out within minutes.

"You deserve answers, my sweet Fia. And I'll give them to you. I'm simply trying to find the right words to make it as painless as possible," Brigid explained.

Fia crossed her arms and chewed on her lower lip, attempting to give Brigid the benefit of her silence while she composed what she needed to say.

"The best place to start is often in the middle of the tale and work back to the beginning. In this case it may be the middle for me but the beginning for you." Brigid looked up at the ceiling then at her son. "Glendon, this may be difficult for you to hear as well. Please know, everything that has happened, everything your father did, everything I did, none of it was your fault."

Glendon frowned as the words sank in. "Well, that's an ominous start if ever I've heard one."

"Unfortunately, it's often darkest before the dawn. This story is no exception." She turned and looked at Fia once more. "I won't bother to ask if you were in possession of a green leather tome when you were a child. The headmistress we spoke with told me you were. She is an interesting woman. Capable and calm in the face of all the wonders surrounding her. You don't find that every day." Brigid placed her chin on her laced fingers and leaned over the table.

"What I will ask is this—have you read it?"

Fia nodded, eyes wide.

"And you gather what it means?"

Another nod.

"So you understand that you are a leanan sidhe. Good. That was the first difficult bit." Brigid sat forward and reached her hands across the table. Reluctantly, Fia placed her own in the other woman's. She had a feeling where this might be going, and it made her stomach roil and churn. "The fey muses are powerful, Fia. It's a wonderous power and a terrible one. Men change when they are near it."

"Some men," Tieg interrupted. "Some men change, Brigid. Not all."

"Yes, Tieg. Thank you. You're correct. Some men change."

"You know this how?" Fia asked.

"I know because I've experienced it. The euphoria of the magic and the despair of it too." Brigid held Fia's hands tightly and looked at her unblinking. Brigid had lovely green eyes. Nearly the same hue as the ones Fia saw each day in the mirror.

And there it was. The bottom dropping out from beneath her. Fia's heart beat in a wild erratic rhythm and her breath came fast. She felt as if she might vomit. She wanted to say so many things, but all she could muster was, "Tell me."

Brigid's eyes limed with tears but they didn't spill—not yet. "Perhaps the beginning is best after all.

"When I was young, the world was not quite as it is now. Feyport was just a town on the coast, and the people there were superstitious and foolish. They didn't understand or welcome magic and didn't understand or welcome the fey. Most refused to even believe we even existed. Some still don't I suppose.

"I was raised by my mother in the woods just to the east of the town. We stayed away from people mainly. Magic was not a gift to be shared but a treasure to hoard and to hide. She taught me the ways of her magic, not so I would use it, but so I might keep it and hand it down. It had been that way for hundreds of years. Ever since the fey went into hiding. I could let it out in small bursts and wield it only in the most cautious of ways. A passing potter who needed a boost or a lonely child who wanted to sing would be the recipients of my gifts. Never enough to make them suspicious, but enough so I could learn. She gave me a book of instructions. The same one given to her by her mother and her mother before.

"I was warned to stay away from the town and its people. To never dream of traveling to the city. I was to be happy and content in my life in the woods. She warned me of the wickedness I might encounter. Strangely enough, it wasn't the townspeople I wanted to spend my time with. It was a witch.

"Carman lived in the woods near our home with her three sons. She was everything I wished I could be. Brave. Beautiful. Confident. She didn't hide her magic or her beauty. She taught me many things. How to laugh, how to dance, how to enjoy each day as the gift it was."

Brigid's voice was thick with emotion as she spoke about her friend. She stopped talking long enough to take a sip from her mug. "I had a misguided belief that because Carman appeared to be no older than me, she would share the same views on life as I did. Obviously, she wasn't my age, seeing as her sons were all men grown. And of course it didn't hurt my interest in her that her sons were by far the most gloriously handsome beings I'd ever encountered. Never mind that they paid me no interest at all. To them I was just the young fey woman their mother had taken an interest in.

"I was young and foolish, and I thought Carman had things so much better. The day she told me my mother was right and I needed to be cautious with my magic, I thought my heart would break in two. Here she was all power and magnificence and she was telling me I needed to hide away in the forest. It didn't seem fair. I convinced myself she must be jealous of my youth. My beauty. My magic." Brigid let out a low self-deprecating chuckle and shook her head at her own foolishness.

"I couldn't fathom a life staying in the cottage— hidden away in the emptiness of the forest—for even another day. Not when the one person I thought understood me was also trying to keep me in check. I did the worst thing I could have at the time. I ran." She took another sip from her mug. "At first it was wonderful. I flitted from town to town up and down the coast. I made men fall in love. Not with me, but with what I could give them. Fame. Wealth. Respect.

"Each time I'd grant them just a small piece of my magic, and in return, my vain soul was rewarded. I was worshipped and adored. They were happy with me because they were happy with themselves. It didn't matter if it wasn't really me they wanted. Me they needed. Me they loved. I could always escape just before they got too close and realized where their sudden inspiration was coming from. But eventually it got tiring. I longed to go back to the small stone cottage I'd shared with my mother. I longed to see Carman and tell her she was right. So, I got on the road and headed back toward the life I'd so easily given up.

"Unfortunately along the way, I met a traveler. He wasn't much of anything special. Just a sad and lonely thing, barely more than a child really. He was leaving the town he'd grown up in to make his name in the city. For what, not even he could say. As we walked along the lane, I caught a glimpse of someone in the trees. A snow white head accompanied by a man with hair the color of flames—Dain and Dother, Carman's sons. I should have gone to them, but I wasn't ready. I still had yet to plan the words to explain myself. So instead, I asked the young man to stop with me for the night at an inn nearby. I had no intention of sharing my magic with him, only a warm spot by the fire in some run-down inn on the side of the road. But as we sat together he began spouting beautiful prose. In truth, he was just as surprised as I was.

"His verse, his words, they were for me. Not only *because* of me, but *for* me. And like a moth to the flame, I was drawn in. He wasn't bothered by my appearance. In fact, he seemed thrilled with the idea of my otherness."

"This was Father?" Glendon asked, but it was clear he already knew. Everyone at the table already knew.

Brigid nodded and wiped a tear from her eye.

"I wish you'd never met the bastard." Glendon's normal jovial demeanor was nowhere to be found as he spat out the words.

"Don't say that, love. Without your father, I never would have had you or—" She pursed her lips. "I'm getting ahead of myself.

"My feelings were fickle, and despite my intention to return home, he'd won me over in one short evening. I went with him to the city. And there I stayed. I was enamored with his words, if not the man himself. He didn't start out cruel. That came later. But even in my youth and with the pretty lies pouring from his lips and onto the page, I knew he wasn't the type of man I really wanted. Just like he didn't really want me. But still I stayed, because of the things he created. The poems and sonnets. The prose of love and devotion.

"But like all good things, those sweet words soon came to an end. He began writing his verse for others. Not for me. And once again, it became evident it wasn't really me he'd ever loved, only what I could do for him. I wanted to leave, but by this time he'd realized what I was. He'd always seen my hair and known I was different, but after a time, my antlers could no longer be hidden. He put it all together and then I was no longer his lover and friend. No longer his wife. I was simply his muse, and he swore he would never let me leave."

Fia squeezed Brigid's hands and gently pulled away. She couldn't sit at the table any longer. She was feeling ill. Was this her future then? To be wooed and then caged? She didn't think she would be able to live like that.

This was what she feared. While she could never imagine Tieg being anything close to the monster Owen was, she worried. How well did she know him? More importantly, how well did he know her?

You have a dozen different smiles for just as many occasions.

"I don't mean to upset you," Brigid said as if reading her thoughts. "My story need not be your story, Fia. But the two are intertwined."

"I understand. It's all just so. . ." Fia didn't have a word for what it was. Sad was too mundane. Tragic? Infuriating?

"Yes." Brigid smiled sadly. "It is. I do so hope however it will eventually have a happy ending."

"As do I," Glendon muttered.

"As you can imagine, given my handsome and unusually quiet son here, I eventually became pregnant. The idea of bringing a child into the mess I'd allowed was mortifying, but I couldn't help being elated all the same. I resolved to find a way to take my child and leave for good. To make my way back to my mother and my life hiding in the forest. I knew Dother and Dain had seen me with Owen months before, and I hoped they might tell their mother where I was. That somehow she might come to me and help me. It wasn't to be, however.

"Owen was never a man to care about society or others' expectations until he felt the fawning of the crowd. The adulation. Something as simple as a family or society's expectation of him weren't on the top of his priority list. We weren't even officially—never mind. That isn't important." She gave a small tight smile in Glendon's direction. "Owen was happy enough I was with child, though he fretted over whether it would be fey like me."

"Well, he needn't have worried," Glendon said. "I haven't a spot of anything so interesting in my blood."

Brigid smiled sadly at her son. "The leanan sidhe share their magic only with their female babes. It isn't the same as the selkies or the faeries. Only women can wield the magic of the muses."

"Shame. I think I could bring out more than a little beauty if given the chance."

"I'm sure you could." Brigid's smile fell completely. "This is the hard part of the story."

The hard part? Fia thought the entire thing had been dreadful from the start.

"When it came my time, I delivered not one beautiful babe, but two." Her words were quiet and raw. Tears streamed from her eyes and landed in a small puddle on the table before her.

"Wait. What?" Glendon asked.

"You are a twin, Glendon."

"There's another handsome bloke like me out there somewhere?" Though he tried to joke, his voice was brittle.

His mother shook her head. "No, you sweet man. You have a twin sister."

TWENTY-SEVEN

The entire room fell into a quiet so deep, the only sound in Fia's ears was the hammering of her heart. A twin sister. A girl to carry on the fey muse magic. A girl born to a woman with deepest green hair and pale ivory skin. A woman who would now be the same age as the slight dark-haired man next to her.

"Are you saying. . . ?" Glendon looked to Fia and back to his mother.

Brigid's nod was barely a movement at all.

Even as Fia was processing what she was hearing, Glendon was on his feet and scooping Fia up into his arms. "I have a sister! Fia! I have a sister! I've always wanted to be a big brother." He crushed her to his chest and spun around, lifting her feet cleanly off the floor.

When he stopped moving, Fia gently extricated herself from his grip. "I . . . Glendon. I already have a brother. His name is Oscar. I'm not your sister."

She turned toward the door. The door to her home. To her childhood. The other three didn't belong there, yet she was the one leaving.

"Fia, wait." Just like the day in the bookshop, Tieg made to grab her arm to keep her from going, but she spun around and faced him.

Tieg had been suspicious of something all this time, and now Fia knew. Not just that she was fey. Not just that she was a leanan sidhe. He had insisted they go to see Owen Johnston, a man he hated. He had convinced her she could read the green leather book. He had come to Bodkin Green and sought out her old boarding school and headmistress without her knowing. All of this because he must have suspected he knew not only what she was, but who she was. But how? Even Glendon seemed shocked by the idea he had a sister.

"All this time you knew. You knew and you never told me."

"I didn't know, Fia. I suspected—"

"Right. You suspected. That's all you ever tell me. You suspected I could read the book. You suspected I was fey. You suspected I was a muse. And obviously you suspected I was your friend's long lost sister?"

"No. I didn't even know he had a sister. This is just as much news to me. I just thought you might be related somehow." He seemed to realize how pathetic it sounded. He ran a hand through his hair, a helpless look on his face.

"Why would you keep something like this from me?"

"Because I wasn't sure. I know how much Oscar means to you, and I still don't understand how you came to be in his family. I just wanted you to know about your past before we started thinking about the future."

"What future? I work for you."

"Please. Fia," Brigid interrupted. "Before you leave, let me tell you the rest. You need to know. You and Glendon both. You need to know."

Brigid had stood and was wringing her hands. Fia couldn't look at the woman without her heart squeezing. For all that this upset her, Brigid Johnston seemed to have a much worse lot in life. The least she could was hear her out.

"You're right. I'll listen."

Tieg made to grab her hand, but Fia jerked it away from his grasp. His lips tightened in a firm line, but he didn't speak.

Glendon was staring at her like he'd never seen her before—his eyes wide and full of wonder. "Is Fia a changeling then? No, wait, that can't be right, am I a changeling?"

She couldn't help the slight exasperated smile she cast his way. His answering grin had her shaking her head.

Brigid gave her son a look of such long suffering love, it made Fia's heart ache for the mother she didn't have.

"Neither of you is a changeling—if such a thing even exists."

Fia knew the stories. Faeries stealing ordinary babies away in the night and replacing them with faerie children. What purpose this could possibly serve she'd never understood, but clearly there was so much in the world— herself included—that she couldn't comprehend; she could not disregard anything out of hand.

"In my youth, I knew Owen could be cruel and selfish. As I got older, I learned firsthand of his brutality. But I don't suppose I ever really grasped just how vile a person he was until a few years ago.

"After I gave birth, I was told only one of the babies survived. Owen wouldn't even let me hold her. Said it would be too hard on me. I had no reason to think he'd lie to me over something like that. He had to travel for a reading and left me to care for Glendon. He was my solace and my joy. I threw myself into motherhood but thought about the baby I'd lost every day." Her eyes pled with Fia to understand. Brigid loved the child she'd never known.

"I should have taken Glendon then and there. I should have escaped. But my heart was broken, and I lost sight of all my previous plans. When Owen returned, things became more difficult. Anytime he thought I might defy him, hold back my gifts, or threaten to leave, all he had to do was threaten Glendon and I would crumble."

Glendon rose and stood behind his mother, wrapping his arms about her shoulders and lending her his strength. "I would gladly have taken a beating if it had prevented what he did to you."

"What do you mean?" Tieg asked. "What did he do?"

Brigid's shoulders became tight.

"Go ahead, Ma. Show them," Glendon urged.

She sighed and stepped away from her son. She turned away from Fia and Tieg, as if embarrassed by what she was about to reveal, then reached up and unpinned the beautiful scarf wrapped around her head.

Fia's breath left in a rush and curses flew from Tieg's lips as they took in the sight before them. Presumably, Brigid's hair had once been long and lustrous, but now it was shorn and barely reached her ears. This however wasn't the worse of it. From spots above each of her ears, the flat, filed nubs of what must have been thick antlers peeked through the strands.

Fia reached up to her own head and gently rubbed the horns sprouting there.

"He did this to you?" Tieg hissed.

Brigid nodded. "He said we couldn't risk anyone finding out what I was. His reputation would be ruined."

"They used to be the most beautiful thing I'd ever seen," Glendon said. "You have no idea how many times I've thought of killing the man myself."

Fia had a hard time reconciling the normally happy and easygoing Glendon with this version of him. He clearly loved his mother very much. It also made his childhood faerie hunts make so much more sense.

"Will they grow back?" Fia asked.

"Perhaps they would if I shared my magic again. That, however, is extremely unlikely. I should have listened to my mother all those years ago."

Tieg scrubbed his hands over his face and leaned back in his chair. "You said you realized how vile he was a few years ago? What happened?"

"We were living in Feyport at the time. Owen thought getting out of the city would be a good idea while Glendon was still small. I think he felt the fewer people we came in contact with, the better. He could still travel to his publisher and to do signings and readings—always taking us with him but keeping us away from prying eyes. I came home one afternoon to find Carman waiting on my doorstep. It was a blessing to see her after so many years, although the news she brought me has haunted me every moment since.

"I'll never forget what she said. 'The one you lost can still be found. Return to the city of smoke and iron. Bestowed with the knowledge of your mother—a gift from her and me together—she waits.' I puzzled over it for days. I hadn't seen my mother in nearly two decades. Then it hit me. Could she have meant the baby I'd lost? Could she actually be alive and Carman had somehow found her? I confronted Owen. Glendon was nearly a grown man by this time and I knew his father couldn't really harm him any longer, so I told him I would leave and take my magic with me unless he told me the truth.

"He broke down, sobbing. It was disgusting. He knew the muse magic was carried from mother to daughter. He claimed he'd been scared that having two powerful fey in his household would attract even more unneeded attention. He couldn't bring himself to kill the child directly, so he traveled to a small village and found a family willing to take her in and raise her as their own. A family who desperately wanted a daughter to love."

Fia felt all the color drain from her face. If Brigid was to be believed, her entire life had been a lie. Her parents weren't her parents at all. Brigid and Owen Johnston were. This time, she couldn't control the nausea sweeping through her. She just made it to the basin before she was sick.

Tieg came to her and placed a hand on her shoulder. She allowed it, wanting to seek a small measure of comfort even if she was still angry at him.

When she returned to her seat, Brigid asked, "Was that part true at least, Fia? Did they love you?"

"They did." And that was its own small miracle, wasn't it? She could have been raised right alongside Glendon, but it would have meant living with a terrible man. Instead, she'd been given the gift of love and acceptance by the two most amazing parents she could have ever dreamed of. She had Oscar as well. He would always be her brother. No matter what she learned about the circumstances of her birth.

"The headmistress at the school you attended told us of your loss. I'm so very sorry, Fia," Glendon said.

"Thank you."

"I assume Owen didn't tell your, um, your parents what secrets you carried, Fia, but if he did. . . Well they must have been the best sort of people." Brigid cleared her throat. "The horror I felt when he confessed—I can't tell you what it was like. All this time you'd been out there. I didn't know."

"That was the night we left, wasn't it? When you dragged me to the Connollys without an explanation." Glendon's green eyes flashed.

"It was. And I wish to everything that is good that we hadn't stopped there. I had no idea his ire would encompass people so kind. I'm truly sorry, Tieg."

"So you believe he caused my parents' death as well?"

"Unfortunately, it seems far too coincidental to believe otherwise."

"I don't blame you in the least. I only wish it hadn't been in vain," Tieg said.

"In hindsight, I wish I'd gone to Carman. Perhaps Dain or Dother could have dissuaded him from accompanying us to the city. But, like a fool, I went running to the city, thinking we could be lost in the crowd. It didn't take him long to find us. Neither of us left the loft for over a year."

Glendon hung his head. "It wasn't a pleasant year. I can tell you that much."

"I couldn't look for you. Couldn't even ask about you. But I knew you were there and that gave me hope. The day Tieg arrived with you alongside him, I nearly wept at the sight of you. One look and I felt it. You were mine. I still don't know how the saints were able to bring you two together, but I am most ecstatic they did."

Fia was at a complete loss for what to say. How to act. What to think. It was all too much to hear and process and believe. Her world had been upended in the span of a few weeks. "If anyone has any other great secrets or life-altering declarations, please can we get them out now? I'm not sure my heart will be able to take any more surprises." She tried for a light tone, but no one laughed.

"I understand this is a bit much. And I don't want you to feel overwhelmed, but I would very much like the opportunity to get to know you better," Brigid said. "As I'm sure would Glendon."

"I know all I need to know, Ma. Fia, I hope you don't mind a shadow. I plan to hound you for the rest of your life." The wonderous smile was yet to leave his face.

"Which leads me to ask," Tieg interjected. "You do plan to return to Feyport, don't you, Brigid? The witch has made it clear, it is her hope you do. If that isn't enough to persuade you, I'd love to have you there as well."

"That depends. Fia, what would you like?"

Fia's eyes widened in surprise. She hadn't thought that far ahead. It was the task she'd been sent here for, but that was before Brigid had shaken her very identity to the core. And what of Owen? Would that not lead him straight back to the tiny town she'd come to love? Plus, she still needed to see Oscar. She doubted she could divulge much of this to him, but it felt like too great a secret not to do just that.

Bending forward, she placed her elbows on her knees and her head in her hands.

"I don't know. I mean yes, I'd like to get to know you as well, but what about your husband, I mean my—" She refused to say the words. Despite what Brigid had told her, Owen Johnston was not her father and never would be. "What about Owen?"

"He will need to be dealt with, I suppose."

At the words, the memory of Darkness's words came back to her. *Let your mind be still. Dain likes his fun, but he'll not harm the man too severely. His fate lies in another's hands.*

Perhaps Brigid and Glendon returning to Feyport was for the best. She could write again to Oscar to see how his work was faring and invite him to town for a spell.

"All right then. I suppose we could rest tonight and get back on the road home tomorrow."

TWENTY-EIGHT

"Told you, Tieg. I told you!" Glendon was nearly giddy as they traveled along the lane heading into Feyport three days later. It had been an uneventful journey if not somewhat boring. The rails should have been cleared and the travel much shorter. Tieg had suggested a quicker route of one day back to the city then catching the train north for Fia, Brigid, and Glendon. He would take the wagon on from there and meet them all in Feyport, but all three of his companions had declined the offer. Glendon said he wanted the time to not only get to know Fia better, but also spend it with his friend whom he'd missed over the past years. Brigid was in no mood to be away from either of her children, and Fia was in no mood to return to Feyport and the possibility of encountering Owen Johnston or the witch and her sons. So the four of them piled into the little wagon and headed back together.

"All that time I *knew* something else was out there and you wouldn't believe me."

Fia was walking ahead of the wagon, enjoying a bit of quite time, and Brigid had fallen asleep in the back. Tieg and Glendon sat side by side on the driver's board, making the quiet conversation easier.

"To be fair, Glendon, I didn't know you were living with a leanan sidhe all the while." Tieg stared ahead at the lithe form of the beautiful woman walking twenty yards ahead.

"Nor did I Tieg, but I certainly didn't let it stop me from desperately seeking what I felt in my soul. All that time. I felt her out there somewhere. Missing." Glendon stared at the same woman, but Tieg knew it was a different kind of longing he felt for her. He couldn't imagine the other man's pain. If Niall or Candice had been removed from his life now he would feel the deepest grief, but what that grief would be if he'd never known them at all, he couldn't say. "I just thought it was me who was lacking. Damn the bastard. If I didn't already hate the man so much, I certainly do now."

"When did you realize your mother was fey? Surely it's been some time."

Glendon nodded. "Sure it has. Years back I suppose. She was different from all the other ladies in town. Different from your ma. When I was small, I just thought it was the color of her hair and such. Before he got it in his head to start cutting it off, she'd leave it uncovered when we were home, and I loved running my fingers through it when she told me nanny stories before bed."

Tieg nodded. "I saw it once myself. I was coming to fetch you for some outing and I don't think she expected me. When I came into the yard, she was coming round the back with a basket of linens. I was struck dumb by the sight of it."

"She never mentioned that, but then again she wouldn't. She has no problem with her appearance. It's him that does. He's clipped her horns for as long as I can remember.

"Anyway, after a particularly grueling month when I was maybe twelve or thirteen, her antlers had started to show again. I begged him not to touch them. They're just so"—he waved his hands, looking for the right word—"majestic, maybe? I don't know. Well, he didn't even acknowledge me there, groveling at his feet. Just took out his file and set to work on them. She didn't make a sound, but I cried enough for both of us."

"What do you think will happen to him?" Tieg asked.

"I honestly don't know."

"The books say he'll be driven mad by her absence."

"Good. I hope it's slow and painful." Glendon's face was severe, and his voice held not a bit of remorse.

"You'd let him end his own life?"

"I'd rather take it myself, but then I'd just be easing his misery. So no. I'm not kind enough to let him take it himself. I'll ensure he lives. Alone. Without a drop of talent or a dime to his name. That would be the best punishment."

Tieg didn't answer. He only nodded in silent agreement with his friend.

Although Fia insisted they could make it to town that night if they just pushed on, Tieg and Brigid wouldn't hear it. The night was full of dangerous things, and both seemed concerned she hadn't yet figured that out for herself. So rather than getting back to the comfort of the inn she called home, they paid for rooms at an inn she didn't.

Fia had been given her own space each time they stopped. It wasn't necessary, she'd told them, but Tieg and Glendon were happy to bunk together, and Brigid felt it would be intrusive to ask her to share in light of the recent revelations. The truth was, she liked Mrs. Johnston just fine and was eager to learn everything she could from the woman, but despite this, she couldn't bring herself to think of the muse as her mother. Her mother had raised her, and her mother had died when she was just a child. It would take more than a few nights to convince her heart otherwise.

Sitting in the common room downstairs, the four of them shared a warm meal of roasted quail with hazelnut and mushroom stuffing. It tasted wonderful, but not as wonderful as it would have if Candice had prepared it.

After several long stretches and more than a few yawns, Glendon announced he was heading up to retire. Brigid stood to join him. After bending to place a kiss on Tieg's forehead, she turned to Fia but didn't repeat the motion. She fell in step with her son. "You two enjoy yourselves. I'll see you both in the morning."

"I should be heading up soon as well, I suppose," Fia said.

"Can you sit for a moment first?"

Fia had an uncomfortable feeling she knew what he wanted to discuss but forced a small smile and nodded.

"Don't look so terrified, I only want to talk."

"I'm not terrified."

"That is most certainly your I'm nervous but can't show it smile. I told you, Fia, I know all of your smiles."

"Nervous isn't the same thing as terrified," she countered.

"Point taken." He sat back in his chair and took a long sip from the frothy ale in his hand. He huffed a breath. "This isn't exactly the setting I wished to have this conversation, but as I never know what the next day will hold with you, I can't keep this to myself any longer."

Fia's heart began to beat double time. "Please," she whispered. "Please don't dismiss me from the shop."

She hadn't realized how much she wanted to keep in his employ. Not just because it afforded her a living wage. Not just because she loved the shop and library, the people who visited, or sweet little Arthur. Not just because she'd come to love Feyport and the people in the quaint seaside town or how easily they accepted her. Most of all she didn't want to leave because despite all he had kept from her and all he had done which frustrated her, Fia didn't want to leave Tieg Connolly.

She wanted to see his scowling face each day and wait for the occasional smile. She wanted to hear his voice in the mornings and wait for the occasional laugh in the afternoon. She wanted to sit beside him as she quietly read and walk beside him as she reshelved books.

She was terrified she might hurt him but more terrified of never seeing him again. And so she said the word again. "Please."

The furrow between his brows was deeper than she'd ever seen it. "Why on earth would you think I plan to dismiss you, Fia? Bindings and Baubles wouldn't survive without you."

"But you said—"

"What did I say?" He seemed genuinely confused.

"You said we needed to discuss my position and that was before all of this came to light. Now I can only imagine you'd like to have any threat removed from your business."

"Threat? Fia. You are not any sort of a threat."

"Did you not hear any of Brigid's story? What if you come to rely on my fey gifts? What if you feel like I can never leave? What if one day it's you keeping me locked away and filing off my antlers? Shearing my hair like one of the sheep in the pastures? All because if I leave it might end you?"

"You can't possibly think I'd ever do any of that. I'd never hurt you, Fia. Never."

"We can't know the future. What if it's I who hurt you?"

"Fia. I am not an artist or a wordsmith. Not even an artisan. I don't paint pots or create epic works. I don't pen anything more than the daily tally in my journal, and the only literature I care about is that which is written by others. I don't need a muse to make me a success. But even if I did, I'd die a thousand deaths if it meant I got to spend just one more day in your presence. Not because of what you are, but who you are. I don't need Fia Walsh the leanan sidhe. I don't need Fia the iridescent-haired muse. I need Fia the woman. Fia who enjoys making me smile. Fia who would rather read a book than convince men of her beauty—not that they need convincing, mind you." He paused long enough to catch his breath. "Fia who my miserable heart longs to see each and every day."

He reached out and took her hand. "I've been trying to tell you this for weeks and failing so profoundly it's a wonder you haven't run for the sea yet." Fia thought about telling him she'd considered running—just not to the arms of the sea—but elected to keep quiet on the subject. "I needed you to know who you are so you can make all the right decisions for yourself. And not look back and wonder if you gave up too much to be here in Feyport. With me. And Arthur. What you are does not bother me in the slightest, just as it shouldn't bother you."

Fia couldn't think. She couldn't even breathe. This was what she'd just admitted to herself. What she'd wanted to hear, and yet... And yet. Something still bothered her about it all.

"So why can't I still work for you?"

"You can't work *for* me because I want you to work *with* me."

"But I already work with you."

Tieg smiled and shook his head. It was one of those rare—but ever increasing—smiles Fia adored. "You do. But I want it to be official. An actual partnership. Not me paying you and you doing what I tell you because you have to as my employee."

Fia thought for a moment. Her eyes glowed with an inner light and she asked, "I'd get to help make decisions about everything?"

"Everything."

"Even about Arthur getting to sleep inside on occasion?"

"Maybe I should reconsider my offer."

She grinned. "You can't. It's out there now."

"I suppose it is." He leaned forward and dragged the hand he still clasped up to cradle against his heart. "I want you with me, Fia. For all of it. The shop. The library. The hedgehogs. All of it. I know each of your smiles, and I wish for nothing more than to see only the genuinely happy one alighting your face for years to come."

Her grin broadened. She knew she was teasing him but couldn't help herself. "What are you saying, Tieg?"

"I thought I was being rather clear. I'm saying I'm falling for you. And I realize now is probably the worst possible time to tell you this. Everything that's happened. Everything you've been through. It's a lot to process and I don't want to muddle things or add to your worries, but I need you to know how I feel."

The grin dimmed just a touch. "I might be falling for you too, Tieg. But you're right. I need to figure out exactly who I am, just like you suggested. I'm willing to take things a day at a time if you are, though."

"I am *more* than willing." A look of relief washed over his face, and Fia giggled quietly.

"Good." She kissed the tip of his nose. "And you said hedgehogs. Plural." She raised her eyebrows and gave him her most mischievous grin.

"I suppose I did."

TWENTY-NINE

Several weeks passed in tentative comfort. Fia remained at the inn with the Bryans, though Candice refused to accept any sort of rent for her lodgings. She showed up at Bindings and Baubles each morning with energy and enthusiasm, often poring over catalogs and receipts with Tieg late into the evening. Arthur continued to delight her with his severe nonchalance. Glendon and Brigid settled into the home they'd once shared with Owen Johnston. Glendon took a position at the distillery and was hoping to start as an apprentice in the cooperage in the fall. Rupert Camden thought he had the perfect eye for making barrels. Owen, thankfully, remained unaccounted for. Perhaps whatever Dain had done convinced him to stay far away from Feyport. As for the witch and her sons, Fia hadn't seen them again.

Brigid came to the transformed barley house every day at noon without fail. She stayed for an hour or two and tried to help Fia understand her nature a little more. Short of the time she spent alone with Tieg, when he stole her kisses and she stole his smiles, either in the shop or exploring the town, these afternoons with Brigid became her favorite part of life in Feyport.

The subtle magic she possessed was so intwined within her, it became a wonder to her that she hadn't ever acknowledged its presence before. She began to learn what it felt like in her blood and in her soul. She experimented with casting it with intent and purpose, but given the lack of true artists in town, she had to rely on creativity when choosing whom to share it with. It was agreed that she should be judicious with those she gifted, sticking mainly to her small circle of relatively close friends.

Niall was the most willing participant in these little experiments, but as his artistic ability was limited to crude drawings in the wet sand of the beach, this was of little help but immense enjoyment for both of them. Tieg had been right, and he lacked almost any artistic ability. Fia was able to influence him once, and the result was a rearrangement of the library books from anything useful into a rainbow collage of spines on the shelves. While it was pleasing to look at, he grumbled for half a day after as he meticulously rearranged them all to a more appropriate organizational system. Most interesting of all were the two people she wouldn't have expected to benefit from her fey magic—Candice Bryan and Rupert Camden.

For Candice it was in the form of pies and Rupert in the flavor blending of his whiskeys. Candice, always an excellent baker, was now producing pies with intricately carved and woven crusts, so beautiful it was hard to justify eating them. They got eaten nonetheless. And Camden, always a fine distiller, was now making blended bottles to rival any for miles around. With each of them, however, Brigid insisted Fia share only droplets of magic and never twice with the same person in a week. It seemed an easy balance to maintain, and no one pushed her for more.

Fia felt a satisfaction in all of this, but the one person she was most concerned about was Oscar. She'd written to him the first day she'd arrived back in town but had yet to hear any reply. With each day of silence her apprehension grew.

After closing up the shop early one Friday afternoon, Tieg and Fia met Brigid and Glendon outside. The four of them were heading to the pub for dinner and then planned to enjoy a walk along the beach to watch the summer sunset over the water.

The town was full of locals and visitors alike. Travelers were beginning to get word of the magical little town by the sea, and with the weather being so nice that time of year, the inn was almost always full. Fia tried to help Candice out when she could, but often she felt more in the way than anything. Ned had even talked about expanding the place and building another few rooms to accommodate the demand.

As they approached the pub, Fia began to feel as if eyes were on her. She adjusted her cap and looked at Brigid who had also gone still. To their right, a small alleyway sat recessed next to the pub's stone façade. Despite the sun still hanging high in the late afternoon sky, the shadows of the small alley were thick and black. The noise from the street dimmed, and a soft hush dripped over Fia's ears. Glendon and Tieg both came to a halt at the opening.

Fia didn't need to be fey to know Dub waited in the alley. Steeling herself, she turned toward the opening and stepped into the shadows, dimly aware of Tieg barking her name as she did so.

"Hello, little foundling. Not many come to me so willingly. Are you brave or are you foolish?" He was just as wickedly gorgeous as she remembered and just as terrifying.

"I suspect a bit of both." He smiled and tilted his head to her in acknowledgment. "But you've not harmed me yet, so hopefully that holds a little longer."

"I've no wish to harm you. Your mother travels with you?"

Although Fia still couldn't outwardly acknowledge Brigid as her mother, she knew better than to say so now. "Yes. Should I fetch her?"

"There is no need. Mother sends an invitation and a warning. This time free of charge."

"How kind of her." Fia said the words as sweetly as she was able, not wanting to raise his ire in any way.

"First, she wishes Brigid to know of her mother's passing. It was several years back but likely she will not have heard."

A lump rose in Fia's throat. Not only because of the tragedy of anyone losing a parent, but also Fia now realizing she might grieve for a grandmother she'd never know. Even more so, however, was the idea Darkness expected her to give Brigid the news.

"In addition, should Brigid seek her, Mother will be waiting at the cottage of her youth. But you all need be wary. Dother senses the man who sired you. He is foolish, that one, and does not know when he is no longer welcome."

All thoughts of the uncomfortable conversation to come fled her mind. "Owen is here? In Feyport?"

"If Dother says it, it is so. He is more akin to the man's heart than even Dain."

Of course he was. Dain being Violence and Dother being Evil. Fia's heartbeat quickened. "Might I ask you something, Dub?"

He dipped his head, the predatory gleam never leaving his eye.

"Your mother, Carman, she brought my grandmother's book to my par— to the people who raised me?"

He nodded but did not speak.

"Were you with her when she did?"

Again a silent nod.

"Thank you for that. And please thank your mother as well."

He blinked at her, all expression gone from his painfully handsome face. "Your gratitude is not needed."

"Oh. I didn't mean to offend you."

"It would take much more to offend me, little sister."

"Will I see you again?"

"Most would not wish to." He cocked his head at her. "Do you?"

Fia wasn't sure why—she should be running in fear—but she nodded. "I suppose I do."

"Perhaps you are indeed both brave and foolish. But if you wish it, I suppose we shall see each other again."

Fia blinked and he was gone. Her friends rushed to her side, Tieg surrounding her with his arms and pulling her in close.

"What in all the hells was that then?" Glendon asked. "You just walked into that shadow and disappeared."

"That, dear man," Brigid said, "was Darkness."

The food at the pub was good, but the ale was better.

The room was full and raucous. Several patrons enjoyed cards or dice. They tapped their feet to the pair of men playing the fiddle and bodhran in the corner. Tieg greeted many of the patrons like old friends, and more than a few stopped by their table to clap Glendon on the back and welcome him and Brigid home.

Soon they were joined by Aylee Garrow and her sister Maeve, as well as Dee and Robbie. They all crowded around a sticky rectangular table. Fia and Glendon sat at one end on either side of Brigid, with Tieg to Fia's right.

Brigid for her part didn't look worried exactly, but neither was she comfortable. It had been some time since she'd openly sat among so many. She followed Fia's lead and kept her small cloche on but didn't go to great lengths to otherwise conceal her hair. The locks were already growing back in a beautiful shade of emerald shot through with the occasional silver strand. It would take time, but Fia hoped Brigid would come to be comfortable just as she was. Fia thought it much more likely to accomplish this if she wasn't constantly looking over her shoulder for the man she was married to.

"So what will you do?" she asked Brigid.

"Go to her, I suppose. "

"How far is the cottage?"

"Not even a day. I can go tomorrow and be back by the time the work week begins again." She looked both excited at the prospect and scared. "I'm sure she'll have some things to say to me just as I've things to say to her— not all of them glowing. But I do hope to repair the friendship we once shared. I'm older and much wiser now than I was when we last parted."

"You'll go with her?" Tieg asked Glendon.

"I'm sure it's not necessary." Brigid spoke first, earning a severe frown from her son.

"I beg to differ, Ma. That man is still out there. Did you not hear the warning Fia delivered from the witch herself?"

"I just long for the day when I can walk about on my own. I crave my independence and now that it's so near, I crave it all the more."

"I understand how you feel," Fia said, nibbling on a bit of bread she'd torn from the loaf on the table. "But for now I think caution should win out, don't you?"

"You're right I suppose, it's just. . ." Brigid stood from the table, wiping her hands on the bit of linen serving as her napkin. "I think I'll be outside. It's a tad on the noisy side in here for me. Glendon, you can pay our tab?"

"No need," Tieg said and rose to pay the publican.

Aylee and Maeve waved their goodbyes as the beautiful woman scooted around the outside of their chairs.

Fia looked at her brother. For some reason, it was easier for her to accept Glendon as a sibling than it was for her to accept Brigid as her mother. Perhaps it was because he wasn't displacing Oscar in any way or because he did look so much like her. Where she and Oscar shared no traits at all, Glendon was the male version of herself minus the dark green hair. In certain light, even that trait was easy to miss. His tall and willowy build in combination with his porcelain skin and green eyes were twins to her own. And while Fia lacked an overbite, his smile creased his face in the same crinkles and folds as hers did.

She couldn't help but find joy in his expression as he continued to flick charming smiles and winks at Aylee. No matter she was a handful of years his senior and clearly in love with someone else. Fia supposed he might not have known that bit though. She'd have to get him up to speed in the near future.

"Should I go after her?" Fia asked Glendon, nodding toward the exit at the front of the pub.

"No, she just needs a minute, I'm sure." Her brother paused his unrequited flirtations long enough to press his thumbs into the bridge of his nose. "She's prone to bouts of melancholy. With obvious good reason. I'd hoped her return to Feyport and finding you would help ease it a bit, but I'm worried."

"Perhaps Dub was mistaken," Fia offered. "Perhaps the books are right and he couldn't live with himself without her."

She didn't like the hopeful tone in her voice when discussing such a dark topic, but she too might rest easier if she knew the man was no longer a threat to the people she cared about.

"I doubt we'd be so lucky."

As if the stars or saints had listened in on their conversation, the wail of a loud cry could be heard even over the din of the pub. A shiver raced down Fia's back. The voice, distorted though it was, had sounded very like Brigid's.

Glendon shot from his seat and was out the door in blink. Tieg, having dropped the coins for their meal on the bar, was right behind him.

By the time Fia—not slow by any means—raced out into the street, Aylee, Maeve, Dee, and Robbie, as well as several of the other patrons were reacting to the commotion as well.

Fia didn't really know what she was expecting to see outside, but the sight before her was almost too absurd to be believed.

Brigid stood tall and regal in the road, looking down on a decidedly disheveled and clearly unwell Owen Johnston bowing before her. He'd gone so far as to latch himself onto her shoes and was sobbing uncontrollably into the leather and laces.

"I've told you. I'm done with it all, Owen."

"You can't. You're my wife." His face was a bright persimmon, snot flowing over his lips and dripping from his chin.

Brigid tilted her chin. "Am I though? I recall no service. No vows. Nothing."

"We didn't need vows or a church. You loved me." His eyes were pleading as he stared up at her.

Glendon grunted as if he'd been struck. Fia was stunned. They had never been married? All that time and he really did just treat her as a possession. Nothing more.

Brigid would not be swayed. "Maybe I did, but you never loved me in return. You took from me and took from me. And never gave me anything."

"I gave you my name."

"I never asked for your name," she hissed at him. "All I wanted was your respect. Your attention."

"And I gave you them." He pointed to where Glendon and Fia stood among the small crowd witnessing the spectacle.

"Don't you dare." The ice in her voice was chilling even to Fia. "Don't you dare. You took my daughter from me and you used my son to keep me in line. All those years ago. And for what? A few meaningless words and the attention they brought you. Without me you aren't even a man, much less a genius."

"I know. I know, Brigid. Please. Please come back to me." Fia felt a nauseas sort of pity for the man. While she wanted nothing more than to have him disappear from all of their lives and pay for all of his crimes, watching him grovel and weep in front of the growing audience was unexpectedly painful. "Please."

Glendon stepped forward and placed a hand on the shoulder of the man who was both father and captor. His face held nothing but contempt. "Come on now. Leave her be."

The words from his son seemed to instill a new energy in Owen. He flinched away and rose to his feet in a motion that was surprisingly agile given his state. "Get your hands off me."

Glendon jumped back, and Fia gasped when she saw the knife in the older man's grip. Fia's brother moved quickly to stand between Owen and Brigid, but he needn't have bothered. It wasn't the leanan sidhe or her son the poet turned the weapon on. It was himself.

Placing the serrated edge to his own throat, he looked to Brigid one more time. "Don't think I won't do it."

She only shook her head sadly at him and looked away.

"You've done this to me and you can't even watch as I end it all." He cried the words in disbelief.

"Put the knife down now," Tieg said evenly as he stepped closer to Owen.

"You think you're so much better than me, Tieg Connolly. Just you wait." Tipping his head toward Fia he added, "Sooner than later that girl will eat your soul just as her mother ate mine."

Tieg shook his head. "I'd wager you didn't have much of a soul to begin with. Now put down the knife."

"I never meant for them to die, you know." His words held a manic sort of tempo. "You don't know what it feels like to have all the joy and wonder of your thoughts and words be yanked away like that. There one moment and gone the next. It's torture. And I knew they had been at your home. Your parents never would have turned her away. But I wasn't in my right mind. They wouldn't tell me where she'd gone, Tieg. They wouldn't tell me."

Tieg's entire body tensed, the muscles in his shoulders practically vibrating with the need to remain still when surely he wanted to do anything but.

"So you killed them. Burned them alive in their own home. Just like that." His voice was hollow, betraying none of the hate or grief he was sure to be feeling.

"I didn't. You aren't listening," Owen argued. "It was an accident. I was frustrated and angry, and I lashed out when your father shut the door in my face. The lamp kicked over and there was nothing I could do. Nothing."

"I knew it was you. Brigid's right. You aren't a genius or even a man. You are nothing more than a piece of human waste. And as much as I'd love to see you slit your own throat right now, you don't deserve even that. You deserve to live years yet. Alone with your failures. Disgraced and unloved."

"And you think you can love *her*. She'd just like her mother. I knew it from the moment she was born and then again when I set eyes on her at my reading in the city. Unnatural." The vehemence in his voice hit Fia like a slap to the face. This man had helped to create her, yet he could look at her with nothing but disgust.

Tieg was hearing none of it, however. While Owen had been spewing forth his ugly words—no poetry awards being won today—Glendon had walked up behind him. The young man grabbed at the wrist holding the knife as Tieg wrestled the blade away. Owen pushed off from Tieg and spat in his direction before racing down the lane. Several of the men from the pub followed in his wake. He'd just admitted to murder after all.

Brigid let out a long shuddering breath and hugged her son to her.

Fia went to Tieg and placed a hand on his cheek. "I'm so sorry, Tieg."

"You've got nothing to be sorry for, Fia." He hung his head and wrapped his hands around the back of his neck.

"It all must have been unbearable to hear."

"I knew it all along, didn't I? It was actually a bit of a relief to hear him confess to it after all this time. Candice and Niall will want to know."

"I'll go with you if you like."

"It would be very much welcomed."

He seemed to gather himself and nodded. Before he could head off toward the inn, Fia stopped him with a hand on his arm.

"Listen, Tieg. What he said. About me? He won't be the only one to think such ugly thoughts. Even if others don't say it out loud, some will surely agree with him."

"Fia, I don't know how much more plainly I can say it. I don't care. I would stand beside you and marvel at your unique beauty each and every day if you'll let me."

Her hand rose to her hair again, and he grabbed it with his own.

"Not these bits that everyone can see, Fia. Although you are the most glorious woman I've ever beheld. But the beauty of your soul as well.

"I'll defend you if needed—although I think you're probably tough enough without my aid—and I will support you even if you don't. I won't shy away from who you are. I will love each and every bit of you. And if there is the occasional person who doesn't like it, well, they can go to hell."

"Really?" She beamed up at him.

"Really."

"In that case, I suppose I should tell you there isn't anywhere else I'd rather be. And I'll do my best not to eat your soul."

He chuckled at her words but only briefly. He was much too focused on holding her face in his hands as he brought his lips down to meet hers.

The sweetness of the moment was broken as Aylee and Maeve walked up beside them. Aylee cleared her throat as the small audience began to clap and whistle in their general direction.

"I'll be happy to watch the shop again, when you two are off on your honeymoon," Maeve said with a wink in Fia's direction.

"One day at a time, Maeve. That's how we are taking this. I'll let you know when we need you," Tieg responded as he threw his arm around Fia's shoulder.

THIRTY

A week later Owen Johnston's body washed up on the beach. Great chunks of his flesh were missing in addition to most of his clothing.

Speculation swirled in the tiny seaside town as to the cause of his demise. As no one had gotten ahold of him after he sprinted away from Tieg and the others outside the pub, no one could say for certain if he'd simply walked into the water of his own accord. But tales of kelpies along the shallows weren't unheard of either. Had one of the monstrous fey water creatures risen up and lured him into the sea only to drag him to the depths and feast on his carcass? It was possible.

Fia didn't know how to feel about the news. While she had never thought of Owen as anything more than a vile man and certainly never as her father, she didn't like the idea of death hitting so close to home yet again.

The change in both Brigid and Glendon was evident as the news settled. Brigid looked less haunted each day, and Glendon was downright chipper. Owen had been no more a father to him than he'd been to Fia, despite sharing a roof and a name.

Brigid was able to travel inland to the tiny cottage set in the forest where she'd grown up and had the reunion with Carman she'd been both dreading and anticipating in equal measure. Carman had accepted her apologies in her own way, by offering to forgive Brigid in exchange for some as yet unnamed favor. Brigid was happy to comply.

Glendon continued his work at the distillery and was accepted into life in Feyport as if he'd never been gone. He moved into the shared lodgings with Niall and his friends from the dairy.

Fia spent all of her days at Bindings and Baubles, loving the smell of the paper and ink, the soaps and candles. She loved the smell of the man she worked beside even more. It was what really kept her coming to work each day. That and Arthur.

It was in the small library and shop that she received a letter from Oscar along with a shipment of handblown lamp flues. She couldn't wait to see his words but hesitated nonetheless before tearing open the envelope. She wasn't certain what she would do if he lamented to her again about his lack of creative industry. She'd told herself she wasn't ready just yet to bestow her magic on him should he need it. Her control was much better—the pies at the inn and Camden's whiskey the primary beneficiaries of her practice—but she still wasn't convinced she would do more good than harm by assisting him.

As she sat thinking on it, Tieg came round and placed his hands on her shoulders, lending what strength he could to her resolve.

She pulled the paper free and, despite her trepidation, smiled at the familiar script.

Dearest Fi,

I continue to miss you daily and hope you are enjoying life in your quaint seaside village. From your previous letters, it certainly sounds as if you are.

I am happy to tell you Trevor continues to be the greatest joy of my life. He has such a way of bringing out the good in me. I cannot begin to describe it to you. He grows an inch each day, I'd swear it, and now has such a charming personality. I have daily conversations with him of which I don't understand a single thing, but the way he carries on it is clear he knows exactly what he's saying.

Claire too is well.

And if a joyful baby and a content wife weren't enough, I am happy to report my creative sparks are once again flowing! I've made more paperweights and small glass figurines and will be sending those along soon. In addition, I've had the most wonderful idea for some more whimsical pieces. How would your Mr. Connolly feel about a series of stained glass panes depicting some rather interesting images? I was thinking to start with a few pixies but I've also had the image of a beautifully seductive selkie and perhaps even a banshee in mind. If it sounds too much, I promise not to be offended.

Please do reply and let me know your thoughts.

Missing you,

Oscar

Fia handed the missive to Tieg and bent down and scratched Arthur's soft belly. She heard Tieg's relieved breath as he finished up and handed the folded letter back to her.

She smiled brightly as she reached around his neck, the paper dangling loosely in one hand.

"What do you say, Mr. Connolly?"

"I say you should no longer fear for your brother."

"It seems that way. Any other opinions on the note?" she asked.

Tieg pursed his lips in contemplation. "I think his first pane should be of a muse. The antlers should be easy." His face broke into a grin. "But I fear he'll struggle with glass that adequately depicts the rest."

THE END

ACKNOWLEDGEMENTS

I am going to keep this relatively short, but I just couldn't end this book without thanking a few people. I've shared a few stories now, and as much as I'd love to say it gets easier with each book, it just doesn't. Without the hard work and support of the folks who help me, these fantasies would still be in my imagination or in an unopened file on my computer.

I've been lucky to find some incredible editors—Karen Robinson chief among them. Her gift with the English language is so welcome and so needed.

My daughters are both amazing young women, bibliophiles and writers as well. They remind me every day how much fun this whole wild ride is and I can't wait to see them taking the world by storm. In addition as a developmental editor, Lily Larsen has the ability to tell me what works and what doesn't. She keeps me grounded in my storytelling. Addie Larsen—the most creative among us—just might win awards for her narration and screenplays.

I also need to give a shout out to my husband who helps with all aspects of the technical design. He is also instrumental in encouraging my dream and keeping the occasional spiral into madness in check. I couldn't do any of this without him.

Then of course, there are the readers. I can't begin to tell you how much every kind word, sweet interaction, social media post, shared review and book signing has meant to me. The community of readers, reviewers, and other authors out there has been the fuel that keeps me going. I thought about putting a few names here, but the list is long and I didn't want to forget anyone. You all know who you are. I thank you from the bottom of my heart.

More from Kami King Larsen

A Simple Tale of Water and Weeping
Blood and Wonder (Medicus Corpus Book 1)
Breath and Starshine (Medicus Corpus Book 2)

Writing as Aster Rye

Bittersweet Breadcrumbs
Vespertine Dreams

Let's Connect

If you are interested in the opportunity to receive free Advanced Reader Copies for future releases and keep up with other exciting news, join my mailing list via my website or follow me on social media.
www.kamikinglarsenbooks.com
Instagram @authorkamikinglarsen
@lilyfernbooks
Or find me on Facebook Kami King Larsen Books and Bits

Thank you for taking the time to share in Fia and Tieg's story. I'd love to know what you think. The Best way to support authors is to leave a review on Amazon, Goodreads, your social media channels, or anywhere else you review books!

ABOUT THE AUTHOR

Kami King Larsen is a native of the desert southwest and studied biology before attending medical school. Although she is a practicing pediatrician by training, she is a lover of great stories and all things whimsical by birth. Kami lives in Nevada with her husband, daughters, and two dogs.

See where it all began with Aylee and Cailean's story

Turn the page for a taste of *A Simple Tale of Water and Weeping*

PROLOGUE

Gentle swells made their way toward the sand and pebble shore. The dark water broke on the shallow shelf of rocks, creating a hypnotic lullaby for those who chose to sleep with windows cracked. The mist rising from the salty water mixed in the crisp evening air, a low blanket of fog blurring the atmosphere. As the tendrils reached above the sea, a dreamy veil blurred the full moon's light. Occasionally, a nesting sea bird would call into the gloom.

It was a typical coastal night. Briny and cool. Nothing out of the ordinary to those who lived along the edge of the sea. Perfectly beautiful and perfectly regular.

Some who lived by the sea would argue it was just as it should be; others might notice the sleek bodies swimming near the shore and think perhaps things were not so ordinary at all. Smooth grey and spotted white shadows spun and swirled, gliding through the murky water in a whimsical ballet. To the casual eye they were just seals. Seals were common enough in these waters. To a more gifted eye, they might be something more. And with the full harvest moon shining down? Well, just a touch out of the ordinary for certain.

Black eyes shimmered just above the surface, inky and wet. Long lashes blinked out the salt water. One set.

Then three. Eight. Thirteen. An unlucky number on a night slightly out of the ordinary.

The waves continued the gentle assault on the shore, breaking and running over the coarse pebble-strewn sand. The thirteen sets of eyes peered at the land, waiting and watching for movement. The stillness stretched out, and the waves rocked the sleek bodies slightly—the ballet at an end. Floating in the tide, they waited—and waited some more.

When all was deemed quiet and abandoned, the oldest and most knowing eyes blinked once more. The moon broke free momentarily from the fog, and silver light flashed in the obsidian eyes. Slowly, the face of a harbor seal rose from the water—tilted back as if to observe the stars. It barked and ducked beneath the waves. Water rippled as its head broke the surface mere seconds later. Where spotted fur and whiskers had been, a head of wavy hair and pale smooth skin emerged.

One by one, the other dozen seals did the same. Locks of grey and silver, brown and gold covered the human faces where only moments before the pinnipeds had been. Eyes no longer black—but a myriad of blues, greens, hazels, and browns—peered out of the beautiful faces of men and women. And in those eyes, mischief danced. The exquisite creatures walked rather than swam up the beach to the shore.

Silently they stepped from the frigid water onto the slightly less frigid land. Each body naked and lovely. They seemed not to notice the cold but to bask in the glory of an unseen sun. Behind each one, dangling from a hand with elegant long fingers and comely shaped nails, trailed a flowing skein of seal hide.

Across the beach and down the road, in the upper level of a building, in a small cozy room, a girl slept. She dreamed of fantastic things. All was perfectly beautiful and perfectly unordinary.

ONE

When Aylee woke from her slumber to begin the day's work in the small town without a name, the sun had not yet risen. The vague remnants of a dream floated around in her head—a rainstorm, a dish of cream, and a stray cat.

Her legs were pinned to one side of the bed courtesy of her dog, Pepper. She nudged the lazy beast over, grumbling about personal space. Pepper merely looked at her with mismatched blue and brown eyes but made no effort to leave the warmth of the blankets.

Pushing her mess of copper and strawberry hair from her face, Aylee swung her feet from the warmth of the quilt and shivered as her bare soles made contact with the chill of the floor. Sounds of movement and the clatter of kitchen tools rose from below, indicating her parents were already busy in the shop downstairs.

Washing her face and cleaning her teeth took only a few minutes. Then she donned a simple blouse and wool skirt along with her thick socks and boots. She left her small room after turning out the lamp and walked down the wooden steps, Pepper racing ahead of her, to the back of her family's mercantile. Using her hip, she pushed the door open and entered the warm space, inhaling the goodness of fresh-baked bread and strong hot tea.

Aylee's father was busy stocking cartons of dry goods on the shelves, and her mother was placing warm sweet rolls into a glass case by the register. She looked up as her younger daughter entered the store.

"Morning, Love. You still fine with running the beach this morning? There's a bit of a chill in the air. We could pay one of the Cormack boys to do it if you rather," her mother said.

Aylee loved going to the shore to gather clams in the early morning dawn. It gave her a chance to really listen to the waves and feel the salty kiss of the air on her cheeks. Not to mention, she wasn't sure she could stomach the sight of one particular Cormack boy this early in the morning.

"Of course I don't mind, Momma. I'll be back in a tick. And don't worry, I'll have Pepper with me."

She grabbed a sticky hot bun in one hand and her clamming bucket and shovel in the other, kissed her da on the cheek, and was out the back door before any other discussion could take place.

The short walk from the main street of town took her past the stone walls of the church and small school grounds to reach the rocky inlet that separated the coastline from the bulk of the town. At high tide, the sea water would flow up the ravine, only to rush back out twice a day. It was low tide now, perfect for clamming. By the time Aylee and Pepper crossed over the small stone footbridge to the sand and pebble shore, she was licking the hot bun's icing from her fingers.

Many of the folks from town disliked and mistrusted the ocean. Aside from a few hardy souls and most of the reckless adolescents, they tended to stay away from the beach and the water's edge. Funny for a village built along the coast, but it was as it had always been. Aylee's mother had never feared the sea and, consequently, neither had either of her daughters.

Something about the way the light diffused in the early morning fog had always brought a kind of stillness and peace to Aylee—not just grey and not precisely golden but more of a tarnished silver, warm and cool mingled together to just the right shade of perfect. It was simply her favorite time of day and one of her favorite places to be.

She tossed a stick along the sand, and the shaggy black and brown dog raced to fetch it and return. Aylee grabbed the stick again and laughed as Pepper tore off when she made to throw the stick but did not. The dog gave its owner a baleful look, and Aylee chucked the stick as far as she could. A few more throws and the shepherd lay down on the damp ground near her feet—the sand a cinnamon and sugar coating on her fur.

Inhaling the briny air deep into her lungs, Aylee wiped her hand down her work apron, set her gear on the taupe packed sand, and pulled her unruly locks into a loose tie. The humid air made the strands heavy against her back. She took one long look out at the breakers and set to work.

When the bucket was over half full, a flicker of movement out in the surf caught her eye. Someone was out there, swimming in the frothy waters. Aylee smiled and shook her head. The chill in the air was bad enough, but to be in the water? That was altogether absurd. She walked toward the waves, hoping to catch a glimpse of who would be fool enough to swim this time of year. Some local kid, unafraid in the way only youth can be, most likely. She could just make out sandy blond hair, long enough to brush the tops of bare shoulders, but in this light it was difficult to be sure.

The bare shoulders disappeared to be replaced by a bare backside. She turned away from the sea quickly. She did *not* want to know whom she had glimpsed. She prayed it wasn't one of the local boys who couldn't keep their tongue in check. It would be all over town and would take days for the stories to stop.

"Apologies. I didn't mean to be nosy. I'll just be on my way," she stammered over her shoulder.

When no answer came, she peeked around to the waves once more. No one was visible. Worried the swimmer might be in peril, she turned full around. Still no sign of anyone. After a long minute, Aylee was convinced she'd need to run into town and raise the alarm. Then, above the next swell, a head did emerge. Her eyes must have played tricks on her earlier, for it was not a nude man or woman in the shallows, but a large grey seal. It seemed to regard her directly for a moment, and she had the unnerving sense it would open its muzzle and speak. She blinked and broke the connection. As quickly as it had appeared, the beautiful animal ducked its head back beneath the surface and was gone. Pepper barked at the waves and rolled onto her back, looking for a few belly scratches.

"Apparently I need to get more sleep," she remarked to the dog and began again to fill her bucket with clams.

When it was full to the brim and a fine sheen of

moisture coated her brow and neck, she stomped her way back up the beach toward the footbridge. The sun was making its way above the shops and homes of town. The rays caught the downslope off the beautiful copper roof of the largest residence in town, belonging to the owner of the local whiskey distillery. The orange-gold metal set a pleasing contrast to the green shingled exterior, and Aylee wondered what it might be like to live in such a home. Would she have a maid and butler or would she tend to it herself, holding warm receptions for the townsfolk each holiday season? The idea made her slightly nauseous.

Lost as she was in thought, she almost missed the bit of scarlet amid the brown and tan of the beach. She paused to retrieve a length of wool and was surprised to see a sturdy shawl unfold. Why would someone leave such a nice item on the rocks? Surely they would be missing it. She bundled the fabric under her arm and continued on her way, determined to track down its owner when she had an opportunity.

The air around her grew quiet, and Aylee had the strange feeling eyes were on her. The seal perhaps? What a fanciful daydream. She scanned the beach again, now alight with early morning sun as the fog was eaten away in spots by its rays. Both sand and sea were devoid of spies.

Satisfied, she walked on. Had she taken the time to look beneath the bridge however, she surely would have had a shock. Bright blue-green eyes stared out from the recess of shadows. After she'd passed and left the beauty of the beach behind, someone slipped out from under the bridge. The cerulean eyes, and the man they belonged to, followed her progress toward the warmth of the mercantile where a steamy mug of tea awaited her.

TWO

It was a busy morning in the little shop. Devon Garrow, shop proprietor and Aylee's father, had received a large shipment of dry goods and sundries the day prior. The town's residents were in and out picking up orders and placing new ones—taking the opportunity to purchase fresh clams, baked goods, and jarred jams as well. Aylee and her mother Una wrapped the purchases in crisp brown paper and tied them with sturdy knots or delicate bows depending on the patron and the package. When Mrs. Matlock requested her fabric and thread to be bound with matching ribbon, they obliged. When Mr. Bryan stated he could use some extra twine on his salted cod, they graciously double bound it. When young Ruby Larking asked for a sweet while her mother shopped, Aylee smiled, winked, and handed her not one, but two lemon drop sweets. It never hurt to do a bit extra to make people happy and to be kind. It felt natural to Aylee—like breathing. For her parents it was natural and also good business.

Una Garrow had just finished packing up a berry pie for Mrs. Larking when the bell above the door tinkled, announcing another customer.

Una smiled warmly and turned toward Aylee.

"Now, Love. Why don't you help Mr. Camden? I believe he's here to collect the order he placed last week."

The slight sinking feeling Aylee always had in response to the presence of Rupert Camden did not show on her face.

"Of course, Momma." Stepping over the prone form of her dog asleep behind the counter, she turned to the owner of both the town's distillery and the beautiful home with the copper roof she'd admired just that morning. "How can I help you, Mr. Camden?"

"Ach, Aylee. You know I prefer you call me Rupert," he responded, not unkindly.

Mr. Camden was perhaps a year or two older than Aylee's father but carried himself like a much younger man. He was always cleanly shaven save for a thick handlebar mustache. His hair was trimmed short and thinning on the top. He had the strong hands of a workman, but his nails were always clean and trimmed and his clothes clean and pressed.

"In the shop it's Mr. Camden," Aylee's father called over his shoulder.

"Of course, Devon. Understood."

Turning back to the counter, Mr. Camden smiled at Aylee. "Your mother's correct. I'm here to pick up my order. You should have a dozen glass jars and six sacks of yeast for me. I also wouldn't mind taking a few meat pies home if your mother has any extra."

"I believe she does. Cooked up quite a batch last

evening. We've got both—lamb and beef."

"I'd be happy to take one beef and two of the lamb." He handed her a small stack of coins.

"I'll get those right together for you. It'll only be a minute."

Glad for a task to keep her busy and away from further conversation with Rupert Camden, Aylee gathered the sacks of yeast and wrapped the small savory pies in a tin. The jars, however, were nowhere to be found.

"Da, do you know about Mr. Camden's glassware?" She had to raise her voice to a near yell to be heard over the din and clatter.

"So I do. Those will be out in the storage. Do you mind running to fetch them?" Her father wiped his hand on his apron.

At the moment, nothing would bring her more joy. She yearned for the crisp air to settle her. She needed to be away from Rupert Camden's gaze even more. Every second spent in his presence was uncomfortable, and she feared the rosy blush on her cheeks from the strain would be interpreted as a blush of innocence and admiration. Her words and manner might be pleasant and sweet, but her inner turmoil gave outward signs which might be misconstrued.

She excused herself and stepped from the back of the shop into the alleyway. Pressing her back and shoulders against the oak door, she drew a cleansing breath from the air and closed her eyes. Once she was stilled, she crossed the cobbled ground to a small, separate brick and stone structure. Taking a key from her apron pocket and placing her hand on the small brass knob, she felt the give of the unlocked door. Da must have left it open—unlike him to be sure, but not so much out of the ordinary it brought any alarm to her mind.

The smell of wood and damp earth mixed with touches

of salty sea and spicy cinnamon welcomed her into the dim space. Stacks of crates, cartons, and tins sat neatly organized along the slate and wood shelves. Paper tags with her father's neat penmanship labeled each container with the contents and date received. In an effort to avoid accidents, the storeroom had no lamps, only two large windows to provide light during the daytime. The windows were in need of a good washing. The resulting effect was a dim, weak sort of watery light, making it less than easy to identify the tan and brown packages.

Aylee's eyes adjusted to the gloomy space rather slowly. She skimmed her fingers along the tags, looking for a recent date and "mason jars" inked together. Moving up one wall and then across the back of the shed, she found nothing. Preparing to scan the opposite wall, her eyes caught on a dingy tarp in the corner, heaped atop a lumpy pile of goods. Perhaps the jars were stacked there, waiting with other items yet to be sorted and tagged. Aylee lifted the top edge to peek beneath and shrieked when she saw not bolts of fabric and jars of pickling spice but a man looking up at her.

She stumbled back, hands searching blindly for any weapon she might use in her defense. They fell upon the handle of a broom. The pine was smooth and cool in her hands but likely not sturdy enough to do more than keep dust at bay.

"Da!" she called out, knowing it was likely of little use. The mercantile was busy, and the noise of the patrons would drown out even the loudest of screams. Hers was barely more than a croak.

The man raised his hands in a gesture which implied *she* was more of a threat to him than the other way around.

"Please." The stranger's voice was raspy as if from disuse. He cleared his throat and spoke again. "Please. I seek only the way to get home."

"I see nothing stopping you," she stammered.

He stood, wrapping the tarp around his waist. This time, the rosy flush on Aylee's face was more than discomfort. This man was bare save the tarp—no clothing in sight.

"Da!" she yelped again. The hammering of her heart did little to help her. She had to remove herself from the closed space and close proximity to this unwanted intruder immediately.

Aylee stepped back another foot, inching her way toward the door. She thought to turn and run, but the idea of having her back to him made her shudder. She squared her shoulders and kept her eyes on his face.

"Please. I should not be here. I dram . . . Not dram? Dream?" He shook his head. "I wish or desire or some word I can't place. I need nothing but to return home."

"Whatever word you choose, you are correct. You *need not* be here. I believe *I am* correct in stating nothing is stopping you from going." The tremor in her voice was equal measure fear and anger.

He glanced down at his chest—one hand holding the tarp and the other grasping at the notch above his breastbone. Searching for something, which evidently was not there. "But . . . my coat. . ."

Even in the weak watery light, she could see the pain of confusion and sadness etched on the planes of his face. While he did not appear embarrassed by the lack of modesty, he did seem conflicted—almost as if unsure how to proceed.

"I know nothing of your coat, I'm afraid." Only then did Aylee wonder where his clothing was and how he came to be in their storage shed without a stitch on. Surely parading naked through town would have garnered notice by at least one or two of the nosy residents.

"At the sea. At the shore," he stated as if she should

already know this. "It was there where I left it and then it was gone."

His talking nonsense was doing little to ease Aylee's confusion. "I still don't understand."

As if not hearing her, he asked, "When is this place?"

She frowned at him.

"Not right." More to himself than to her. "When? Not when. Where is this place?"

"My family's storage shed."

He shook his head. "The town. What is this town?"

"Well, it's just . . . *town*." The gloom hid most of his expression from her, but she could sense his growing frustration.

"Just town? No town is just town." This seemed to agitate him more for some reason, the gravel in his voice grinding in the muffled confines of the shed.

"Right." The fear, while still present in her mind and voice, was being crowded out by something like sympathy. Surely this must be some sort of ploy, an act to have her let down her guard, flimsy though it was. He did seem genuinely innocent and confused. Perhaps he had suffered some sort of trauma to his head? Or belonged in an asylum? Neither were happy choices; however, something in his manner sparked that bit of herself which always longed to do the right thing. To help the sad creature was a small task, and she at least owed him for taking her mind off Rupert Camden for the space of a few moments.

The jars! She still needed them and didn't fancy sending her father in here to look for them. That would raise all sorts of questions about her time spent alone with a naked man.

"If you'll wait here, I can fetch you some things and you can be on your way."

Stepping into the light cast by the open door, broom still in hand, she saw the carton labeled "jars" set along the opposite wall. She grabbed the clanking glasses to her chest and returned to the shop.

Having gotten Mr. Camden on his way with a halfhearted promise to see him at the town jubilee later that week, along with his goods packed neatly into his wagon, Aylee ducked back out of the shop and up the stairs to their rooms above. She ran though the apartment, easily finding what she needed: a pair of drab trousers, a well-worn wool sweater softened with time and a hundred washings, a newish pair of thick socks, and an extra pair of not-so-newish boots. Her mother had recently taken up a charity position with the town and had been gathering used items from the neighbors to be distributed by the church to the less fortunate. Aylee had not gotten a good look at the stranger's build. She did recall her eyes, in preserving his modesty, had rested above the shelving at the back of the shed, making him a good head taller than her father, and Devon Garrow was not a short man.

Creeping back into the storage shelter like a thief, Aylee made certain no one was watching. The alleyway was blessedly deserted. Could her luck hold out? Would she find the shed equally empty?

She closed the door securely behind her. Her wariness had less to do with concern for the stranger and more with self-preservation. Being caught with a naked man would do nothing for her reputation or that of her family. Her luck did not stretch, and she found the man standing quietly just as she'd left him—looking dejected, slightly confused, and just as naked.

Taking a deep breath, she took a moment to look at him. Shadows slatted across his face, making it difficult to see. His pale alabaster skin contrasted against the shock of dark hair crowning his head. In the dim light, she couldn't quite make out the color of his eyes, but he didn't appear to be much older than she was.

"I've brought you some things. You can get dressed and be on your way." She reached into her apron pocket and pulled out a small handful of coins. "I don't have much in the way of money, but this should be enough to get a room for a night or two on the road."

He opened his mouth, but she interrupted him. "No need to thank me. It's not exactly summer weather, and I wouldn't want to be in the cold if it were me."

He frowned.

"There'll be a bit of cheese and some fresh bread for you by the back shop door across the alley. I can grab you a flask of cider as well. That should get you on your way to home." She paused a moment. "Where exactly is home? Not town. I know that much."

Silence. It stretched out, the expectation of a response from Aylee and the lack of one from the stranger weighing the space between them.

"Well, then. Good luck." She sighed. "There's an inn at the edge of town—across from the dairy. The Bryans are good people and keep clean rooms. They're fair, and the coins should be plenty for a night or two."

Aylee thought he might speak, but once more he seemed at a loss. She was torn between incredible frustration and feeling overwhelmingly sorry for this man. Perhaps she should fetch her father and involve him in the cause. Fear won out and she elected to keep his peculiar arrival and interaction to herself for the time being. He had not threatened her and did not seem inclined to violence. She vowed silently to keep wary and mention his presence in the future if it seemed prudent.

She nodded once, smiled with a kindness that radiated from her eyes to his, and said simply, "Safe travels."

She returned to helping her mother in the shop but found her focus drifting the remainder of the day.

A Simple Tale of Water and Weeping is

available now!